Books by Adriana L

My Amazon

Signed Copie

Brewer Family Series

The Proposal | The Arrangement

Carmichael Family Series

Flirt | Fling | Fluke | Flaunt | Flame

Landry Family Series

Sway | Swing | Switch | Swear | Swink | Sweet

Landry Family Security Series

Pulse

Gibson Boys Series

Crank | Craft | Cross | Crave | Crazy

The Mason Family Series

Restraint | The Relationship Pact | Reputation | Reckless | Relentless | Resolution

The Marshall Family Series

More Than I Could | This Much Is True

The Exception Series

The Exception | The Perception

Dogwood Lane Series

Tumble | Tangle | Trouble

Standalone Novels

Sacrifice | Wherever It Leads | Written in the Scars | Lucky Number Eleven | Like You Love Me | The Sweet Spot | Nothing But It All | Between Now and Forever

For a complete reading order and more information, visit www.adrianalocke.com.

The Arrangement

Adriana Locke

The Arrangement

Cover Design: Kari March, www.karimarch.com
Photographer: Ren Saliba
Editor: Marion Archer, Marion Making Manuscripts
Editor: Jenny Sims, Editing 4 Indies
Proofreader: Michele Ficht

Created with Vellum

To Marion,
For always going above and beyond, and for your friendship. It means the world to me.

Cast of Characters

parents

Reid Brewer: divorced, in prison awaiting trial

Rory Brewer: divorced, putting her life back together

siblings

Gannon Brewer: President of Brewer Group

Jason Brewer: CEO of Brewer Air, former military/private security

Renn Brewer: [The Proposal] retired rugby player, married to Blakely

Ripley Brewer: exercise physiologist

Bianca Brewer: [Flame] former Interim President of Brewer Group, moved to Florida and married Foxx Carmichael

Tate Brewer: Director of Operations at Brewer Group

Synopsis

Synopsis

The gorgeous CEO of Brewer Air is my boss and, thanks to a bet, my new husband for six months.

Why? Because I begged.

I have a grandmother to support, a stack of bills higher than my five-foot frame, and as a cherry on top, I need to find a new place to live. *Soon.*

Sure, Jason Brewer's bright green eyes and chiseled jawline steal my breath. His smirk makes me weak. The former military hero's protective nature is as sexy as watching him control a boardroom or fly a plane.

But none of that matters. I'm desperate—not foolish. I know forever-level commitments aren't real. This is simply a business transaction with a billionaire.

It's too bad we didn't consider all contingencies.

Our first kiss was to seal the deal. The second was in front of an Elvis impersonator. The third kiss led to a honeymoon that was so hot it burned into my memory.

I tell myself it's okay because there's an arrangement in place. It's a—*very*—enjoyable means to a much-needed end. There's nothing to worry about.

Except there is ...

Jason is determined to prove that we could be more. When he proposes a new arrangement, it changes everything in ways I never saw coming.

Chapter 1

Chloe

"That'll teach you to lick my muffin!"

I hold the last crumb-topped blueberry muffin in the palm of my hand. "Do you really think that telling me you licked this will stop me from eating it?"

Nickie laughs, setting her coffee mug emblazoned with the Brewer Air logo on the corner of the table. "It should. I'd be grossed out if I ate a muffin that someone had slobbered all over."

"Did you have to say it like that?"

"Hey, I'm just telling it like it is," she says.

I sit in the break room, gazing out the window overlooking the putting green the Brewer executives installed last spring. It's a much better view than the picnic tables no one used that were there before—especially when the executives gather outside to shoot the shit.

The view is exceptional on those days.

"Listen, I live for Muffin Day," I say. "And I put a lot of work into securing this small piece of heaven. I'm not afraid of a little spit."

"*Ooh*. Sounds interesting. What are we talking about?" Jake from accounting stops beside us, stirring his coffee even though it's black. I only wish that was his most annoying trait. "Swapping stories? I have a few if you want a threesome."

He wiggles his brows as if we don't get the innuendo.

"Keep walking, Jake," I say, making my exasperation with his presence loud and clear.

He mutters something under his trademark garlicky breath and continues down the hall.

Nickie takes a seat across from me, grinning. "I can't tell if Jake fears or is infatuated with you. Something tells me his dreams start with you climbing naked on top of him and end with visions of knives."

"I have the same dream about him, minus the naked part."

I push all thoughts of Jake out of my mind and sink my teeth into the top of the sweet, fluffy muffin. I struggle not to moan.

Few things are better than gourmet baked goods—especially when they are entirely out of your budget. I can barely afford cheap ramen and tap water at the moment. Nothing, not even Nickie's threat that she licked my muffin, will stop me from enjoying it.

"How did you even get that thing?" she asks, watching me with amusement. "Weren't you in the morning meeting when the muffins were delivered?"

I hold the bundle of goodness to my nose and inhale the sweet aroma. *So, so good.*

"It's moments like this that I worry about you," she says.

I peel the wrapper away from the side. "Yeah, I was in the meeting. But I slipped out at precisely ten after nine and intercepted an unsuspecting Wendy as she carried the Rolling Scones box from the front desk. I swiped the biggest muffin, hid it in the cabinet under the coffee pot, and returned to the conference room, no one the wiser."

"You have it timed that perfectly?"

"Nickie, this blueberry muffin is the highlight of my week."

"That's sad."

"You're telling me."

I take a giant bite, lifting a brow in response to her perfectly arched one.

My life is hard for Nickie Kennedy to comprehend. But I get it. It's a series of unfortunate events over here. And for someone like Nickie, who leads a very full, charmed existence, imagining that someone could look forward to a muffin must be baffling. It probably seems exaggerated—like I'm making it up for a laugh.

But it's the truth.

I'm this pathetic.

"What was the meeting about, anyway?" She dusts a strand of red hair off her shoulder. "It looked tense."

"I don't know. It probably was. A lot of scowls were worn today."

She laughs. "What do you mean *it probably was*?"

"Jason had two of his brothers with him."

"*Oh*. Which two?"

"Gannon and Tate, and they were oozing alpha male vibes. The Brewer Trifecta of Power was in there, and concentrating on anything besides them was rather difficult."

"Well, that explains why half our department milled around all morning instead of logging invoices. They were trying to get a glimpse of *The Trifecta*."

I poke at a blueberry. "I will admit, *The Trifecta* is a bonus of working here. I came for the paycheck. I stay for the view."

"As we all do. But you ducked out on the view for a muffin. That says a lot about you."

I laugh. "That says Tate's analogies were boring, and my stomach growled. Remedying hunger and saving myself from mental anguish comes first on the hierarchy of needs. That's true even if the view is spectacular. Tate is gorgeous ... when his mouth is shut."

She shakes her head as if I'm ridiculous and watches me savor what's left of my breakfast.

The Brewer men, all five brothers, are the most stunning family in the universe, and no one will convince me otherwise. Even their sister and mother are beautiful. But one of them outshines them all—my boss, Jason.

Jason, the CEO of Brewer Air, is arguably the most attractive man of all time. Sandy-blond hair. Bright green eyes. High forehead, strong brow, and solid jaw. He's remarkably intelligent, a powerhouse in every right, and confident yet somehow not arrogant. Getting to know him takes some effort, but Jason is a lot of fun once you do.

And I think about the fun part. *A lot.*

"Speaking of things that say a lot about you," she says, resting her chin in her palm. "Did you call Bodhi back?"

"*No, I didn't call Bodhi back.*" I mock her, earning a roll of her eyes. "I told you I wasn't calling him back when he asked for my number."

"Look, I get that he is a busboy at twenty-five, but he has potential. And with all the running around he was doing during the lunch rush, his stamina must be great."

"My failure to return his call has nothing to do with his place of employment. Actually, I like the idea that he's out there hustling his ass off."

"Then what's the problem?"

I sigh, sitting back in my chair. Nickie sighs right back.

We have this conversation at least once a week. My friend has decided that I cannot possibly be happy and live a fulfilling life without a man. She's projecting. I've known her for three years—we started work at Brewer Air the same day—and I've never known her to go more than a week without a boyfriend.

On the other hand, I just passed the six-month mark of complete singledom. The guy before that wasn't exactly a winner, but he did get the important job done. Mostly. I did learn to fake orgasms throughout that experience, which is a silver lining. I think.

"What will you do?" she asks, sounding like a broken record. "Stay single forever?"

"I think my relationship status bothers you a whole lot more than it bothers me, Nick."

She leans forward, resting her elbows on the table. "Someone has to worry about you getting laid, and if that someone has to be me, then so be it."

Jake appears out of nowhere, opening his mouth to interject an unwanted comment into our discussion. The mere thought of Jake getting laid makes my stomach lurch.

"Keep walking, Jake," I say again.

His head falls forward, and he scoots off toward his office.

"Your relationship status should bother you more. Forever is a long time, Chloe." Nickie doesn't miss a beat.

I cram the rest of the muffin in my mouth.

"That's ladylike," she teases. "Go out this weekend and swallow like that at the bar. You won't be single for long."

I laugh, nearly choking on the last bit of blueberry muffin. "*Stop it.*"

"No, I won't stop it until I'm satisfied that you remember that you're a whole person who deserves love and affection and a big hard cock."

I wipe the corner of my eye with a napkin and try to rein in my laughter.

"Do you have a secret boyfriend?" she asks, crossing her arms over her chest. "I'm starting to think you do. It's the only answer that makes sense."

"Trust me. If I had a boyfriend, you'd be the first person to know, so you'd shut up about it."

She nods, smiling in satisfaction.

It's easier with Nickie to pretend I'm not interested in dating at all. I once made the mistake of being open to the idea, and she came to work the following morning with a photo album on her phone filled with men she thought might be a good match for me. That morning, I learned that Nickie is a one-woman matchmaking company. She memorized their bios and statistics and rattled them off like a game show host.

It was as impressive as it was alarming.

But the truth is that I'm not anti-dating. I'm anti-relationship. *Anti-marriage.* When coupled with the fact that I only attract men who I'm not interested in and that I have zero free time thanks to a mountain of debt that'll wind up crushing me at some point—my life is lonely.

I'd rather it be lonely than miserable.

"You have to make time for what's important to you," she says.

I hold up the muffin wrapper and grin. "I made time for this little nugget today, didn't I?"

She groans, making me laugh.

"Look, my neighbor's grandson is coming to town this week," I say. "Thomas and I have a little friends-with-benefits thing going on, which will hold me over for a while. It's the best I can do."

"That's absolutely *not* the best you can do."

"Even if I wanted to meet someone—which I don't—there's no time. During the week, by the time I get home, I've been gone ten hours, and I've started picking up shifts at Fika's if someone calls off in the evenings. I also need to spend time with Mimi since she's alone at our apartment all day—which I feel terrible about, by the way. I barely have time to bathe and sleep, and I feel guilty when I do that."

"Feeling guilty for taking care of yourself is ridiculous."

I shrug. "I'm struggling right now thanks to a crap ton of debt, sky-high rent, and trying to keep Mimi out of a nursing home—all while managing not to get offed by the nasty guy on the first floor of my apartment building." I pause while Nickie glares at me. "But my life is built on a precarious set of needs that must be met, and mine must be last right now. And that's okay. It won't always be this way."

"I told you the Pliny Building wasn't safe."

"And I told you the Pliny Building is cheap. Get over it."

"What does the cost matter if you wind up dead?"

"Listen," I say, "choices were made. I could starve to death and live somewhere nicer or take my chances with the guy in 1B." The memory of the slimy prick who lives conveniently by the exit, so I must pass him every time I leave the apartment, makes me shiver.

"Getting whacked is faster and less depressing, and at least I'd go out on a full stomach."

She makes a face. "That's not funny."

I chuckle, tossing the muffin wrapper on the table. "Relax. I'm kidding." *Kind of.*

She blows out a breath, wanting to cling to this conversation. But the look on my face must convince her otherwise.

"I was asking about the meeting this morning because of the gossip going around the building today," she says. "Did you hear the rumors?"

"I generally try to avoid them."

"Well, you might want to hear this one."

I lift a brow.

"The word in accounting is that we're downsizing, and they're going to eliminate a bunch of positions soon," she says, her eyes wide. "Everyone is panicking. And since you're Jason Brewer's executive assistant, I thought maybe you had a little insight you could share with your work bestie."

"You know I'm under a nondisclosure agreement."

"Yeah, but there are ways you can tell me without telling me. For example, blink one for *yes* and two for *no*."

"No," I say, laughing.

"*No,* as in we aren't downsizing, or *no,* as in you're a terrible friend?"

"I can't tell you anything for certain, but you know how rumors go."

"Don't you worry something will go wrong, and we'll all be jobless?" Nickie asks.

"In theory, of course. But over this? No."

She stands, smoothing out her skirt. "Walter asked me to give him my stapler this morning. It feels like a sign. *Give me your stapler because you won't need it—you're out of here.* I almost fought him over it, as if possessing office supplies is nine-tenths of employment law."

I laugh.

"He's an asshole. He orders me around like I'm a peon. You should've heard how he ordered me to give him my stapler." She pauses dramatically. "That's a problem for me. *Ask, don't order.* I don't want to give him anything now—not my time, my skills, or my fucking stapler."

"Sucks to be you." I grin. "I'd give Jason Brewer whatever he wants."

Someone clears their throat behind Nickie. I groan, sure that it's Jake in another attempt at weaseling his way into our conversation. I peer around my friend to send him on his way for a third time but stop.

My irritation fades as my lips part with a one-liner and my gaze focuses on the man in the doorway.

And my embarrassment grows.

It's not Jake.

Jason stands in the break room entrance like he's been there a while ... long enough to have heard my seven-word sentence.

His sandy-blond hair is sun-kissed to perfection. It's styled back off his chiseled face, giving me a better view of his bright green eyes and thick, heavy brows pulled together as he watches me ... and smirks.

"I'd give Jason Brewer whatever he wants."

Dark dress pants fit his muscular thighs. A thin brown belt cinches his narrow waist. A crisp white shirt is cuffed at his elbows, displaying the ends of the tattoos etched into his upper arms that peek out the bottom of the sleeves.

My God.

I melt in front of him in a mix of surprise, concupiscence, and deep, *deep* mortification from being overheard.

Nickie fights a laugh. "I'll talk to you later, Chloe." She turns for the door, smiling cheekily. "Good morning, Mr. Brewer. How are you today?"

He nods, never taking his eyes off me. "It's been an interesting day so far."

She laughs. "So it has. Have a good one."

"You too," he says, crossing one ankle over the other. His lips twist in amusement.

"*So*," I say once my traitorous friend abandons me and leaves the two of us alone. Despite the look in his eyes, I try to exude cool, calm confidence. "How long were you standing there?"

He holds my gaze for a moment, then two. Finally, he presses away from the doorway.

"Chloe, may I see you in my office for a moment?"

Shit.

Chapter 2

Chloe

T*hree ... Four ... Five ... Six ...*

The elevator dings, and the doors open to the executive level.

A rush of sandalwood-scented air floats into the lift and guides me onto dark hardwood. An oversized desk anchors the space, and a copper-colored airplane hangs from the ceiling by an invisible wire. It's classy with a touch of fun.

"Did you get your muffin?" Brandi asks from behind the desk.

"Is that a serious question?"

She laughs. "Jason came up a few seconds ago and said not to let you get distracted. You're to go straight to his office."

"I'll take that under advisement."

Her eyes sparkle as she settles against her seat, awaiting the next move in my latest situation involving my boss. Our back-and-forth amuses Brandi. It amuses me, too.

Jason and I met the summer I turned seven. My parents had just divorced, and my mother began housekeeping for Jason's mother, Rory. Rory was kind enough to allow Mom to bring me with her. I spent those long, sunny days romping through the vast Brewer property with the two youngest kids, Bianca and Tate.

It was the best summer of my life—especially one scorching July afternoon.

Tate was making me pitch a baseball to him in a grassy area next to the pool. My arm was getting sore, but I wasn't about to complain. I wound up, launched the baseball at the makeshift plate, and stepped on a bee.

I screamed bloody murder.

Then, out of nowhere, one of Tate's older brothers scooped me up in his muscled arms and carried me like a princess into the kitchen. Through my tears, I committed everything about Jason to memory—the scent of his sweat, the kindness in his eyes, and how safe I felt with him. He was my hero, and I've been slightly smitten with him ever since.

I tap my raggedy fingernails against Brandi's desktop. "What are the odds that I could get you to lie to him for me? Tell him I had to go to HR for an emergency. Or that I got up here and got violently sick and had to head home for the greater good of humankind?"

"What in the world did you do this time?"

I grimace at the memory. "Can't tell you. But rest assured, it was something I'll have regret dreams about for the rest of my life—"

A buzzing sound cuts me off. Brandi snickers as she pushes the speakerphone button.

"Yes, Mr. Brewer?" she says.

"Don't tell him I'm here," I whisper.

"Did I just hear Chloe?" he asks.

My eyes go wide. "What the hell? Do I not have any privacy today?"

"Get back here," he says.

His tone is firm and rough. Yet a hint of mischievousness is embedded in the words, making me smile—and raising my temperature.

"*Yes, sir*," I say sweetly, turning toward the hallway leading to his office. I'm stopped by a tissue being thrust at my side.

Brandi hits a button, and Jason's call is disconnected.

"Wipe your mouth. You have a tiny blue stain in the corner right there." She touches the side of her lip. "I can't let you go back there looking like you sucked off a cartoon character."

I take the tissue from her. "This is why you get paid the big bucks."

"Sure." She laughs, holding out a small wastepaper basket. "You can repay me by telling me what this is all about."

I drop the tissue in the trash and head down the corridor. "I can't do that. Think the worst, and you're probably on track."

"You're no fun."

Jason's oversized door looms ahead. But instead of going straight to the end of the hall, I make a slight detour and stop in my office. Jason is silent on the other side of the wall connecting our spaces.

I flip on the light and pull a mirror from my desk. I'm ready to see him after a quick once-over and a fresh coat of lip gloss.

A pulse of excitement races through my veins. It doesn't matter that I've worked for Brewer Air for three years, spent seven months as his EA, and have known him most of my life—or that I consider him as much a friend as I do my boss. There's no real way to prepare for those green eyes and sexy smile.

I smooth my dress, straighten my powder-pink cardigan, and set my shoulders back.

Here goes nothing ...

"You wanted to see me?" I ask, swinging our adjoining door open without so much as a knock.

He leans against a wide desk crafted from the same dark wood as Brandi's, with one arm crossed over his thick chest. The other hand reaches his mouth, his thumb feathering against his lips as he waits for me to approach him.

My God, he's handsome.

His expression is controlled and unreadable. It's a game he plays. He tries to throw me off with his aloofness.

He should know by now that it won't work on me.

"You're already getting on my nerves today," I say.

This earns me a slight, crooked grin.

"Nickie says there's a rumor that we're preparing for a layoff," I say, moving across his office to the windows overlooking Nashville. "I assured her it was just gossip."

"I heard."

I look at him over my shoulder. "You heard the gossip?"

"No, I heard you telling her it was gossip."

"Eavesdropping is a nasty habit, Mr. Brewer."

He smiles cheekily. "So is telling your coworkers you would do *anything* for your boss."

My core melts as I absorb the heat in his eyes.

"Is that what you think I said?" I ask, lifting a brow. "Because I think you're hearing what you want to hear."

"Are you saying you wouldn't do anything I asked?"

I grin. "Are you saying that's not what you want to hear?"

The air thickens as we let the tension settle around us.

Our relationship is unusual, but it works. Sure, working so closely with an old friend that I'm crazily attracted to has its drawbacks. I'm jealous when women flirt with him. I worry about his well-being. And I've considered packing an extra set of panties in my purse for the days he wears my favorite black suit and tie.

But it also has its perks. I know Jason well enough to anticipate his needs. We trust one another, which provides a more relaxed working environment. And Jason and I communicate effortlessly, respect one another, and value the same things.

We might flirt in private for fun, but when it's time to work, no one is more productive and efficient as us.

I glance over my shoulder into my adjoining office as Brandi sets a vase of flowers on my desk. The burst of color looks pretty next to the iced coffee Jason brought me this morning, although I have no idea who they're from. So I make a beeline for her.

"Are those for me?" I ask.

"Yes. Wendy just sent them up from the front desk," she says. "They're freaking gorgeous, Chloe. Who are they from?"

"I have no idea."

She peers around me, then speaks in a hushed tone. "Do these have anything to do with why you were summoned to Jason's office?"

I laugh out loud. "Definitely not."

"Well, they smell amazing. Enjoy them," she says before disappearing around the corner.

Orange and pink roses, yellow carnations, and bright greenery fill a small, square vase. I find the card nestled in the petals and pull it out.

Friday at seven. See you then.
Thomas

Thomas? I roll my eyes but mentally applaud the effort.

"Who are those from?" Jason startles me.

I turn to find him leaning against the doorframe between our offices. He's trying to appear nonplussed, but I see through the facade. He's annoyed. *Good.*

"It's none of your business," I say, grinning at him.

He steps out of the doorway, motioning with his arm for me to return to his office. He snatches the card from my hand before I get past him.

"*Hey,*" I protest, although I don't try to retrieve it from his palm. The invasion of my privacy is worth his reaction.

The darkness sweeping over his features pulls at a knot in my stomach, releasing a burst of hormones to flood my system. I imagine him grabbing me and shoving me against a wall, his eyes burning into mine. His fingers biting into my flesh as he lifts my shirt—

"Who is Thomas?" he asks, interrupting my fantasy.

"A friend."

His jaw sets as he looks up, narrowing his eyes at me. "What's Friday at seven?"

I narrow my eyes back but fail to remove the puckish smile from my face. "What do you think is Friday at seven?"

"I thought you weren't dating."

"No one said anything about dating, Jason."

He takes a deep breath, his fingers flexing around the thin paper, then marches back to his desk.

I quickly gather my wits and move as confidently across the office. My heart thumps with each step I take. His voice is liquid fire as his words ring through my mind. *"I thought you weren't dating."*

I try to hide my grin. *This is way more fun than Thomas is going to be.*

"Can I have the card back?" I ask, stretching my hand across his desk.

He makes no move to return it. Instead, he deliberately places it beside his phone. Then he sits down and rocks back in his chair, daring me to take it.

"I didn't think you were seeing anyone," he says, resting his chin on steepled fingers.

"I'm not seeing anyone." I grab the card before he can stop me and then sit across from him. "But just because I don't want to date anyone doesn't mean I don't have needs."

"And Thomas meets those needs?"

"He's going to on Friday."

I smirk. Jason is unamused.

"Did you decide whether to draft a contract to Rigglen Aeronautics?" I ask, circling back to a safer topic—work. "Jerry Rigglen calls me daily, and I promised him an answer this week."

"You would know if we were drafting a contract to Rigglen if you hadn't snuck out of the conference room this morning."

"I had something to take care of."

He hums, eyeing me suspiciously. "Should I find it coincidental that my EA slipped out of a meeting at the same time the morning pastries arrived?"

I smile. "No, because that's exactly what I was doing—and I'm not sorry. I had a morning from hell, and I needed a little pick-me-up."

"Why was this morning so bad?" His features shift immediately, switching to genuine concern in a snap. "Did something happen?"

My heart softens as I stare into his flecks of jade.

I consider telling him about Mimi's recent falls—like the nasty one this morning—and how I'm scared she's declining quicker than I anticipated. I think about sharing that I don't think I'll ever get on top of my bills. I nearly explain that down deep, in the darkest hours of the night, I fear that every choice I've ever made is wrong, and I'll regret it all at some point in my life.

Jason would be empathetic, jump into action, and try to help me. And sharing my reality with him would be a relief. I have few friends and no family beyond Mimi, so being honest with him would be nice.

That's precisely why I don't say a word.

At Brewer Air, I'm not the girl living in one of Nashville's shittiest neighborhoods. My circumstances don't color my coworkers' perception of me because no one besides Nickie knows them—and she knows only the bits and pieces I choose to share with her.

I'm a normal twenty-five-year-old woman with everyday problems at work. And I want to keep it that way.

I don't need pity or a knight in shining armor. I need to figure out a way to solve my problems myself.

"Tate's analogies almost killed me," I say instead. "That's what happened this morning. I adore your brother, but his analogies are horrendous."

Jason sits back, watching me curiously—not quite believing my about-face.

"If you aren't a golfer, the terminology doesn't translate," I say, talking fast to distract him. "It took me too long to realize that a caddie wasn't a Cadillac. He said the caddie was carrying his clubs, and I sat there trying to figure out why he didn't just use a golf cart. Then I started wondering what kind of Cadillac, and I started humming this song about a Cadillac ranch my mom used to listen to when I was a child."

"I'll talk with Tate and tell him to ease up on the analogies."

"On behalf of the staff that were present, *thank you*." I lick my lips, needing to fill the void and control the conversation before he digs deeper into my morning. "Did you beckon me to your office to discuss Tate's analogies, or can I return to work? I need to confirm a few appointments for next week and follow up with Gannon's office about using one of our jets for meetings in New York on the fifteenth."

"Can we accommodate that?"

"Yes. I had to shuffle a few things around, but we made it happen. Also, while I have you, Ford Landry moved your call from two this afternoon until the day after tomorrow, and I scheduled a massage for you at home tonight at seven."

He looks at the ceiling and sighs. "I don't need a fucking massage."

"*Yes, you fucking do*. You've had a headache all week."

He focuses his attention on me again. "How do you know?"

"Because you've had a bottle of acetaminophen on the corner of your desk since Monday, and you've been more difficult than usual."

His gaze softens, going from slight irritation to unguarded ease in seconds. I watch as his shoulders fall and the lines across his forehead relax. A small smile ghosts his lips.

"I'm sorry if I've been difficult," he says. "I don't mean to be."

I stand, fighting a smile. *He really is such a good man*. "I know you don't. And you haven't been *that bad*. I've seen you much grumpier."

"Yet you still work for me."

"It will take a lot more than you being grumpy to make me leave." I wink at him and turn to my office. "I need an answer on Rigglen. Today, if possible."

He doesn't reply. So I pause with a hand on the doorframe and look at him over my shoulder. He's watching me curiously, as if uncertain what to say.

"What?" I ask.

"I'm the boss around here. But when I'm with you? I question it."

"Smart man." I smile at him. "You have a call in ten minutes with Towlin. Don't forget."

I hold my breath, anticipating Jason's grimace—my heart hurting for him. Calls with his attorney always increase his stress, and I hate adding them to his calendar.

"Thanks," he says, sighing. "What are you working on this afternoon?"

There are a hundred things I need to do this afternoon, and I could rattle them off with ease. But if I do that, Jason will start worrying about it all. Instead, I decide to tease him and take his mind off his problems for one more moment.

"The first thing I'm going to do is thank Thomas," I say, grinning.

"Not on my fucking clock."

I giggle and swing the door closed.

"I mean it, Chloe," he says, the words sneaking in before the latch shuts.

My giggle turns into laughter as I toss the card on my desk.

I will get more enjoyment out of jealous Jason this week than with try-hard Thomas this weekend. And if things were different—if I wasn't working for Jason and actually believed in happy endings—I could get a lot more enjoyment out of Mr. Brewer.

But that's not life. I've learned that the hard way. Life is the opposite of what they dangle in front of you in the movies. Sure, it has happy moments and good things, but the ending always looks more like a drama than a fairy tale.

The only happy ending I'm going to get out of Jason, or anyone else, will happen in my dreams.

Chapter 3

Jason

I wait for the thud of Chloe's door closing before I lean back and expel the air from my lungs.

That woman is going to be the death of me.

I massage my temples as the recurring pain I've been fighting rears its head again. A massage sounds fantastic, and the fact that Chloe noticed I needed one—and went ahead and scheduled it—is par for the course. It's also one of the things I love most about her.

One of the many things.

When we met, she was a child. I vaguely remember her tromping around the house with my youngest siblings. I left home when I turned eighteen, heading to college and then the military—anything to avoid living in the same house as my father. I didn't see Chloe again until we met at a coffee shop four years ago. I don't like coffee but was there to get my mother a drink. Yet after seeing Chloe there? I've been there every day since.

For a solid year, we were coffee buddies during the week and eventually expanded it to coffee shop breakfasts on the weekends. I looked forward to her stories much more than the black coffee I ordered so I'd have something to hold. She was playful and witty. So freaking funny. And her curves? *Holy fuck.*

But she'd had a boyfriend and been completely off-limits.

We became such good friends, and even though I'd wanted her then, I accepted our friendship for what it was. If buying her a coffee and listening to her rambles was the only way I could spend time with her, then I'd take it.

Twelve months after we met, she mentioned off-handedly that she needed a job. I offered her a spot at Brewer Air before I realized what was happening. She was the executive receptionist until my EA position opened. Having watched how meticulously and professionally Chloe handled the receptionist role and how she often went above and beyond her responsibilities, I knew she'd be an excellent fit as my new EA. I wasted no time moving her into my adjoining office and promoting Brandi to take her place.

I still haven't decided whether that was my life's best or worst decision.

"Jason?" Chloe says after a short beep. "I have Mr. Towlin on the line for you."

I heave a breath and sit up, pressing the speakerphone button. "Send the call through."

The line beeps as the call connects.

"This is Jason," I say, still massaging the side of my head.

"Good afternoon. How are you today?"

We exchange pleasantries, something I find utterly ridiculous at this stage of the game. Nothing is pleasant about discussing your father's felonies, upcoming trials, and how you will shield your family from it all.

"All right," Towlin says, sighing into the phone. "I have a few things to go over with you."

I take a quick, irritated glance at the clock. "Let's do it."

"Okay. I'll start with the bad news first. I met with someone in the prosecutor's office this morning, and it appears your father is waffling on the plea deal."

I shove away from my desk. "*What*? What do you mean he's waffling on the plea deal?"

"They're still working on it, but the defense now wants less prison time and more time in home confinement."

"The prosecutor can't be considering this."

"It's a work in progress."

I stand and pace the room. Memories of the day my father showed his true evil side flood my mind at warp speed.

Mom's screams as I walked into her house. Her image on the security cameras, kneeling in front of a man with a gun pressed against her temple. Our father's voice booming through the man's phone. Bianca in the background, pleading with Dad to stop as he threatened to have Mom's brains splattered across the living room—and threatening to do the same to my sister's.

My stomach recoils.

Grabbing the assailant from behind.

Shots fired.

The gun sliding across the room.

Fists flying. Foxx Carmichael shouting through the phone as Bianca's sobs grow louder.

Holding my mother in my arms.

Watching a man bleed on the floor, begging me to end his life. Choosing to make him live and suffer the consequences of his actions.

I heave a breath, steadying myself as adrenaline pounds through me.

"I understand your frustration," Towlin says.

"Do you, though?" I stop pacing and stare at the phone. "If this thing goes to trial, my mother and sister will be called to testify. They'll have to relive the day their husband and father tried to murder them. The defense will try to humiliate and vilify them in the media. They don't deserve that."

"Let's also remember they'll do the same to you."

"I could give a fuck about me."

"Yes, I realize that, Jason. But as your attorney, *I* give a fuck about you. Your family does, too. On that note, let me remind you to keep your head on straight until this is resolved."

I glance up at a knock on my door. Tate comes through with a joke on his tongue, but he swallows it once he reads my face.

"You might warn your siblings to keep things a little tighter to the vest. Ensure your employees have strict nondisclosure agreements. Just be smart. Remember, the more they have on you, the more they can muddy the waters. And the muddier the waters, the more likely your father could walk. It's highly unlikely, but we can't risk it. His attorneys have pulled off wilder stunts in the past."

My hand wraps around the back of my neck as I watch Tate close the door behind him.

"If Dad walks, I'll kill him," I say, my eyes glued to my brother. "I will wrap my hands around his throat and squeeze until the last breath leaves his body, and I'll smile the whole fucking time."

Tate's lips press into a thin line as he nods.

"Don't tell me that," Towlin says with a nervous chuckle. "Let's stay focused on getting him locked up like he deserves."

"Anything else?"

"That's enough for today. I'll call you as soon as I have an update."

"Thanks."

"Goodbye."

Tate reaches across my desk and ends the call for me. "It never gets less shocking to recall that your father tried to kill your family." He eyes me warily. "You doing okay, Jase?"

"Yeah, I'm fine." My teeth grind together. "Is it bad that I wish Foxx would've killed Dad? Just put a bullet between his eyes and ended all of this?"

"I'm pretty sure if you put in a request, Foxx could still make it happen."

I grin because he's right. Foxx could make it happen.

Foxx and I met years ago while working private security for a man named Fenton Abbott, who specialized in overseas operations. We were a lot alike—driven and fairly quiet—and we both came from large families where we didn't quite fit the mold. We became fast friends, especially for men who didn't court friendships.

He's the smartest and most capable person I've ever met. He's my best friend and, thanks to Bianca, my brother-in-law.

"What did Towlin have to say?" Tate asks. "Why were you discussing Dad walking? Isn't he taking a plea deal?"

I run a hand down my face, wishing I could shield my family from this—wishing I would've seen the signs and prevented it all from happening in the first place.

"Apparently, our father is considering turning the deal down," I say, watching Tate's eyes widen ever so slightly. "But it'll be fine. We all need to stay on our toes, avoid doing anything stupid, and trust the process."

Even though I don't.

Tate frowns but nods as if he believes me—like he knows it'll be fine ... because I said so. *Oof.*

"So what's going on?" I ask, ready to move on from the topic at hand. "I thought you were going to Gannon's office?"

"I was until I heard Renn is headed that way." He sits in the chair across from my desk. "Have you talked to him today by any chance?"

I sit and stare at my brother. His question is normal, but his hint of concern is not.

Whatever is happening with Renn, I'm going to hate it. I'm sure of it.

"I'll take that as a no," Tate says, moving around in his seat.

"What's happening?"

"Oh, not much. Renn just wants to talk to you and Gannon about buying the Tennessee Royals."

What? "Renn wants to buy the Royals?"

"Yup."

"He wants to buy a *rugby franchise*?"

"Yup."

I groan. "This is the epitome of a bad idea in so many ways. Towlin *just* told me not to make any waves until the trial ends, and Renn wants to buy the Royals. *Wow.*"

"In Renn's defense, he doesn't know Towlin said that."

"Oh, for fuck's sake," I mutter, blowing out a breath. "Renn's a smart guy. He witnessed the disaster surrounding the purchase of the Arrows. Why would he think we need to duplicate all of that now?" *Fucking Renn.* I pace my office again. "Has he even been retired a year? And he hates the Royals' management. They're the reason he retired in the first place. So why would he want to buy it? It makes no sense."

"I mean, if we buy it, we could fire the current management. That would be one problem solved."

"One problem solved while we take on an endless number of others."

Tate shrugs.

This is ridiculous. We have no business buying another sports team, not when our hands are full with the Arrows *and* our hockey franchise.

I scratch the top of my head.

"Come on, Jase. You had to have seen this coming."

No, I didn't ... but I probably should have.

I should've known you can't take a man out while he's at the top of his game and give him nothing to do. Idle hands being the devil's playthings and all. Renn has always been able to find mischief, even if his hands are full.

"Can he put it off for a while? A year?" I ask, groaning. "Maybe two?"

Tate shrugs again.

"Gannon will probably love this. *It's good to diversify,*" I say, mocking our eldest brother's inevitable tone. "Why do I feel like I'll be the only holdout?"

"Because, my guy, you will. I'm with Gannon. I think it's smart to show our investors—and the world—that we're united. That it's business as usual over here."

Dammit.

"Strength garners support," he continues. "Everyone wants to support the strongest. And it's a whole hell of a lot better to walk into a room with everyone talking about your business deals than have them talking about your father's transgressions. That's what they'll remember at the end of the day."

"True." I run a hand down my face. "I hate it when you make sense."

His brows pull together, studying me. "What's wrong?"

"Nothing. I'm just ... tense. I've had a headache for a week."

He stands, yawning. "Me, too."

"You're probably just tired from chasing women all weekend. We are not the same."

He lifts his chin and grins. "You underestimate me."

"Oh, really?"

"Really. But that's an expected take from someone so old," he says, heading for the door. "I'm going to grab another coffee from your break room. It's infinitely better than ours because Gannon is cheap, and then get back to work. I'm heading to San Antonio tomorrow to smooth things with a few Arrows investors. It's a good thing I like golf." He pulls the door open. "I've golfed so much the past six months that I swing in my sleep."

"Must suck to be you."

He winks. "It never sucks to be me. I'll talk to you later."

"Bye, Tate."

I wait until the door latches before I blow out a breath. Then I sink back into my chair and try to sort through my thoughts. But instead of thinking about my conversation with Towlin, Renn's impending proposal, or the hundred calls I need to make, I let my mind flow elsewhere ... to the one place it goes when I need to decompress.

To Chloe.

"I'd give Jason Brewer whatever he wants."

A smile immediately splits my cheeks. Because no matter how shitty or stressful of a day I'm having, Chloe makes it better.

The past three years with her in my office and the past seven months with her as my EA have been the best of my professional life—despite my family drama nearly paralyzing my personal one. Knowing Chloe is here, waiting for her iced coffee and ready to support me through the day, is a relief. It gets me up in the morning.

It's also my last thought most nights before bed.

I didn't give much attention to settling down before all this shit happened with Dad. There wasn't a gaping hole in my life that needed to be filled. I traveled, explored, and did my own thing on my own time—and I liked it that way. Autonomy equaled peace.

But I've started reassessing things.

Dad's failures required us all to step up and work together. We rely on each other like never before. Our bond is tight, our relationships are valued, and I can't fathom going back to only talking to my siblings once a month.

Unbeknownst to me, I've become a man who doesn't feel burdened by family obligations. I don't feel the need to make something of myself. For the first time in my life, my role in the family is clear, and I'm comfortable there.

Maybe autonomy isn't vital to my happiness. The inner tug-of-war I experience daily isn't my gut telling me to retract from others. It just might be telling me to lean into it.

To start a family of my own.

But therein lies the problem. The only woman I can imagine in my world every day is Chloe.

And that can't happen.

Not only would I never risk our friendship and working relationship, but she and I don't want the same things. She's young and beautiful—and at the age to have fun and discover what she wants from life. That isn't a man ten years her senior who's eyeing marriage and children in the near future.

How do I know? She's said so.

And that fucking sucks because I'd give Chloe Goodman whatever *she* wants.

And that's not me.

Chapter 4

Chloe

I shove the key into the lock and rattle it around a few times. It takes a certain finesse—a jiggle to the right while lifting the knob until it's pointing at my boobs—to free the door. It swings open like it's waited all day for the opportunity.

"Chloe? Honey? Is that you?"

Mimi's voice travels through the small apartment. It's weaker than I'd like it to be. But the fact that I can still hear it, that she's still here—both alive and at home with me—is a blessing. It's a blessing I don't take for granted.

"It's me," I say, locking up behind me. "I'll be right there."

I slip off my shoes and set my bag and keys on top of an old dresser I refurbished from a salvage store. After some elbow grease and tender loving care, the piece of furniture doesn't look as good as new, but it gets the job done. And I'm pretty freaking proud of it.

"How do you feel?" I ask, coming around the corner.

Mimi looks up from her soap opera and smiles. There's a cut on her forehead from her fall in the bathroom this morning. The immediate area surrounding the burgundy line is turning a nasty shade of purple and her hair has seen better days. Out of all the damage from this morning's incident, the hair would bother her the most if she could see it.

The two-bedroom, one-bathroom apartment is ... humble. The paper-thin walls are peach, but I'm pretty sure they were white at some point in the distant past. The brown floor would've been an odd choice in any era, but the yellow appliances are straight from the seventies. That they work—most of the time—is a small miracle.

The biggest issue I have with this unit is the bathroom tile. They're uneven, and a few are broken. Mimi has fallen three times since we moved in a year ago, each incident ending a little worse. I'm scared shitless there will be a fourth time ... and what that might look like.

"Let me see you," I say, reaching for her chin.

She swats my hand away like a toddler. "I'm fine. I told you that this morning."

"Your head says differently."

"I've kept ice on it most of the day," she says. "Greta has come by every couple of hours and checked on me, swapping out my cold compress." She rummages on the table beside her until she finds an ice pack shaped like a heart. "She brought this about an hour ago. Before that, I was using a pack of frozen carrots."

I laugh, kissing the top of her head and sitting on the couch beside her. "Your color is back in your face. That's good."

She tosses the heart down on top of a crossword puzzle book. "I feel fine, Chloe. You act like I jumped off the Grand Canyon. It was a little stumble. No biggity."

"No biggity, huh?"

"Yes. That's right. No biggity, boo." She wiggles her shoulders and makes a kissy face.

I snort so hard it hurts. "No biggity? What's that mean?"

"You were listening to it the other night. *No biggity. No doubt. Boo.*"

I try not to laugh, but I can't help it. I let loose a flurry of giggles.

She settles back in her recliner, grimacing as she gets comfortable. "I really am okay. Just a bit sore."

"How did it go with Greta?" I ask, knowing Mimi isn't a huge fan of our nosy neighbor whose grandson sent me the gorgeous flowers I left on my desk.

"She was her typical cheery, lovely self," Mimi says, rolling her eyes. "We played cards a little while this afternoon, and she told me about how you and Thomas would make a great couple."

"No." I shake my head, resolute that Mimi will not find out I occasionally bang Thomas. "I'm not dating. You know that."

"I agree that you aren't dating Thomas. You can do better. But I do think you should let me set you up with Sherry's grandson. We talk about it all the time on Social. You'd make the cutest couple."

"No blind dates, Meems. We tried that once before, and the guy you hooked me up with wound up puking off my roof at three in the morning. I'm still not sure how he got up there in the first place."

She laughs. "He was singing love ballads in your honor. How mad can you get?"

"Very! He woke up the whole neighborhood with a terrible rendition of 'Always.' He wasn't exactly a Romeo, but we almost saw his blood when he slipped on his puke and almost fell off the house."

Her face lights up. "He was cute, you must admit. And he was *spi-cy*. I guarantee you would've had a more exciting time with him than you did with that last dud you had. What was his name? Harrison?"

Her ability to recall names might be rusty, but her instincts haven't faded a bit.

If there's one thing you can't get past my grandmother, it's a bad character. She can sniff out an asshole from a block over. I should've listened to her when she warned me that Harrison was a bad seed, but in my defense, he did have great shoulders.

When he broke up with me, I told Mimi that I caught him with his physical therapist even though that wasn't true. I didn't have the heart to tell her that Harrison made me choose between them. He was tired of me giving so much time to Mimi.

Mimi was right. He was a dud.

She shrugs and affixes her attention back to the television. "I guess Harrison was spicy too. He just got his spice on with the physical therapist, not you."

My jaw drops. "*Mimi.* That's not nice."

"Honey, what do you expect me to say?" She lifts her slightly bruised chin. "That's the best damn thing that man ever did for you. What would've happened if you hadn't walked in on them?" She jams a bony finger my way. "You would've married him. That's what you would've done. Better know now than regret later."

"I wouldn't have married him. We weren't even seriously dating. And you could be a little softer with your opinions. That delivery was harsh."

She rests her head against the chair. "How was work, sweetheart?"

"Oh!" I spring off the couch. "Hang on."

"I'm hanging ..."

I return to the entryway and grab a white paper bag from my things.

Greta called me a couple of hours ago and said that Mimi was doing better, but her spirits were a little down after her accident this morning. She tried to have fun with my grandmother and take her mind off things, but she sensed that Mimi's loss of mobility and independence was starting to get to her.

And it broke my heart.

"Look what I got you," I say, entering the living room again. I drop the bag on Mimi's lap and sit on the couch. "Open it."

She eyes me skeptically. "Are you trying to soften a blow I don't see coming?"

"Mimi, just open the bag."

Instead of doing as I ask, she clasps both hands on the top. "You're acting odd. What's going on?"

"Nothing is going on. We just had a rough morning, and I wanted to brighten your day a little bit."

"What are you not telling me?" Mimi asks, fear flashing momentarily through her eyes.

I pull my feet up and under me. "Nothing. *I promise.*"

She is uncertain. It hurts my heart that she expects every good thing to be tempered with something bad—even if I do the same thing. *Always waiting for the other shoe to drop.*

I motion toward the paper bag. "*Open that.*"

"It is getting warm on my legs." She unfolds the top and peers inside. "Is this ..." She jerks her face toward mine with eyes as wide as saucers. "*You didn't.*"

She digs inside the bag and pulls out an Italian beef sandwich from Stupey's, a little boutique sandwich shop. It has the best sandwiches I've ever eaten, and the Italian beef is Mimi's favorite. But as delicious as they are, they're equally expensive. We've not had food from there in months.

"What did you get for you?" she asks.

"I wasn't hungry."

"Chloe Grace ..." She watches me sternly, almost as if she will refuse to eat because I don't have something. "You must've spent fifteen dollars on this sandwich."

She looks at the ceiling, perhaps considering her next words. Pride is a dreadful thing for strong women. There's something about watching her react, *watching her struggle*, that settles a lump in my throat.

We sit quietly. The only sound comes from the couple above us getting into one of their typical afternoon arguments. It'll last twenty minutes, and then they'll have make-up sex so loud that we'll turn the television up to drown them out. Mimi used to take a broomstick and hit the ceiling, but they didn't care. It only seemed to make them louder.

"I know you don't want to hear it, Chloe, but thank you for taking such good care of me."

I gaze at the bump on her head. *Yeah. It looks like I'm really taking good care of you, Mimi.*

"This isn't easy. I know it isn't," she says. "You should be out there having fun instead of worrying about an old fart like me."

"Are you saying you aren't fun?"

She laughs. "I was fun once. And I wish with everything in me that I could've been young at the same time as you. Oh, the fun we could've had together."

I reach for her wrinkly hand. "You're my best friend, Meems."

She squeezes my palm before I pull it back.

"Tell me about your day," she says, lifting her sandwich and unwrapping the foil around it. "What happened? Give me all the details."

I pull a throw pillow over my stomach and slow the smile stretching across my face.

"I had a good day," I say. "I got a blueberry muffin from a bakery downtown, and it was divine."

"Nice."

"I'm finally caught up on work."

"Because you're brilliant."

"And Jason might've overheard me talking about how hot he is—more or less."

She grins wickedly, reading between the lines. "I knew a pilot once," she says, taking a bite of her sandwich. "My gosh, Chloe. This is just what the doctor ordered."

Watching her savor her dinner is the most satisfying thing I've felt in a long time. She's been losing weight and has had too little joy. This moment means more to me than any moment of the day.

"It was in the sixties," she says, opening a small container of peppers she prefers on the side. "He was so handsome. The studliest of the studs. He had that rugged hero thing going on. Do you know what I mean? Sharp jaw. Cheekbones to die for. The smile that melts your panties right off ya."

I burst out laughing. This story changes slightly every time she tells it, but I'm not about to stop her.

"I can't remember his name." She thinks about it for a minute. "Anyway, you could look at him and just know he could handle anything that came his way. It was so damn sexy. If I hadn't been engaged to your grandfather, I would've rocked that man's world."

"There's no doubt."

She grins. "Show me a picture of Mr. Brewer again."

"*Mimi* ..."

"Use your phone and get me a picture. I wanna see him. I don't get to see hotties anymore, and I want to remember what it feels like to be alive."

I groan—not at the words, but at her tone. "Let's not."

She takes a bite, watching me while she chews.

Mimi is entirely too enthralled with my work life ... and my hot boss. But it's all my fault. The day I ran into Jason after several years, I sprinted home to tell Mimi all about it. It all came pouring out of me —how Mom had worked for them for many years until she took a job as a nurse's aide to help take care of Mimi. I told her about the Brewer family and how Jason had always fascinated me.

And how he was even more fascinating now.

"Guess I'll find a picture myself," she says, reaching for her water bottle.

The last time I tried to tell her I wouldn't look Jason up online, she got my phone while I was in the shower and tried to do it herself. That only cost me three hours of my life and a factory reset.

I huff and get up to retrieve my phone from the hallway. When I return to the couch, I pull up Jason's photo from the company website and hand it to her.

She takes one look at him and drops the phone in her lap. "I think he gets cuter every time I see him."

"Yeah," I say as nonchalantly as I can manage.

"How on earth do you get a thing done in the office aside from staring at this man all day? I'd be jumping his bones in the conference room."

I hold out my hands and shrug. "I have good self-restraint."

She peers at his picture again. "I don't know why you don't make some moves on him. You're beautiful and smart. There's no way he doesn't have a thing for you."

"Mimi, stop."

She hands me the phone with a warning written on her face. "Why?"

I sneak a final peek at Jason before turning off the screen.

Mimi is just like my mother was—a firm believer in love. I've never been able to wrap my head around that fully. I've never had the guts to ask about it, either.

My granddad, despite his faults, was a decent man. I have a few nice memories of him as a child. But his vice was a screwdriver cocktail, and his outlet was my grandmother. I've heard enough stories to wonder why she stayed with him until he passed away the same summer my parents divorced.

On the other hand, Mom didn't stay with Dad—but it wasn't by choice. Dad left us without so much as a reliable car. Despite her heartbreak, she never gave up on the idea of a happy ending. She passed away from colon cancer two days after my eighteenth birthday with me and Mimi by her side.

But I can't tell my grandmother that even if Jason was interested in me—something I'm not conceited enough to believe—I no longer believe in fairy tales or magical endings.

"Jason is too busy to date," I say, grabbing her remote. "He's the CEO of one of the largest boutique airlines in the country, remember?" I point at the ceiling as a thump rattles the room. "That was the headboard against the wall, wasn't it?"

She rolls her eyes and sighs. "Turn it up."

I whisper a silent thanks to the universe, turn up the volume on the TV, and settle in for some good soap opera drama.

Chapter 5

Jason

My stomach growls, breaking my concentration—something I've battled to retain all afternoon and evening. Focus isn't something I struggle with. If there's work to be done, I can tune out a marching band. Hell, I can even ignore Tate if it means completing a task.

But the one thing I can't keep from infiltrating my thoughts is Chloe.

Friday at seven. See you then.

I straighten my desk, make notes for later—leaving off a reminder to have Chloe work late on Friday—and then rise to my feet. My stomach reminds me that I haven't eaten since morning's breakfast bar, so I make my way to the kitchen.

The sun hovers on the horizon, bathing the house in a warm, muted light as I make my way through the foyer.

Chloe hasn't mentioned dating anyone in a long time. I usually try to avoid those discussions, knowing they'll wind up pissing me off. The two guys I know she's dated haven't known their ass from a hole in the ground. How do you manage to get her to date you and then fuck it up?

I don't know what makes me want to fuck them up more—the fact they didn't treat her right or that they're obviously too stupid to have deserved a chance with her in the first place.

"Not my problem," I mutter, opening the refrigerator. I find leftover chicken breast, brown rice, and vegetables and pop them into the microwave. The plate spins in a circle. My thoughts spiral, too, reminding me of all the contracts I need to peruse before morning.

But before I can retrieve my plate and return to my home office, my doorbell rings.

"You good?" Tate shouts before the door closing echoes through the house.

"In the kitchen."

Steps tap across the hardwood, getting louder as they grow closer. Tate and Renn round the corner and grab seats at the island.

The two of them together are hell on wheels. They're the same height and mostly the same build now that Renn has lost some of his rugby muscle, thanks to his retirement. I'm not sure who is cockier between them, but I know that I'd call Gannon or Ripley if I had an emergency. By the time Renn stopped trying to be a hero and Tate had taken enough selfies to post on Social, I'd be dead or in jail.

"Calvin was in the guardhouse and said you were home," Renn says. "Do you know what I don't understand?"

"Mathematics? Tact? How to properly eat spaghetti?" I ask, taking my plate from the microwave.

He rolls his eyes. "I don't understand how Calvin works in personal security. Where did Landry Security find that guy? He just tried to big dog me."

Tate snickers at Renn's annoyance.

"I really think he expected me to cower to him," Renn says, pointing at himself. "*Me.* A professional rugby player. What does he think is gonna happen? Nothing his little lanyard can save him from, I'll tell you that."

"*Former* professional rugby player—*ow*!" Tate says, rubbing his shoulder where Renn punched him. *Hard.*

I chuckle at them.

"I mean it," Renn says. "The only scary thing about Calvin is that he might just be dumb enough to think he could take me."

"Have you been talking to Foxx?" I ask, getting a fork from the dishwasher.

His brows pull together. "No. Why?"

"Well, Foxx isn't a big fan of Calvin's either," I say. "I guess Bianca used Calvin to make Foxx jealous, and although she was kidding, Foxx doesn't kid."

"*Ooh*. Bet that went over well," Tate says.

I shrug, pouring myself a glass of wine. "Considering Foxx doesn't joke around about anything, let alone our sister, let's just say Calvin is lucky he can still form words."

"Foxx Carmichael." Renn laughs, shaking his head. "That's one motherfucker I wouldn't want to fight."

"Do you two want a drink?" I ask.

They shake their heads and follow me to the table. Renn sits across from me, and Tate takes a chair beside him. There's a twinkle in Renn's eye that makes my stomach tighten.

"You okay?" Renn asks. "You look a little putrid?"

"Learn a new word today?" I ask, spearing a broccoli floret.

"Yesterday, actually." He stares holes through me. "Have you talked to Mom lately?"

Tate's words from this afternoon ring through my mind as I take a bite of my dinner. *"He just wants to talk to you and Gannon about buying the Tennessee Royals."*

This isn't about Mom, and we all know it.

I stare at Renn and take another bite.

Tate leans back in his chair with a shit-eating grin. "This is about to get interesting."

"Is this about the Royals?" I ask, watching him over the rim of my glass.

"Who told?" Renn groans, looking at Tate. "*Fucker*. I wanted to be the one to bring it up to him."

"Why? So you could blindside him, and he could tee off on your face?" Tate asks.

Renn laughs. "You think that old man could hit me?"

The glass clinks as it touches the tabletop. The sound causes my brothers to stop squabbling and look at me. I lift a brow.

"Kidding." Renn clears his throat. "But, yes, it's about the Royals. I want to buy the team."

"And I want—*a lot of things*," I say, catching myself before Chloe's name pierces the air, and I can't take it back. "Doesn't mean either of us will get those things."

And neither will Thomas if I can help it.

"I was on board with you starting an airline," Renn says.

"I had a business plan and no reason to have Towlin's number on standby."

Renn rolls his eyes. "Will you just think about it? I can get everyone on board but you."

I sigh and watch my brother squirm like a little boy in his seat.

Renn and I have never been wildly close—mainly because I was the kind of person he liked to pester, and he was the kind of kid I wanted to throttle. I wanted to read books; he wanted to kick a ball at my face. So I'd challenge him to combat or a test of physical fitness, and all he'd run was his mouth. Despite being a physical phenom, he knew I'd kick his ass.

But it's different now—for all of us. Gannon gets the calls about finances. I get the calls about safety and logic. We all call Bianca for strategy sessions, and Tate provides entertainment. Ripley is always there to ride for any of us.

But Renn has seemed to turn to me even more over the past few months. He had me help upgrade his security system. He wanted my advice on what car was safest for Blakely. He had me help him hang a television in his living room—something he would've paid someone to do a year ago. Now that he's married, he's suddenly Mr. Fix It ... with my help.

I want to blow him off, but the look on his face stops me. I can at least hear him out ... then tell him no.

"Would you manage it?" I ask. "Does Blakely's brother want to be involved? If so, what roles do you and Brock want to play?"

"We want to be involved. We don't know much about running a professional sports organization, but that didn't stop Gannon from buying the Arrows."

I roll my eyes. "Which is why I suggest holding off for a while. Let's consolidate what we already have and give ourselves time to breathe."

"*But I can't breathe.* That's the thing. I need something to do, or Blakely is going to kill me." His bottom lip sticks out. "She told me yesterday that if I didn't find a hobby, she'd get a job."

"What about your charity program?" I ask.

He makes a face at me. "I have a lot of energy, Jase. And you don't know what it's like being married."

"Of course, he doesn't," Tate says, snorting. "Jason will never be married."

The tone, coupled with the assuredness of his statement, hits me sideways. I set my fork on the edge of my plate.

"What's that supposed to mean?" I reach for my glass.

"It's pretty self-explanatory, isn't it?" Tate asks. "You'll never marry and know what having a wife is like. Period."

"What makes you say that?" I ask.

Renn leans forward, resting his elbows on my table, and grins. *Heathen.*

"I'm sorry," Tate says, amused. "Is there something I don't know? Did you suddenly decide to be social enough to meet a woman, ballsy enough to do something as crazy as fall in love, and then have the guts to agree to be with her for all of eternity?"

Renn's grin widens.

My cheeks heat as their gazes fix on me. I'd blame it on the wine, but I'm pretty sure it has more to do with the questions than the two drinks of alcohol.

My brothers and I have never discussed my relationship status, mostly because I avoid discussing anything too personal with them. Even if they didn't require every moment to be about them, I still wouldn't talk in-depth about how I feel about women or my private life. Giving them too much information is akin to handing them the knife to torture you.

And they would because they're assholes like that.

But something about their quick assumption that I don't have the guts to be married irks me.

I take a long drink and absorb their amusement. Then I do something I never do. I let them get to me.

I sit back, narrowing my gaze. "What makes you think I'll never get married?"

"Seriously?" Tate asks, on the verge of laughter.

"Yeah, seriously. I'm dying to know why you think I'll never have a wife."

"Do you want the list or a quick synopsis?" Tate asks.

I lift a brow.

"For the record," Renn says, his eyes darting between us. "I'm the Switzerland here. If you two start fighting, I'm taking no sides. Only videos so the family can enjoy watching Tate get pummeled."

Tate gasps. "I'm hurt."

"You will be if you fuck with Jason."

"You have such middle-child energy," Tate says, glaring at Renn.

I sigh. "Can we get back to the topic at hand? I have shit to do tonight."

Tate rips his attention from our brother and turns it on me. "If you're serious and have never realized that you're not marriage material, let me break it down."

"Here we go," Renn mumbles, scooting away from Tate.

"You're hardheaded as fuck," Tate says. "You're used to being in control ... of situations, airplanes, and corporations. We don't help your hero complex because we defer to you, too." He groans. "Of course, we can't help it because you generally know how to do everything, and Foxx is the only person I *might* call before you in an emergency."

I shake my head. "You're full of shit."

"Fine. You're also too busy for a woman, and I've never seen you with someone for more than two months—three at best. You're decent at interpersonal skills but suck at intrapersonal ones."

"Not true," I say.

"How do you figure?" Tate asks.

I sweep my hand across the room. "Take this situation as an example of my intrapersonal skills. You two came here because you value interacting with me. I must be decent at it if you want it so bad."

"If we don't come here, we won't see you." Tate gives me a fake smile. "And Renn needs you to sign off on moving forward with the Royals acquisition."

I want to pause and remind Renn that I am not signing off on his fuckery but am too invested in this conversation with Tate. I shift in my seat, focusing on my youngest brother.

"Why does this bother you so much?" Tate asks.

"It doesn't bother me. It's just annoying that you seem to think I'm incapable of finding a wife because ... why? I work too much? I like things orderly and planned? I'm intelligent?" I smirk at him to get under his skin. "I know you tell yourself that women don't like intelligent men to make yourself feel better, but that's not true, Tate."

Tate folds his hands in front of him and settles in. "So this means you think you will marry someday?"

My insides twist as his words fall on my ears.

He has no way of knowing that I've been considering this question a lot lately, nor does he realize that the idea has been weighing heavier and heavier on my mind. I should blow him off and get on with my night. But his conclusion that I'll be alone forever ticks a fear I only recently discovered.

It's not one I really want to face.

"Yes," I say, my voice void of the rising emotions welling inside me.

"Interesting," Tate says.

He leans back and exchanges a look with Renn—one full of bullshit and mischief. *Fuck*.

I steel myself for what's coming next. I don't know what it is, but I know, yet again, that I won't like it.

Tate licks his lips. "Do you remember how we bet fifty thousand dollars a few years ago that Gannon would wreck his sports car within six months?"

"I still feel bad about that one, but yeah. Why?"

"And then you had to donate it to a charity of my choice because ... who won? Oh, right. Me," Tate says.

I hold my hands out, hurrying him along. We seem to be on a meandering path to nowhere, and I want to get to the end as quickly as possible.

"Do you remember when we also had a wager that Renn would be the leading scorer on his team in his last season?" Tate asks, side-eyeing him.

"What?" Renn sits up, his eyes wide.

Tate grins. "Jason bet you wouldn't be the leading scorer, and I bet you would. Because I believed in you."

"And I won," I say, rolling my eyes. "Can we focus here?"

"You bet against me?" Renn asks, mouth hanging agape.

"Yes, and you came in second, just like I predicted."

"Fucker," Renn says, crossing his arms over his chest and shaking his head.

"So ... wanna have another little wager?" Tate asks, smiling cockily.

Renn stands and plants both hands on the table as if bracing himself.

I take a deep breath. "A wager for what?"

"I bet you one hundred thousand dollars that you won't get married and stay married for six consecutive months," Tate says. "I'll give you three years to make it happen. Winner gets the money deposited into their preferred charity, per usual."

"You're out of your mind," I say, standing and collecting my dishes.

"Is that a *yes*?" Tate asks, following me into the kitchen.

I place my plate and glass beside the sink and spin around to face my brothers. Renn stands behind Tate, mouthing something to me I can't understand. The two of them together are like two errant toddlers in adult bodies.

I'd laugh if I weren't annoyed.

"I would never marry someone to win a fucking bet," I say, exasperated with the conversation. "Who does that?"

If I weren't so determined to end this conversation with Tate, I'd warn Renn to wipe the smug look off his face.

"I'm not saying to marry someone to win a bet," Tate says like I'm a child. "I'm just saying that in three years, you'll almost be forty."

"Your point?"

He laughs. "If you haven't found someone, fallen in love, and married them by then, my point stands. And, therefore, I win."

The swipe at my age—something Tate loves to point out at every opportunity—isn't lost on me.

Bastard.

"I have work to do," I say. "Scram."

They head for the door, chuckling to themselves. I follow them to ensure they actually leave.

"I'll let Gannon know the Royals is a go," Renn says.

"Waste his time. That'll be fun for you," I say.

Renn groans.

"Be nice to Calvin on your way out," I say. "Otherwise, I'll have Ford assign him to your details."

The sun dips behind the trees as my brothers step onto the porch. I gaze across the lawn, inhaling a lungful of clean air. Renn and Tate chatter back and forth as they head to the driveway.

"The bet stands," Tate says, opening his car door. "I'll be

researching charities. I might go for something new this time. Maybe an animal rescue or a clean water initiative."

"Fuck off," I say.

"Love you, too." He laughs. "See you later."

"Later."

"Bye, Jase," Renn says.

"Bye."

I shut the door and lock it, wishing I could lock out the non-possibilities from floating through my head ... along with Tate's words.

"You're hardheaded as fuck. You're used to being in control ... of situations, airplanes, and corporations. We don't help your hero complex because we defer to you, too."

This is true and not new information. I've known this for years. But what gets me—what rubs me the wrong way—is that Tate seems to think I'm destined for a life alone. *Does he think I'm incapable of love? Or unlovable?*

I hate that it bothers me, but it does. And I can't deny that I wish this were a bet I could win.

I groan and head back to my office.

But I can't deny it's impossible to win this one, either.

Chapter 6

Chloe

"No, Mr. Rigglen, I'm sorry. Mr. Brewer is unavailable next week," I say, glancing at Jason's calendar again. "The only dates available are the ones I included in my email."

"None of those work for me. I suggest Monday the thirteenth or the following Thursday. Pick one."

Excuse freaking me? "Your suggestions have been noted," I say, looking up as Jason waltzes through the door. I press a finger to my lips and then point at the glowing speakerphone light on my phone. "I apologize for the inconvenience, but the thirteenth and the following Thursday don't work with Mr. Brewer's schedule. I know this meeting is very important to you, and I'm doing my best to squeeze you in as soon as possible."

Mr. Rigglen sighs roughly, making his displeasure clear. I want to worsen his displeasure by shoving his suggestions where the sun doesn't shine. Instead, I paint a smile on my lips because it's harder to be mean when you're smiling, and I take a long, deep breath.

Jason leans against the corner of my desk and watches me with bright, assessing eyes. He sets an iced vanilla latte next to my cell phone.

"Thank you," I mouth to him. He winks at me in return.

"Listen, Miss Goodman, I understand your boss is a busy man," Mr. Rigglen says. "We all are. But he rejected our proposal, and I'm entitled to an explanation."

Jason's brows lift. Something about his reaction—how he steels himself in place—makes me fidget.

"Again, I apologize for the inconvenience—"

"It's not a fucking inconvenience, and you better—"

His words are cut off by my office phone scraping against the desk as Jason drags it to him.

"Do you want to say that again?" Jason's jaw flexes as he stares daggers into the poor handset.

"Mr. Brewer?" Rigglen's voice is full of surprise. "I didn't know you were there."

"Listen to me," Jason says, his words pulsing. "Don't *ever* call my office and talk to my assistant like that again."

"I ... I'm sorry. My emotions got the best of me."

Jason's fingers flex against the desktop. "I was going to call you this afternoon and offer you an alternative contract that doubled the scope."

If a pin dropped, it would sound like an explosion.

I lean back, my heart pounding.

"But now?" Jason's hand hovers over the phone. "You can go fuck yourself."

"Mr. Brewer, I—"

He punches the button to end the call and slowly moves the handset back to its original position.

"Well, okay then," I say, unsure how to break the tension. "Bad morning?"

"Great morning, actually. You?"

I giggle, thrown by the sharp change in direction. "The word *great* is a bit much, but I could say *good* and feel solid about it."

He stands, gives me a killer smile, and rolls his sleeves to his elbows. The sight of his thick and muscled forearms makes my mouth water.

Something is inherently sexy about a man's arms. That's especially true when they're strong enough to throw you over their shoulder and carry you to bed but gentle enough to cradle a baby in the middle of the night. I'm not sure I'll ever be in my baby era, but his arms make my ovaries ache.

And, for some reason, I think he knows that.

"It's been a very productive day so far," I say, focusing on his schedule and not his arm porn. "Your travel arrangements are set for Vegas this weekend. Renn's penthouse was available, so I arranged for you to stay there. The aviation maintenance reports came in. I organized them and put them in a folder on your desk. I don't know why they can't start filing those electronically." I make a face in exasperation but keep moving. "Tate was here. I tried not to let him enter your office, but he's stronger than me. He started talking about all sorts of things to distract me, and it worked. So Godspeed on that."

Jason shakes his head.

"The safety manuals are ordered," I continue. "Landry Security sent updates to your family's security plan. I gave it a quick once-over, and you'll want to take a closer look at Ripley's detail before your call with Ford tomorrow morning. They have Calvin assigned to Ripley for the next ten-day stretch, and that always ends ... spectacularly."

"Good catch. Thank you."

I laugh. "Also, your schedule for next week has been confirmed, and I got you in for a haircut next Thursday."

A slow smile slips across his lips. It tugs at the corners of mine.

I would never admit it, but doing these small, personal things for Jason is the favorite part of my job. He never asks me to do any of them—massages, haircuts, or having groceries delivered when he's been working late all week. But his appreciation when I spot a need and work to meet it makes it worth it. Those things matter more to my boss than the safety manuals, even though I don't think he would admit that either.

It surprises me how well I fit in at Brewer Air and, quite frankly, how well I do my job. I was nervous when I accepted the promotion to executive assistant. But Jason's belief in me—his assurance that I could do this job and would excel at it—made me believe it, too.

"Also," I say, ignoring the butterflies in my stomach. "Your mother emailed you this morning. I marked it urgent. You'll probably want to look at that sooner rather than later."

"Why?"

I grimace and stand. "It seems she wants to cut her security detail in half."

"*What?*"

"*Yeah.* I slowly backed out of that one and left it for you."

He runs his hands down his handsome face. "I'm convinced my family is trying to kill me this week."

"I—" My cell phone rings next to the coffee. Greta's name flashes on the screen, making my stomach drop. She doesn't call unless something is wrong with Mimi, and with Mimi's recent falls, I'm scared. "I'm sorry, Jason. But can I take this? It'll only be a second."

"Absolutely. Want me to come back?"

"No. Just wait right here," I say a little too quickly, bringing the phone to my ear. "Hey. Is everything okay?"

"Hi, Chloe. I hope this isn't a bad time."

"What's up?"

"I just checked on your grandmother. We played a little gin rummy, and I took her some banana bread I made for breakfast."

"That was very nice of you," I say, lifting my eyes to Jason. His eyes are filled with curiosity and concern.

"She's a sweetheart, and I'm happy to do it. She still has a pretty big knot, but I think she's feeling better, and her spirits are better today, too."

I exhale a hasty breath, saying a quick prayer of thanks that this call was a good report and not a bad one.

"I'm happy to hear this," I say. "But I'm at work right now, and my boss is here. So I'd really like to finish this conversation tonight when I'm at home."

My cheeks burn under Jason's watch as I try to get her off the phone.

Greta has never called me in the middle of the day to chat, and I've never accepted a personal call unless I'm on my lunch break. I'm sure Jason doesn't mind, but I still don't like looking so unprofessional.

"Oh, of course," she says. "By the way, before I let you go, Thomas told me you were seeing him this weekend. I'm thrilled, Chloe. Absolutely thrilled. He's coming in tonight for a conference tomorrow and I can't wait to see him."

"I'm excited, too. But I really do need to go."

Jason's brows pull together.

"I'm sorry—one more thing now that I think about it. Was that Friday or Saturday night you're seeing him?" she asks. "I'm supposed to play bingo on Friday night and bridge on Saturday, and I can't remember which to cancel."

I wince. "It's Friday night. But I do need to go. I'll talk to you tonight. Goodbye."

"Goodbye, sweetheart."

I look up to find Jason crossing his arms over his chest.

My smile is weak as I set the phone back down. "I don't normally answer personal calls at work, but my grandmother hasn't been feeling well. I was afraid it was about her."

"So how's Mimi?"

His curiosity piques a certain curiosity in me, too. It's not until his eyes narrow ever so slightly that I realize what he's really asking—*who was on the phone*? It would be so easy to tell him it was Greta. But his nosiness is too entertaining to simply give in.

"Mimi is fine." I take a sip of the coffee he brought me and shuffle through a stack of papers. "Thanks for the coffee, by the way."

"Do you and Mimi have big plans for Friday night?"

I laugh. "You really need to rein in the eavesdropping habit."

"You really should rein in the talking about shit you don't want me to hear."

"I'm not an attorney, but I think I'm afforded an expectation of privacy in my office."

He holds my gaze, opening the door between our offices with a flick of the handle. "Pretty sure this is still my office."

I fire him a playful look.

"Excuse me." Brandi pops her head around the corner. "Finance just called, and they need you in the conference room, Mr. Brewer."

Jason and I exchange a grin. *Saved by Brandi.*

"Come on," Jason says, motioning for me to follow him.

We follow Brandi down the hallway, and then the two of us step into the elevator. He doesn't say a word until the doors close.

"Are you going to tell me about Friday night?" he asks, looking at me over his shoulder.

"Nope."

He nods, turning his attention back to the front of the elevator. "Is it a secret?"

"Why do you care?"

"I don't."

"Seems like you do to me," I say as the bell dings. I step off the elevator first and walk shoulder to shoulder with Jason down the hall. "What does finance want? I didn't even grab my laptop."

He swings the conference room door open. "Doesn't matter."

Then why in the world are we here?

When we enter, three men and one woman from finance are rising from their seats. Gannon, Tate, and a handful of staff from Brewer Group, the holding company for all Brewer companies and interests, are on a large screen at the front of the room. All heads turn to Jason as he walks in.

The respect he garners when simply entering a room is a match to my libido every freaking time.

"I tried to catch you," Gannon says to his brother. "We're going to have to reschedule this for tomorrow morning. This system keeps freezing and glitching; the tech team doesn't know what's happening. Hang on. The connection is flickering again. *Fuck ...*"

The screen goes black.

Jason approaches the computer beneath the screen and turns the volume down. He hits mute before minimizing the screen. He answers the goodbyes from the staff leaving the room.

And then we're alone.

The energy in the room shifts as he faces me again. The air is thick and warm, perfumed with his cologne. It's a woodsy scent offset by a slight citrusy note.

It smells like possibilities and danger.

He slips his hands into his pockets and saunters around the room. He nibbles on the inside of his cheek, his brows pulled tight as he thinks.

"If you need me to attend tomorrow's meeting in your place, I can," I say. "I don't have anything that can't be moved."

"Are you sure you don't have any personal calls about Friday that you might miss?"

I laugh, my face flushing. "Are we still discussing this?"

He stops on the other side of the oversized table and plants both palms against the stone. He levels his sights on me.

Something is brewing behind those gorgeous green eyes. Whatever it is, it's causing a storm to roll across his features. The intensity in his gaze makes me shiver.

"Why are you looking at me like that?" I ask, keeping my attention pinned on him.

"You signed an NDA to work here, Miss Goodman."

"Yeah." I make a face at him. "What does that have to do with anything?"

"Well, if you're dating someone new, I need to be sure you're not dating a competitor. Could be a conflict of interest."

My chest shakes as I try to hold back laughter. "He's not new."

"Oh, really?"

"And he's not a competitor, so no worries there."

"You never know someone's connections."

He's prodding, and it's obvious. It's also … interesting. We've had discussions before about dating—mostly that neither of us date much. But he's never been so insistent on getting details.

Even though he's digging in an area that doesn't concern him, and I'd be pissed as hell if my former bosses acted this way, I don't mind. Maybe it's because our relationship is more personal than professional.

Or maybe it's because the twinkle in his eyes makes my heart skip a beat.

"What are we going to do?" I ask, placing my hands on the table and mirroring his posture. "Are we going to stand here until I break it all down for you?"

"Depends on how long it takes."

"Might take all day."

He drops a shoulder and tilts his head as if I'm deliberately being difficult and he doesn't understand why.

"Who is he?" he asks.

"Do you really want to know?"

"How do you know this guy? How do you know he's going to be nice to you? Is he safe?"

I sigh, rolling my eyes in frustration. "He's my grandmother's neighbor's grandson. He's an EMT if it matters. He has no interest in you or your business." I can't help myself. "He's only interested in saving lives and giving people mouth-to-mouth."

Jason's eyes blaze.

I've hit a nerve. Unintentionally, I've struck a chord—one that I believe will have consequences. And by the heat radiating off him, I'm not sure what those consequences may be.

Or what I want them to be.

"Is that what you want?" he asks carefully.

We're treading into new territory, and every sentence intensifies the tension in the room. My dress clings to my body, stuck to my skin by a sheen of sweat, and my palms slide along the cool stone of the table. The weight of his gaze makes me feel powerful—*beautiful*—and it's heady.

"Well, it *has* been a while," I say, leaning forward. "Thomas is the perfect candidate to give me what I need."

Jason licks his lips. "And what do you need, exactly?"

"Do you really want to know?"

Jason moves slowly around the table, his fingertips dusting along the top of the quartz.

Excitement blooms in my stomach, causing my heart to race, and I wonder if I might've bitten off more than I can chew. My brain hurries to keep up with my body—to settle down the hormones that have flooded my system. But there's no stopping my attraction to Jason. And, by the looks of it, there might be no stopping his attraction to me.

A thought in the back of my brain warns me not to go any further. Jason is my friend *and* employer—this situation could quickly get out of control. But instincts take over as he stops inches from me and peers at me from nearly a foot above.

We aren't friends. We aren't coworkers. We're a man and a woman.

"Does that bother you?" I ask, my stomach clenching.

My voice is breathier than I'd like—softer and more intimate than it should be. But his vulnerability, the unguarded way he's looking at me, screws with my head. It sure as hell screws with my libido.

"I'm bothered, all right." He takes a measured breath. "I'm also your boss."

"And you're absolutely not my type."

"*Oh, whatever.*"

I laugh, the moment broken. Relief washes over me as Jason steps back, running a large hand over his head.

"Not being egotistical or anything," he says, smirking, "but I'm *absolutely* your type, Chloe."

"Hate to break the news to you, but you're not."

He watches me out of the corner of his eye and pauses as if he's about to say something. Instead, he fights a smile and heads for the door.

I follow him, knowing he knows I'm a liar. But I also wonder if he realizes that if I had to describe my type, I'd say his name.

Chapter 7

Chloe

"Good night, Mimi," I say from her doorway. "Do you want me to turn on a fan to help with the noise?"

She's propped up in her bed, an old Western playing silently on the small TV across the room. Her hair is in rollers, and a fresh coat of pink nail polish shimmers on her fingertips. She smiles with freshly sugar-scrubbed lips.

"Yes, and I'll turn my television up, too," she says. "If you don't mind turning on my fan, I'd appreciate it. Someone's smoking something somewhere, and it's starting to make me a little woozy."

"Do you need a pain reliever or a drink of water?" I ask, switching on the fan.

"Oh no. I'm fine." She holds up a shaky hand and gingerly explores the knot on her forehead with her fingertips. "Just a little purple."

"If you start to have a headache again, you better tell me."

She snorts. "I'm not telling you. You'll let Greta's grandson in here again, and I'll wind up breaking his fingers if he wags them in my face one more time."

"*Mimi.*" I laugh, shaking my head. "Be nice. He's an EMT. Greta offered to send him over to check you out—*for free.* I couldn't turn down the offer."

And I wanted a quick meetup with him to make sure he still passed the vibe check. Unfortunately, I'm not sure. It's not his fault because I know I was comparing him to Jason Brewer, which is wholly unfair. No one would stand a chance against Jason. But that doesn't mean I can override my squashed interest in Thomas and pretend I want him to bend me over the hood of his car again.

Dammit, anyway.

"I'm just old, Chloe. I'm not deaf. I don't need him in my face and yelling at me like I'm hard of hearing. I can hear just fine." She clenches her jaw and turns back to the Western. "And he's gonna hear me give him a piece of my mind if he tries that shit again."

I sigh. "Yell if you need me."

"You know I have a cell phone, right? I can text you. Or call you. I don't have to yell."

"What is wrong with you tonight?" I ask, laughing. "You're ornery as hell."

"I just got pissed off again thinking about Thomas and his skinny little finger shoved in my face." She looks at me out of the corner of her eye. "Next time, I'll take it and shove it up his—"

"*Good night, Mimi,*" I say loud enough to drown out her rant. "I love you."

She smiles. "I love you, too, honey. Sleep tight."

I pull her door closed and take the few steps to the kitchen.

The air is scented with the popcorn I had for dinner and the sauerkraut the people across the hall apparently had for theirs. I flip on the light, waiting for it to finish flickering before plucking the papers I hid from Mimi off the top of the refrigerator.

My stomach sours as I reread the return label. *Marquis Morrison Insurance Co.*

"How can they get away with this?" I whisper, releasing a long, hard breath. I tap the envelope against my palm and sigh.

The letter was at the bottom of the stack of mail delivered today. I almost mistook it for junk and tossed it in the garbage. A part of me wishes I had.

I scan the letter once again, looking for their contact information. Thankfully, I spy a twenty-four-hour customer service number.

"Mimi?" I poke my head into her room, working hard to keep my tone light. "I'm going to go for a quick walk. I'll be back soon."

"Okay."

I turn for the entryway, open the envelope, and type the customer service number printed at the top of the letterhead into my phone. Then I slip into the hallway and lock the door behind me.

Sitcoms and music drift out of each apartment as I pass. I take the stairs quickly down one floor, my finger hovering over the phone but wait until I reach the entry before pressing the green button.

The doors to the Pliny Building squeal as they open. Cigarette smoke clouds the steps, the inhabitants of the complex not giving a crap about the sign forbidding that exact behavior that hangs behind them. I fan my face, trying not to breathe in the putrid smell, as I find a relatively quiet spot next to a tree in the vacant lot beside our building.

Car alarms and sirens wail in the distance as I work through several prompts, and it takes a few minutes to wade through the questions before I get a human.

"Thank you for calling Morrison Insurance Company. This is Savannah. To whom do I have the pleasure of speaking with today?"

"Hi. This is Chloe Goodman." I swallow a lump in my throat. "I received a termination letter today for my car insurance, and I'm unsure what happened. I sent my payment in on the seventh."

"I'm happy to look into this for you, Ms. Goodman. May I get your birthdate and the last four digits of your social security number, please?"

"Sure." I rattle off the information. "This has never happened before. I don't know what's going on."

She clicks away on a keyboard. "All right, Ms. Goodman. It looks like your monthly installment was due on the first. We offer a ten-day grace period, as stated on your bill. But your check wasn't received until the twelfth."

"Okay. But you did receive it?"

"Yes, ma'am. But unfortunately, it was two days beyond the grace period, and your policy went into automatic termination."

Fuck. Fuck, fuck, fuck. I pace around the tree trunk.

"One easy way around this is to sign up for automatic bill pay," she says, like I'm unaware of the marvels of modern technology.

"I know. I switched banks recently and am moving everything over slowly," I say, trying to keep my voice even. "Look, I've been a customer with you for three years, and I've never missed a payment. I mailed it on the seventh. It'll say that on the envelope."

"I understand. However, it was due on the first. It was still technically six days late if you mailed it on the seventh."

"So what do I do now? Do I have car insurance?"

"You do not."

"*Oh my God,*" I groan, stopping in my tracks and looking up at the darkening sky. "Can you just reinstate it then?"

"That is possible, yes. But, because this policy was terminated for nonpayment, we'd need the remainder of the balance to do that. And, unfortunately, there are fees associated with the nonpayment."

Tears fill my eyes. "How much are we talking?"

"That's six hundred forty-two dollars and thirteen cents."

I gasp. "You're saying I need to pay six hundred-whatever dollars before you reinstate my insurance?"

"Yes, ma'am."

I blow out a wobbly breath.

"Would you like to make that payment? I can take it and get you back on track if you'd like."

The thought of shelling out most of my savings because the postal service apparently chose to deliver my payment via the Pony Express makes me nauseous. My chest burns, tightening so fiercely that I press on it to try to relieve the pressure.

I have scrimped and saved every nickel to get us out of this hell-hole. Even though my salary at Brewer Air is good, money doesn't go far—especially when rent is sky-high, there are bills to pay, and every month presents a new unforeseen expense like tires for my car and a hospital visit for Mimi's bronchitis three months ago.

That six hundred-whatever dollars is a quarter of my savings. That could be the difference in getting out of here in six months … and not.

A solitary tear trickles down my cheek.

There's no use in shopping around for prices. This was by far the cheapest company for the bare minimum coverage.

"Yeah," I say, my voice cracking. "Please take it out of the bank account on file ending in 1122."

She reads off a script, and I confirm payment.

"That does it," she says. "You'll receive an email confirmation shortly. Please read it, as there may be forms you need to fill out and return to us."

"Lovely."

"Is there anything else I can do for you, Ms. Goodman?"

I shake my head in frustration. "No. Thank you for your help."

"You're very welcome. Have a good night."

"You, too."

Blowing out a breath, I pull myself back together. "This wasn't the energy I was supposed to be attracting."

The ridiculousness of the statement makes me laugh. One of the men standing beside the door yells something my way, but I ignore him.

It will take me months to catch up to where I was fifteen minutes ago. All for nothing.

The temperature drops as the sun makes its final descent behind the horizon. The voices coming from the newly formed shadows are louder, and the sirens seem to get closer. At least if someone jumps me, I could get a few punches in. I could use an outlet tonight.

I move toward the building, and as I take my first step, my phone rings.

"Hello," I say, not bothering to glance at the screen first. I keep my eyes up and scan the area.

"Chloe? Hey, it's Jason. I hope it's not too late."

My steps falter at the bottom of the steps. *Shit.* "Hi, Jason. No, it's fine. What's up?"

"I was hoping you could pull a few reports for me as soon as you get into the office and email them to me. I'll send you a list of what I need. The finance meeting is at Gannon's office in the morning, and I'm going to head straight there before coming into the office."

I flip off one of the smokers in response to a lewd comment and swing open the door. "Of course."

"Hey, little mama." The man from 1B steps into the hallway. "Have you been cryin', sweetheart? Come inside and let Daddy wipe those tears."

"Chloe? Who was that?" Jason asks.

"Hang on," I say into the phone before turning to Mustache Man. I slide my key between my fingers. "Why don't you fuck all the way off?"

His belly bounces while he laughs. "Let's do that together. You can hold on to these handlebars and ride me as long as you want."

"Chloe!" Jason yells, his voice barreling over the line.

My neighbor reaches for me. I jerk my arm back, hitting my elbow on the wall. My phone goes flying down the hallway.

Mustache Man's eyes glimmer with something I can't name—something I'm too scared to identify.

"Don't touch me," I say, squaring my shoulders to his. My knees tremble from the adrenaline coursing through me. "If you ever try to touch me again, I'll spoon your eyeballs out and feed them to you. Got it?"

"Ooh. I like 'em feisty." He licks his lips in a vile manner. "You know where I live, baby. Come on over anytime and ride Daddy's dick."

I walk backward until I pass my phone. Then I scoop it up, jog up the stairs, and down the hall. I quickly let myself in the apartment, locking all three locks. *Click. Click. Click.*

"*Chloe*!"

"Oh shit." I fumble with my phone and bring it to my ear. "Jason! I'm sorry." I get a quick glimpse of my flushed face in the mirror. "You caught me at a bad time."

"*What the fuck was that*?"

His words, *his tone*, send a shiver snaking down my spine. Each word is sharp enough to cut through glass.

I don't want to have this conversation with him, not tonight, not after the insurance company's highway robbery. If I talk about it, I might cry. If I cry, there will be hell to pay.

"It was nothing," I say.

"Don't bullshit me."

I laugh angrily, slipping off my shoes. "Jason, with all due respect, please let this go. I'm not built for this tonight."

The line quiets, but that doesn't mean it's still. His energy ripples silently through the phone. I know the exact face he's making right now, and while it's hot as hell, it's also scary.

It's a good thing we aren't face-to-face.

"Are you safe?" he asks, the edge blurred from his words.

I sneak down the hallway to my room. "Yes, I'm safe. I'm home."

"Who are you talking to?" Mimi shouts from her room.

"Was that Mimi?" Jason asks.

I sigh in defeat. *I can't handle these two at the same time.* "Yes. Will you hang on again?"

"Do I have a choice?"

"I'll assume that's rhetorical," I say. "Mimi, I'm back."

"I heard ya," she says. "Did you lock up?"

I hold my phone behind me to prevent Jason from hearing and pop my head in her bedroom door. "Yes. I locked up. We're as snug as a bug in a rug."

She lifts a brow. "Who are you talking to?"

"No one. If you get up tonight, yell for me, text me, call me, or do whatever techie thing you're capable of doing. *Do not get up by yourself.* The landlord didn't fix the bathroom tile, and I don't want you falling again. I mean it."

"Is it a man?" she asks, smiling wickedly.

I laugh. "Yes, actually, it is. I'm going to go to my room and have a conversation. Turn your television up and give me some privacy."

"That better not be Thomas!" she yells as I close her door.

"Can this day be over yet?" I mumble, finally entering my room. I leave my door cracked to hear if Mimi gets up and then crawl into bed and collapse. I need a shower and to brush my teeth, but I don't have it in me. "Jason? I'm sorry. Again."

"Did you talk to Thomas today?"

"Yes." I smile weakly. "He came by this afternoon to chat with my grandmother."

"He knows your grandmother?"

I grin. "This conversation is stalling." I snort. "Stalling. Get it?"

"I'm not in the mood for aviation jokes, Chloe."

"I'm not in the mood to talk to you either, but here we are."

He mumbles something that I'm sure I'm better off not hearing.

"Do you need anything else?" I ask. "I'm exhausted and just want to try to get some sleep."

I close my eyes and imagine Jason calling to say good night instead of asking for files. *How would he say good night? Does he like to talk on the phone? Is he the kind of man who would remember to call before bed, or would he get lost in his work and forget?*

"Look, you're going to have to give me something," he says, softer this time. "Are you all right?"

The genuineness in his voice hits my heart ... and causes my stupid tears to well up again.

We are friends. But this? I don't want him knowing that professionally I'm rocking life, but personally? *I'm drowning.* And, if I tell him the night's activities, he'll never look at me the same way. I'll be the helpless woman failing at life. I'll be pitiful. A charity case.

"I'm fine," I say. "It's just been a day, and you caught me at the climax."

He hums. The sound travels to my core and sets it on fire.

I close my eyes. "I'm too tired to care that I just walked into a climax joke."

"Who were all of those people?"

"My neighbors and Mimi."

"Those were your neighbors?"

I nod, even though he can't see me. "Yeah."

He pauses as if he's mulling over that information. Finally, he clears his throat and seems to let the non-neighborly neighbor thing go. *Thank God.* "How is Mimi? You said she's been sick."

The kindness in his tone hits me right in the heart. It's likely because I'm overly emotional tonight—which I hate. But his compassion means a lot.

I swallow a lump in my throat, reminding myself why I don't open up to Jason about Mimi and my financial situation. I don't want his pity. But it feels so nice to have someone on my side that I give in.

"She's not sick, really," I say. "She just forgets she's not in her thirties anymore, and her legs give out. She's fallen a few times recently. I have to sleep with one eye open because I'm scared to death that she's going to fall in the dark."

There's a long pause—an extended, comfortable moment that feels like a hug. I sink into my mattress, my muscles relaxing for the first time all day. My mind is quiet, even if only temporarily, while I listen to him breathe.

"If you need anything, Chloe, you can call me," he says quietly.

"I appreciate that. Let's talk tomorrow, okay?"

He sighs. "Okay. On that note, thank you for answering my call. Good night, Chloe."

"Good night."

The call ends and I set my phone beside me.

It's still too early to fall asleep, but I hope lying down translates into some form of beauty rest. Otherwise, I'll be pacing back and forth across the kitchen. That would result in stress lines and an anxiety attack, for sure.

And God knows I don't need more of either of those.

The apartment is fairly quiet this time of night, all things considered. An occasional raised voice or screaming television show rattles through the walls. I'm used to the amalgamation of smells—tobacco, curry, *varnish*. But those seem to be lesser than usual tonight, too.

I close my eyes and let my mind wander to Jason.

What would life be like with someone like that in your corner? Not just as a boss, but as your partner?

Your lover?

I pull a pillow to my chest and hug it tightly.

"If only fairy tales were real," I whisper.

I force all thoughts out of my mind of bills and bank accounts, nasty neighbors, and broken floors. Instead, I fall asleep thinking about a man with striking green eyes holding me in his arms.

Chapter 8

Jason

"Are you good with that?" Ford Landry asks, his voice filling my car as I fly down the expressway.

I flip the visor down to spare my eyes from the bright morning sun. "I mean, I don't love it. I get her point, and I respect it. But I don't love it."

"At what point do we compromise?"

With Rory Brewer? Good fucking question.

I glance at the time on my dashboard and wonder how the hell things got so complicated before eight in the morning. If my life weren't already full of situations like this, like my mother calling our security company and demanding her detail be cut in half, I'd be worried. At least they're consistent.

"She's not going to want to compromise," I say, passing a pickup truck doing forty-five miles per hour in the fast lane. "I'd be a lot happier about her having one security guard if it could be Foxx."

"I'm pretty sure he's happy right where he is—at home with your sister."

I roll my eyes. "What about that Erickson guy you were telling me about?"

"Give me a second." The sound of him tapping at his keyboard comes through the speakers. "I have an interview with him tomorrow. My buddy, Cane Alexander, gave him a stellar recommendation, so I can't imagine I'll have a problem with him. Cane likes five people on a good day."

"Any chance Erickson will work out of Florida?"

"Maybe. Let me talk to him tomorrow and run a background check. If we hire him, I'll consider assigning him to your mom."

"Good. Tell her to sit tight until we can get a plan in place."

"Will do. Other than that, I'm good on this end. Renn did send an email last night with explicit instructions not to have Calvin on his detail."

I shake my head, remembering my conversation with my brother last night. "Renn's surprisingly emotional right now. It's probably a good idea to keep him and Calvin apart."

"Did something happen?"

"No. And I don't want it to," I say, chuckling.

"Me either." He sighs. "Do you have any questions before I let you go?"

I tap my fingers against the steering wheel and take the exit toward the office. Soft classical music drifts from Ford's office through my car speakers. His wife makes him play it to help his blood pressure—something that all his friends know, and none of us let him live down.

I've known Ford Landry for a decade. We served two tours together in the military before he got out and went home to Savannah. I was discharged and went to work for a private security firm, Mandla.

Ford and I kept in touch. When the government shut down Mandla after a bold rescue operation in Africa went sideways, Ford asked me to work for him. I chose to go home to Nashville and start Brewer Air instead.

Our paths crossed again when I took over the security operations for my family and our businesses. Naturally, I hired Landry Security because Ford is one of only a few people in this world I trust implicitly.

Besides Foxx, Ford may be the only one.

"No questions from me," I say. "Let me know if Erickson is a viable candidate."

"I will. If he doesn't pan out, I have ten or twelve interviews next week. With business booming like it is, I could hire twenty people if I could find twenty decent options."

"Good luck with that."

"Right?" He groans. "Okay, I gotta get busy. I have a meeting with Troy Castelli in five minutes. Talk to you later."

"Later."

I press a button on the steering wheel, ending the call.

My car's engine roars as I press the accelerator and overtake a minivan, passing it safely to the right. I set aside Mom's security situation, knowing Ford has it handled. Then I click on the navigation screen before my phone connects to Brandi.

"Brewer Air, this is Brandi. How may I direct your call?" she asks.

"Hey, it's Jason."

"Good morning, sir."

"Good morning. Is Chloe in the office by any chance? I've called her phone several times this morning, and she hasn't answered."

Last night was long. I couldn't sleep for shit. I kept replaying our exchange—the strange man's voice and Chloe's pitch as she responded. Her grandmother telling her that she better not be talking to Thomas. The stress and exhaustion in Chloe's voice.

It bothers me.

A lot.

I feel like I know so much about her, and I'd describe our relationship as *close.* Yet after last night, I realize there's a lot I don't know about Chloe ... and I wish that weren't true.

I tap my fingers against the steering wheel and exhale.

"Actually," Brandi says, "Chloe called in and said she'd be late."

My stomach drops. "She did?"

"Yes. She said something happened at home and she'd be in by lunch. She had me pull a few reports and email them to you. I hope that's all right."

Fuck. "Yes. Thanks for doing that, Brandi. I'll see you in a few hours."

"Of course, Mr. Brewer. Goodbye."

The call ends, and I ease up on the gas pedal.

A swell of anxiety rises in my chest. I can't fight the feeling that something's wrong.

Maybe something happened to her grandmother.

"She's not sick, really. She just forgets she's not in her thirties anymore, and her legs give out. She's fallen a few times recently. I have to sleep with one eye open because I'm scared to death that she's going to fall in the dark."

A chill races down my spine as her neighbor's voice echoes through my brain.

Waves of concern wash over me for the millionth time. *Who the hell was that, anyway? And what was he saying?*

I stopped myself several times from finding out where she lives and checking on her. A part of me thinks it's overstepping my role as her boss—and that's probably true. But a bigger part of me thinks it's the right thing to do because I'd do it for any of my friends.

I stop at a light. Using the pause in activity to my favor, I slide my phone out of the holder and tap on Chloe's name. It rings three times before her voicemail picks up again. This time, I leave a message.

Fuck.

"Hey, Chloe, it's Jason," I say, running a hand through my hair. "Call me back when you can, please. Thanks."

Where is she? She's never late and rarely calls off from work—and she wouldn't have had Brandi pull those reports for her if it wasn't necessary. That I know for a fact.

Every time she takes a personal day, she lets me know at least a week in advance. And if she doesn't answer when I call, she calls me right back.

I glance down at my phone. No return calls over the last hour.

This is so unlike her ...

I take a hard right into a parking lot. I barely stop the car before I call HR.

"Brewer Air, Keisha speaking," she says.

"Morning, Keisha. It's Jason. Can you get an address for Chloe Goodman for me?"

"There are laws about who and why I can release personal information, Mr. Brewer." She laughs, not knowing I'm about to lose my patience. "I'm assuming you're using this for some super important company project."

"I don't see why else I'd need it."

"Me either." She clicks away on her keyboard. "It's 8901 Lang Avenue, Number 4A. Want me to text that to you?"

I activate the navigation system and pop the address into the search bar. "No. I got it. Thanks, Keisha."

"No problem. Have a good day."

"You, too."

I end the call quickly.

Anticipation surges inside me, mixing with irritation and a touch of adrenaline. I'm still trying to understand why I asked for this information. *What can I really do with it?*

What do I want *to do with it?*

I haven't found an answer to either question before the navigation displays the route to Chloe's house ... a whole seven minutes away.

An internal war brews over whether I take this information as a *good to know*—or if I use it. Before the arguments can be played out, I slam my car into drive and follow the prompts to get into the left turn lane.

Fuck it.

I slow my speed as I draw closer to my destination.

I've only been to this part of town a few times. No business happens here. There aren't meetings or restaurants, and there are no parks for a nice afternoon jog. It's not a place to be if you don't have to be here.

So why is Chloe?

The buildings on both sides of the road have seen better days. Chain-link fences separate lots and grass and weeds run rampant through broken sidewalks. Litter and debris have accumulated in dusty front lawns and empty spaces between complexes.

Heads turn as I crawl through the neighborhood, searching for address numbers on the buildings. Most have no numbers at all. Some have a few. But only one building—8901—has all four.

Even if I didn't recognize it as the infamous Pliny Building, the faded block letters on the top, minus half of the *L*, would be my first clue.

"You have reached your destination," the car chirps as I stop in front of the large brick structure.

"Hey, fucker. Move it or lose it," a man shouts from the sidewalk. He holds his arms to the sides of his dingy white tank top as if he owns the space.

I hold up a hand in a semblance of a wave and press down the street.

My jaw clenches, and I rub it absentmindedly while taking in the neighborhood. Every block, every turn, is more of the same. Car alarms. Windowless buildings. Doors boarded with plywood and covered in spray paint.

Logic says to return to the expressway and head to the Brewer Group for my meeting with Gannon. I'm already behind schedule, and there's work to be done. Instead, I whip a left and circle the block, finding a parking spot a short distance from Chloe's building.

Chloe's building.

Why in the world does she live here?

I rack my brain, wondering how much we pay her. Surely, it's enough that she doesn't have to live in this neighborhood. If it's not, I just added another task to my to-do list. *Pay people better.*

I grab my phone and leave Gannon a message. "Hey, it's Jason. I'm not going to make it over there this morning. Something came up. Have your assistant send me notes, and I'll respond by the end of the day. Thanks."

My breath is measured as I stare at the building. I give myself a final chance to back out. But even as I consider it, I know my decision's already made.

I must make sure she's okay.

Warm air hits my flesh as I step out of the car. I press the remote on my keychain, and the lock's beep catches the attention of a small group of men gathered around the back of a blue pickup truck. They cast glances at me and then at my vehicle as I pass.

Please don't be ballsy enough to try to break into my car. I don't want to kick your asses today.

I make eye contact as I walk by, giving them the slightest nod. It's enough to acknowledge their presence and not enough to warrant a conversation. The look should be sufficiently pointed to keep them from getting too bold while I'm gone.

I'm bold enough for all of us, it seems.

What am I doing? I have enough problems on my hands. I need to get out of here.

Yet, I keep walking toward the Pliny Building.

My jaw sets as I correct myself.

I'm not walking toward the Pliny Building. I'm walking toward Chloe ... because there isn't any other choice.

Chapter 9

Jason

Despite its bleakness, the Pliny Building is a sensory overload.

Whiffs of stale cigarettes and burnt food overtake me as I enter the foyer. Canned sitcom laughter pours through the walls, drowning out the meows of the cat darting through my legs. Trash spills onto the floor from the bin in the corner.

I stand in a mixture of shock and awe at my surroundings—and at the fact that Chloe lives here.

This isn't safe.

What the actual fuck?

My anxiety level rises, and my instincts kick in. I want to check for threats and secure the premises. Then I want to get my target out of here.

I rarely fight my instincts. But, today, I must.

The door swings shut in the distance, the sound rattling through the empty lobby. A long hallway extends before me, and another lies to my right. A front staircase splits the middle but is blocked off by yellow caution tape.

I spy a laminated map of the building tacked to the bulletin board by the stairs.

4A. Down the hallway and then up the back stairwell.

My senses heighten as adrenaline pulses through my veins.

Nothing about this feels right—the building, the man with a mustache watching me through an open door on my left, or the fact that I'm showing up to Chloe's uninvited.

But the idea of Chloe being here feels wrong, too. And that propels me down the hall and up the rickety stairs until I'm standing in front of apartment 4A.

A wreath wrapped with pink flowers and vines hangs in the center of the door. It's a startling contrast to the surrounding gray walls. It's so Chloe.

Before I can decide my next move—something I should've already done—the door opens, and a woman with short, unnaturally black hair is staring at me.

"*Oh.*" She looks me up and down. "Who are you?"

Fuck. "I was just, uh ..."

"Are ya lookin' for Chloe?"

"What makes you ask that?"

"Because who else is a man like you coming around here to see?" She chuckles, aiming her head into the apartment. "Heya, Mabel. There's a man here to see Chloe."

"A man? What kind of man?" a voice calls from somewhere in the distance.

"A cute one."

"Well, what are you waiting on, Greta? Send him in."

"All right. I'm heading out now. See you tomorrow. Call if you need me." Greta holds the door wide open. "Go on."

I start to object and blurt out that I am leaving but stop short of it. *I've come this far. I have to know Chloe and her grandmother are okay.*

"Thank you," I say, slipping by her.

I take a deep breath and assess the situation. A picture of Chloe is on a little table beside the door. In it, she sits next to two women and wears a happy, carefree smile.

"I'm in here," a woman's voice calls from around the corner.

Here goes nothing.

My heart pounds, at war with my brain, as I slide farther into Chloe's space.

There is no going back now.

"Well, look at you." A woman sits in a brown recliner with a quilt over her lap and a book of crossword puzzles in her hand. Her purple shirt matches the bruise on her head. *The infamous Mimi.* "Have a seat."

She motions toward a sofa, so that's where I sit.

"I'm Jason Brewer, Chloe's boss. I apologize if I'm interrupting."

"I know who you are. I've heard much about you and seen your picture a few times." She grins. "I'm Chloe's Mimi, and you're not interrupting anything. You saved me from Greta. She just drones on and on about her grandson and my granddaughter." She rolls her eyes. "That coupling will happen over my dead body."

That makes two of us.

I chuckle, mostly at the way her eyes sparkle with mischief.

"Now," Mimi says, setting her crossword puzzle on the tray table beside her. "What are you doing here? I don't reckon you were just in the neighborhood."

Few people in the world can read others as well as I do. Mimi seems to be one of those people.

"You're a straight shooter, aren't you?" I ask, appreciating how her eyes light up like Chloe's when she's ornery.

She laughs, warm and unguarded. "You aren't going to hit a target if you shoot sideways."

"That's true." I clear my throat. "Chloe didn't show up to work this morning and hasn't answered my calls. I was nearby and concerned. So I thought I'd stop by and check on her."

Mimi smirks before I can backtrack or attempt to smooth over my admission.

"Do you go to all of your employee's homes when they miss a day of work?" she asks.

A slow smile graces my lips. Mimi winks in return.

"She ran to the pharmacy for more ... oh, whatever you call the stuff for swelling," she says, frowning. "I fell again this morning. Got a knot on my knee to match the one on my head."

I lean forward, resting my elbows on my knees, and study Chloe's grandmother.

She's thin and frail, with pale skin and silver hair. There's a pride about her—a sense of unapologetic dignity—and despite her stature, she has a maternal presence that steals your attention.

She reminds me a lot of my grandmother.

"Are you okay?" I ask her. "Did you see a doctor?"

"Nah, I'm fine. I mean, I won't win any beauty pageants for a while, but I'll survive."

I grin, nodding at my realization. "I see where Chloe gets it."

"What? Her beauty?"

I laugh. "That and her stubbornness."

"Well, maybe." She chuckles but places her palm lightly against the bump on her head and winces. "It's hell getting old, Jason."

A piece of my heart splinters, hurting for this woman.

I imagine seeing my mother like this someday—a strong, vibrant person weakened to a ghost of herself. It kills me. At least I'd have my siblings there to shoulder some of it and share the experience.

Chloe has no one.

As if she can read my mind, Mimi nods knowingly. "I wasn't always a broken old lady, you know. I wasn't always a liability."

"I'm certain Chloe wouldn't appreciate hearing you talk like this."

I glance at the door. *How long until Chloe returns?*

Now that I know what's going on, that Chloe isn't sick and no one's hurt, the part of me focused on protecting her switches back to protecting my own skin. Because if Chloe catches me in her apartment, talking to her grandmother, I'm not sure what will happen.

With the adrenaline from earlier now dissipating, I'm not sure I want to know.

But I can't interrupt Mimi.

"And I'm certain you're right. Chloe wouldn't like this one bit. But that doesn't make it any less true," she says. She sits back, resting her head against the chair. "I've lived a good life. Married a decent man. Raised a daughter who made me proud. Got a brilliant granddaughter who I love with all my heart. I worked hard. I traveled. I did some things that I sit around now and think about and wonder how the hell I didn't get murdered."

She laughs softly, gazing off into the distance.

I don't know her well enough to discuss her life and feel awkward getting so personal. But something tells me she needs to talk about it. And I'm already here.

"It sounds like you enjoyed yourself," I say.

"Oh, I did." Her gaze pulls to mine. "Do you have a girlfriend?"

She watches me intently, pinning me to the sofa.

I begin changing the subject, but her mouth presses into a tight line.

Okay, then. I take a deep breath. "No."

"A boyfriend?"

I catch a laugh before it escapes my throat. "Um, no."

"Why not?"

"Well, I am a heterosexual."

She chuckles. "Good to know. But why don't you have a girlfriend?"

I'm knocked sideways by this line of questioning. I definitely didn't see it happening today, let alone from her. But the question is direct and matter-of-fact, and Mimi clearly expects an answer. I'm not about to disrespect her by evading it.

"I don't date," I say, going with an easy excuse. "I don't have a lot of free time."

She smiles to herself. "That's a lie, but I won't press you on it."

"What do you mean I'm lying? You just met me ten minutes ago," I say, amused.

"Honey, I didn't get to be my age and not learn anything about people. A man like you? Everything you do is intentional. Am I right?"

I don't know what to say, but I feel it's a rhetorical question, anyway.

"So let me ask you this," she says. "If everything you do is intentional, why are you really here?"

The room stills, and her question hangs in the air. It's like a grenade spiraling toward the ground, ready to explode on impact.

"I talked to Chloe last night," I say, my voice low. "I heard a man yelling, and she sounded upset."

Mimi's expression darkens.

"And she mentioned you'd fallen yesterday," I add. "When she didn't answer me this morning, I had a bad feeling. I guess I just wanted to know what was going on—that you both were okay."

"Why did you care?"

The smugness in her tone pulls at the corners of my mouth.

"I'm nosy," I say, grinning.

"Curiosity can do more than kill a cat, you know." She leans back again. "I think you're a good man, Jason. So I will tell you something, but you can't tell Chloe."

I flinch.

I didn't come here to get in the middle of family secrets. God knows my family has enough of them for the whole city. But despite my hesitation, I also can't get up and leave. I'm rooted on this sofa, at Mimi's mercy.

"Chloe has the best heart of any person in the world," she says. Her words are somber but tinged with an unmistakable tenderness. "She's stronger than I ever was."

Mimi closes her eyes briefly and sighs softly.

"Her mama, my daughter, was sick with colon cancer for three years," Mimi says. "Chloe took care of her. She took classes when she could and worked two jobs when she had to, but that little granddaughter of mine never complained. Not once. And when my Beatrice passed, *God love her soul,* Chloe was holding her hand and singing to her."

Fuck. My hands wring together as I endure the wrenching in my chest.

"Then she moved me in with her despite my objections," she says, chuckling to herself. "I told her I would go to a nursing home, but she wouldn't stand for it." Mimi's head rolls to the side so she's facing me. "Chloe gives up her life to take care of me. She lives here to make it work. With her debt from taking care of her mama, student and personal loans, and the cost of just trying to live right now, it's killing her. *And she doesn't say a word.*"

The last sentence is nothing above a whisper. Yet she may as well have shouted it.

I knew Chloe was strong and determined. I'm aware that she's sweet, genuine, and kind. But I had no idea that she was going through so much personally.

Guilt riddles me.

How do I call her a friend and not know this about her? How could I have missed the signs? Why hasn't she said anything to me or asked for my help?

I still. *It seems she's used to being the one doing the caring, not the other way around.*

"Greta's helping me get a plan in place to move into a nursing facility," Mimi says, her voice clear.

"Have you talked to your granddaughter about that?"

"No. She'll fight me on it. And I know she'll be unhappy for a while, but it's best for her." Tears gather in the corners of her eyes. "I'm the only person on this planet who loves her and would do anything for her. And the best thing I can do for her is give her life back."

A lump lodges in my throat as I reach across the space between us. I take her shaky hand in mine and give it a gentle squeeze.

"If Chloe's upset in the next couple of weeks, that's why," Mimi says. "I'd appreciate you giving her a little grace."

Damn.

I've fought in wars. Lost friends. Watched a man try to murder my mother.

Through it all, I was as cool as a cucumber.

So why am I fighting back tears over a woman I barely know?

Fuck this shit. I need to get out of here.

"I will absolutely give her grace," I say. "Please don't worry about that."

"And don't let her worry about me. Hell, I'll be able to go outside there and breathe the fresh air. Feel the sunshine on my face. Might even get to smell a flower now and again."

I'm in awe by the simple things that Mimi clearly misses—things I certainly take for granted. *Fresh air. The sunshine on her face. The scent of a flower*. Yet this woman, who is both opinionated and sweet, isn't complaining.

The apple doesn't fall far from that tree, it seems.

Maybe there is something I *can* do.

"Can I do anything for you, Mimi?"

She waves a bruised hand through the air. "Just keep an eye on my sweet girl."

I stand, needing a bit of fresh air, too. I'm not sure what to make of this information. Helplessness is not something I do well.

"I need to get going, Mimi. I have a few appointments this morning."

She looks at me and nods as if she's sad to see me go.

I sigh. *I can't just leave her like this.* "Can I give you my phone number? You know, just in case you ever need anything?"

She points at her crossword book and the pencil beside it. I take it and write my name and number on the inside of the front cover, then I place it back on the table. She gives me her number, and I add it to my phone.

"If you need anything, call me, okay?" I ask. "And I mean that. We're friends now."

"Thank you, Jason. It was nice meeting you."

"You, too."

A lock snapping and a door swinging open rings through the room. Mimi and I exchange a glance.

"Meems, I'm back," Chloe says, her footsteps growing closer. "I found the—*Jason*?"

Her eyes are wide, her mouth open. She drops the small box in her hand.

I shove my hands in my pockets and don't say a word.

I didn't have a vision of how it would look when I saw Chloe, but this wouldn't be it if I did. It would've been easier if she had answered the door or if she had been here when I came inside. At least we could've been surprised together.

"What are you doing here?" she asks, glancing quickly at her grandmother. She returns her attention to me as she picks up the box. "Please. Enlighten me."

"I was worried. You didn't return my calls or show up, and that's not like you."

She laughs nervously. "Yeah, well, sounds like someone has control issues to me." She hands Mimi the box and then squares her shoulders to mine. "Let me walk you out."

"It was nice meeting you, Mimi," I say.

"And you're calling her Mimi?" Chloe lifts a brow before turning to the front door. "I leave for twenty minutes ..."

Mimi winks at me, entertained by the situation. Chloe, on the other hand, is not.

She ushers me into the hallway, letting the door slam behind her. A woman walking our way jumps at the sound.

"What the hell, Jason?"

She's so hot when she's pissed.

I smile at her, hoping for one back. That doesn't happen.

"What are you doing here?" she asks with a hand on her narrow hip.

"Excuse me," the woman says, reaching us. "Are you Chloe Goodman?"

Chloe blows out an exasperated breath. "Yes."

"I have this for you." She hands her an envelope. "Have a good day."

"You, too," Chloe mutters, ripping the envelope open. She unfolds a document. Her brows pull together as she reads it. "*Oh my God.*"

"What?"

She clenches her teeth together and folds the letter angrily. When her eyes meet mine, they're filled with tears—angry ones, I think.

"Is everything all right?" I ask, my head spinning. *Is this her life? One disaster after another?*

"You know what? No. It's not all right. But it will be."

"Can I help?"

She sighs, rolling her head around her neck. "Thank you, Jason, but no. You can't help. How did you even get my address?"

"Keisha."

She makes a face to express her displeasure.

"Maybe I overstepped," I say, holding my hands before me. "But you scared the shit out of me. What was I supposed to do?"

"Wait until I get in the office." She closes her eyes and shakes her head. "You shouldn't have come here."

"Why?" *Because you're not used to people showing up for you?*

"Because this ... This is my life. It's a very different world from Brewer Air. And when I'm at work, I'm not reminded of this. But now ..." She groans, shrugging helplessly.

"But now *what?*"

I want to reach out and pull her into me, promising her everything will be all right. Because I could make it all right. I could fix all her problems easily, and it would please me so fucking much to do that for her. And for Mimi.

She won't accept my help, though. As a matter of fact, I know she'd take it as an insult. She's as prideful as her grandmother. That's an endearing trait most of the time. But right now, it's frustrating.

"You don't want me here?" I ask.

I take in the fear in her eyes. *The vulnerability*. It rips my heart into pieces.

She deserves to have someone protect her—love her. Help her. Cheer her on. *Why can't that be me?*

"No," she says. "I'll come into the office this afternoon. We can talk then."

"All right," I tell her, keeping my hands in my pockets so I don't reach for her. "I'll go."

She nods, her bottom lip quivering.

I turn away before I do something stupid and move silently down the hallway.

Chapter 10

Chloe

"Breathe, Chloe," I whisper to the empty elevator.

I suck in a slow breath and blow it out in an easy, even gush before stepping out of the elevator. Brandi starts to speak but stops when she sees me. Her face says it all.

"Yes, bad morning," I say, moving through the foyer. "I owe you for helping me with the reports this morning. Thank you again."

"You don't owe me anything. It's my job." She narrows her eyes as I scurry by. "Do you need anything, Chloe?"

"I don't know. Does this office have a policy on drinking?"

Her laughter makes me smile for the first time today.

"If not, I'll take two shots of whiskey," I say over my shoulder.

"Whiskey?"

I stop at my door, looking back at her as I reach for the knob. "I told you. Bad morning."

I flash her a half smile, half cringe and enter my office. My shoulders slump before I get the door shut behind me, and a small grin slips across my face.

A coffee has been set beside my computer next to a pastry.

"Damn you, Jason," I say softly, grinning at the result of his thoughtfulness.

I dump my bag into a chair and close my eyes, trying to center myself. My stomach is knotted, and my nerves frayed—not just from Mimi's fall or from finding Jason at my apartment. But also from the notice given to me in the hallway.

Please be advised that the property at 8901 Lang Avenue has been deemed condemned by authorities. Residents have forty-eight hours from the date of this notice to vacate the premises.

My heart sinks. "What am I going to do?"

Tears fill my eyes, welling so fast that I tip my head back to keep them from trickling down my cheeks.

The notice implied I have rights, but none of those rights seemed to cover new housing. I'm not delusional. Our landlord won't give a shit about what happens to us. And I've dealt enough with the court system when my mother died to know I'd rather do just about anything else than deal with red tape.

Besides, none of that will help me find a place to live in two days.

"How is this my life?" I say, keeping my eyes wide so the fluid absorbs back into my body.

I sniffle and look around my office. I'm so discombobulated. I'm unsure whether to jump into work and forget about this for a while—let it calm down before I scramble and make a bad decision. Or, do I begin looking for a cheap place to live and work extra hard next week to make up the time?

My attention settles on the flowers Thomas sent. For some reason, I laugh. "That date won't be happening. Leave it to the government to cockblock me."

Tate's laughter trickles from Jason's office.

I tap beneath my eyes to ensure they're dry, then knock on the door.

"Come in," Jason says almost immediately.

My heart lodges in my throat as I poke my head around the corner. Jason's eyes snap to mine so hard that it makes me breathless.

"I was just letting you know I'm here," I say.

Jason searches me—for what? I don't know. But the assessment leaves me feeling more comforted than anything.

"I was worried. You didn't return my calls or show up, and that's not like you."

I was so bewildered, *and embarrassed*, that I can't remember if I thanked him for caring. That makes me feel worse.

"Hey, Chloe," Tate says, flashing me his million-dollar smile.

"Hi, Tate." I switch my attention back to my boss. "Do you need anything? If not, I have a million emails to return."

Jason's brows knit together, and he rocks back in his chair. "Actually, I do need you for a couple of things. Would you mind hanging out here for a minute?"

"Sure."

My breaths grow shaky as I make my way to stand beside Tate.

"Can I get your opinion on something?" Tate asks me.

"What's up?"

"So there's a woman who I see off and on. It's nothing serious," he says. "She wants me to attend her sister's wedding next month. I want no part of that, and she's pissed."

"Why don't you want any part of that?"

"It's like holding a baby. A woman sees you holding a baby, and—boom! All they can think about is having your kid."

"You say that like you've experienced that a time or two," I say, laughing.

He shivers. "Or three. I don't like babies. None of them. I'm concerned about Renn's kid because I feel obligated to be the cool uncle because God knows I'm the only one available for that role."

Jason snorts, but I don't look at him.

"But what do I do about my actual role?" Tate asks, eyes wide.

"What must a cool uncle do to fill that spot in the kid's life? Do I have to hold it? Feed it? Or can I just buy it tons of presents and call it good?"

"I think you're overthinking it," I say.

"I'm not. I assure you, I mean every word of this."

I laugh again at the look of absolute seriousness on his face. "Babies are magical. You'll love Renn's baby. Trust me."

"Yeah. They magically make others want them. Don't you experience that? If you hold a baby, don't you want one?"

"It's been a very long time since I held a baby, so I'm not sure," I say, grateful for this distraction. "But, yeah, holding a baby would probably naturally make me think about having one of my own. But puppies do that, too. If you see a puppy, you suddenly want one. Right?"

"Maybe other people." He looks at me like I don't make sense and turns to his brother. "What about you? Do you think babies are magical?"

Jason watches me carefully. "Weren't you talking about a wedding?"

"Oh. Right." Tate bumps my arm, drawing my attention back to him. "So how do I get out of this wedding and still get to see her again?"

"I don't know. Have plans?" I suggest. "Make something up. Say you have to go out of town on business. How can she argue that?"

He nods. "That's good. That's very, very good."

"That was pretty obvious, Tate."

"I just get all nervous about these things. I don't want to hurt anyone's feelings, you know? But I also don't want to hurt my own, and if she thinks I think we're more than friendly acquaintances, if you know what I mean, then that hurts me."

I try my hardest not to laugh at him, but I fail. Miserably.

The joyful sound is in stark contrast to the depression settling over my soul. I want to grab on to it and hold it close—to allow it to keep me from descending into a pit of despair.

Mostly because I don't have time to sit in my sads. I have to find a place to live.

Why does life have to be so expensive?

My heart hurts for Greta, and for Mrs. Donaldson on the third floor. *What will they do? Where will they go?*

How is this even legal? How can they make us vacate our homes in two freaking days?

"Do you know who else gets nervous about weddings?" Tate smirks.

"Who?" I ask.

"Jason."

My gaze sweeps across the room to my boss. "Why do you get nervous about weddings?"

Jason rolls his eyes as he sits up, his patience with his youngest brother growing thin.

This is usually the time that I try to segue Tate into leaving to save Jason's sanity. But because I know what our conversation will entail when Tate does walk out, I'd rather him stick around as long as possible today.

So I say nothing to prompt him to go. Instead, I dig my heels in to keep him here.

"I didn't know you had a problem with weddings," I say to Jason.

He glares at his brother.

"It's a new thing with him," Tate says, teasing Jason.

"*Okay* ..." I look at Tate and then Jason. "I feel like I missed a conversation."

Tate sits on the edge of Jason's desk—just out of reach of Jason's right hand.

"I'm about to be one hundred thousand dollars richer," Tate says, needling Jason.

"Why?" I ask.

"Get out of here, Tate," Jason says.

Tate grins like a cat that ate the canary.

"What's going on?" I ask again, curiosity getting the best of me.

"I bet my brother that he won't get married within three years and stay married for six consecutive months."

What? I start to dismiss Tate's words as a joke, but Jason's reaction makes me think it's not.

Tate looks at me over his shoulder. "It's a sure bet if you want in on it."

"I'm sorry," I say, shaking the fog out of my head. "Say that again. You bet one hundred thousand dollars that Jason won't get married within the next three years?"

"Yup." Tate grins. "Easy bet, huh?"

"Tate, *leave*," Jason says firmly.

"You're just mad that you're going to lose," Tate says.

I wave a hand in the air. "Is this real? You really bet on Jason's marital status?"

Tate stands looking pleased with himself. "We bet on a lot of ridiculous things and just give it to charity. We'd give it to charity anyway, so why not have some fun with it?"

Fair.

"Do I win the most?" Tate asks. "Yes. Are my brothers salty about it? Also, yes. But this might be the easiest money I've ever won."

"I bet my brother that he won't get married within three years and stay married for six consecutive months."

My brain starts to spin. Each second that passes by increases the speed ten-fold. The pace makes me dizzy, and I grab the back of a chair to steady myself.

Tate's words echo through my brain like a recording that won't stop playing. *He bet his brother and is donating the money ...*

An idea—a dangerous, wild idea, pops up in my mind. It's risky and silly, but it might just work.

I flip my gaze to Jason and find him watching me.

He did ask if he could help ...

"So you're going to pay the money one way or the other, right?" I ask, gripping the chair. "One of you is paying the other."

"Right," Tate says.

I don't look away from Jason. "And what defines a charity?"

"I don't know. A charity is a charity."

My eyes flutter closed briefly as I try to talk myself out of this. I need to stop talking, go back to my office, and get ahold of myself. But as my eyes open again, I'm reminded of finding Mimi this morning on the bathroom floor in tears ...

"What if you win, Tate, and decide you want Jason to donate his winnings to someone you meet on the street?" I ask carefully. "Would Jason have to give them the money?"

Tate shrugs. "If that person needed it, I don't see why not. The idea is to help others."

You could help me ...

My breathing becomes ragged as I seriously consider the thoughts running through my head. I'm thinking under duress, and I know that. But it also seems like it might work.

I need money.

Jason wants to help.

I'm under no illusion that this will result in a fairy-tale ending —*neither of us wants to be married*—so what can it hurt? I'll happily sign whatever pre-nuptial agreement Jason wants to guarantee that I won't ask for more than half the winnings.

Jason gets to beat Tate. I get to keep Mimi from a nursing home and myself from living in my car.

I gulp as my body temperature rises.

And, if we're married, would it be all that wrong to fuck my husband?

I look up at Jason and find his eyes heated.

Six months. It's only six months.

Oh my God. Am I crazy?

My chest aches from the stress, but my heart races because there's hope. And if I'm anything, I'm hopeful.

Screw it. Desperate times call for desperate measures.

"Tate, I have bad news," I say, grinning. "You're about to lose that bet."

Jason is puzzled. Tate flinches.

"What are you talking about?" Tate asks.

I take a deep breath and turn to Jason. "We're getting married."

Chapter 11

Chloe

"W*hat?*" Tate and Jason say in unison.

They watch me with a mixture of amusement and confusion. When I fail to laugh or crack a joke—and probably from the determined yet frenzied look in my eyes—their reactions shift.

Tate's amusement grows. Jason's confusion deepens.

My awareness of the situation heightens, and my hands begin to shake.

"I'm sorry," Tate says, his words kissed with a laugh. "I thought you just said you were marrying Jason."

It's now or never.

I lift my chin. "Because I am."

Tate nods, disbelief written all over his face.

"What are you talking about, Chloe?" Jason asks carefully.

"You're marrying me."

He's as surprised as I am to hear *those words* come from *my lips* in a sentence *about us*. But I've said them—they're out in the world. And I can't deny that, aside from the tightness in my chest from my nerves, this doesn't feel like a bad idea. It's a bit of a relief, really.

And that might be the scariest part of all.

Jason narrows his eyes, searching mine for an answer to an unasked question.

"What's going on here?" Tate asks, picking up on the tension between his brother and me.

"I'd like to know that myself," Jason says.

I swallow. "I don't know how much clearer I need to be, but Jason and I are getting married." I turn to Tate. "Six months, right? From the date of the wedding, I'm assuming."

For the first time since I've known him, Tate is speechless.

"I'll take that as a yes." I turn back to Jason. "Marry me. I'll be the best wife ever—even though I'm unsure how to be a wife because I've never wanted to be one. But I'll take a course or read a book or watch a bunch of romantic comedies that I usually stay away from like the plague because those happy endings are bullshit. But I can pretend," I add quickly. "I will. I'll do anything. I—"

"Whoa, wait a minute." Tate holds his hands up and takes a few steps my way. "Are you fucking serious?"

I gulp, sweat dampening the back of my neck. "Yes."

He looks at Jason. "You're marrying her?"

"I … don't know what's happening here," Jason says, eyeing me. "Are you okay? Did you hit your head or something?"

I groan loudly enough to snap them both out of shock. "Tate, if Jason gets married and stays married for six months, you'll pay him one hundred thousand dollars, which is completely ridiculous, but who am I to judge? Right? Rich people play rich people games, I guess. But that's the way this bet works?"

"Yeah," Tate says, nodding slowly. "That's how it works."

"Okay. Then we're getting married," I say. "We stay married for half a year from the date we say *I do*, and then you pay me fifty thousand dollars and donate the other half to whatever charity Jason chooses. Deal?"

Tate's shoulders settle back, and he faces me like he does men in business meetings. If I wasn't on the verge of losing everything I have and gaining a mental breakdown, I might find it funny.

"This has to be a real marriage," he says, his voice higher.

"Define that." I look him in the eye. "What constitutes a real marriage?"

"You can't just put a ring on your finger and go through the motions. You must *actually* marry my brother."

"Who is sitting right here," Jason says from across the room.

We both ignore him.

"This wager was to prove that Jason can't ..." He throws his head back and laughs. "Hell, I don't even remember what it was for now, but I want to see this play out."

"Fine," I say. "It'll be a real marriage."

"You have to live with him," Tate says, glancing at Jason quickly.

"Fine," I say again. *Not sure how I'll convince Jason of that, but one battle at a time ...*

"You have to do things together. Spend time together. Wind your lives together and make a real go at this."

"What else?" I ask.

Tate's smile stretches from ear to ear. "Then I got nothing. Game on."

I hold out my hand, and Tate shakes it. His palm is softer and smaller than Jason's, but I don't comment. Not when I'm this close to miraculously solving my problems.

"Okay. Great," Tate says, walking backward toward the door. "I'll be awaiting my invitation."

The door swings shut with a crisp smack.

"What the hell just happened?" Jason asks, making me jump.

"I forgot you were here," I say, turning to him.

He laughs as if he's in shock. "You forgot I was here as you just made a deal with my brother to marry me? What am I? A piece of meat?"

"You could be, but that's not the point." I move to his desk and stand across from him. My gaze levels with his. "You're marrying me. I already shook on it."

"I saw that. May I ask why?"

I hold my breath, deciding how much to tell him. But as I war with where to start and what to divulge, I realize I'm too tired to hold back. And I don't have a lot of time to work with, either.

"The letter I got today during your impromptu visit was a notice that the Pliny Building is condemned. I have forty-eight hours to vacate the property."

Jason's brows shoot to the ceiling.

"If I can even find a cheap apartment in two days, I might be able to afford the security deposit and first month's rent, but my funds are already low thanks to car problems, bills, and loan repayments." I take a shaky breath. "When my mom died, I got myself in a hole, and I'm still climbing out of it. Interest is a real thing."

His features sober. The vein near his temple pulses, and the sight of his jaw clenching makes my heart pound.

"Why haven't you asked me for help?" he asks.

My throat constricts as his green eyes shine. "Because this isn't your problem."

"What you really mean is that *you* aren't my problem, isn't it?"

The lump grows, nearly sealing off my ability to breathe. I become lightheaded as I watch him fight with his emotions. I hope I didn't just make a massive mistake.

"It hurts me that you've been struggling all this time and have never said a word," he says.

"I don't want you to think I'm incompetent, lazy, or needy."

"But you'd rather me think you're a fool for not coming to me? I have resources, and I care about you, dammit."

Tears fill my eyes, and no amount of praying will keep them from falling.

"The last thing I want to do is sully our friendship over money," I say. "I don't want to owe you, Jason, because I don't know if I can ever repay you. And everyone that's ever tried to help me in the past has used that as an invitation to judge me, direct me—to give me ultimatums. And I'd rather live on the street and have a tarp to cover up Mimi with at night than to send her to a nursing home where no one gives a fuck about her. Where they don't know the life she's lived and don't give a shit about how much respect she deserves. I won't worry that she's lying there lonely or cold and no one is there to give her a blanket just so I can live in a better place …"

My voice cracks as the floodgates open. The saltiness of my tears splashes against my lips.

"Come here." Jason marches around his desk and is at my side before the tears hit my shirt. "My God, Chloe."

He pulls me into his chest, wrapping his arms tightly around me. My cheek lays against him as my heart bleeds inside me.

I can't remember the last time someone hugged me like this. *And that's why I finally break.*

His chin rests on my head as we sway gently from side to side. My tears stain his shirt, my sobs whispering quietly through the room. It's the first time I've been able to cry freely for as long as I can remember.

I didn't realize I needed this.

I sniffle as the wave of emotion begins to wane and the haze of feelings lifts. A chuckle slips past my swollen lips from embarrassment, and I pull away.

"My mascara is all over your shirt," I say, wiping my face with my hands.

"I don't give a damn about the shirt." He grabs a couple of tissues from the bookshelf behind his desk and brings them to me. "Do you need anything? A drink?"

"No. I'm good." I still have the coffee this generous, sweet man brought me on my desk. I blow out a breath and sniffle again. "Thank you for that hug."

"Want to repay me?"

I nod, unsure where he's going with this.

He half leans and half sits on the edge of his desk. A small smile dances along his lips. "Then fill me in on this wedding we're having."

My laughter comes unexpectedly, and the sound makes Jason's smile grow wider. I swipe the tissue under my eyes and feel my cheeks flush.

"You know I'll give you the money, right?" he asks. "You don't have to marry me, for fuck's sake."

"You giving me money is not an option. So if you don't want to marry me—"

"I didn't say that."

His words are sharp and decisive, and there's something so ridiculously attractive about it that I nearly lose track of what I'm saying.

"Then I'd rather earn the money somehow," I say. "And I can justify this ridiculous bet if I know Tate will donate it anyway. While it hurts my pride to consider myself a charity, I'm desperate enough to succumb to the definition. So, for the next six months, I'll try my best to make this worth it to you since you're not taking half of the money. I'll cook. I'll clean. I'll do the laundry. If you have a dog, I'll walk it. Whatever you want."

He smirks. "So what you're saying is that you would do anything for me?"

I try not to smile but fail miserably.

He sits quietly, the wheels behind his eyes turning. I'm too nervous, too emotionally spent, to say anything else. Besides, the proverbial ball is in his court.

Finally, after what feels like ages, he licks his lips. A slow smile ghosts his lips.

I hold my breath, uncertain where this is headed.

"I'll marry you on one condition," he says.

"Yes."

"Yes, what?"

"Whatever the condition is, I agree," I say. "Beggars can't be choosers."

His Adam's apple bobs as he swallows. "I'd rather you agree to this because you want to rather than because it's a term in an arrangement."

Oh. "Fair."

He stands tall and straightens his tie as if he can't manage to sit still any longer. "I don't *just* want to get married. I want to prove Tate and Renn wrong. Those cocky little shits run their mouths, and I want to show them that they aren't always right."

"How do we accomplish that?"

"We make it believable." He stops moving, his eyes finding mine. "We make them question whether we're going through the motions or if we've really fallen in love."

"Clearly, we aren't falling in love."

A shadow filters through his features. "Clearly. But they won't know that." He moves around his desk, standing next to his chair. "So you move in with me. We continue working together unless you want to be a housewife."

"I'd like to stay working with you. I hope that after we get divorced, I can keep my job."

"Of course."

I nod, sighing in relief. *I hope it's that easy*. "Good."

"But we'll tell everyone we're married. We'll go to dinners, functions, and family events. We'll move Mimi in with us."

My heart stops. Eyes go wide. My jaw hangs slack.

I didn't dream he'd offer that. I hoped I could get a small advance to cover the housing, but does he want Mimi to move in with him, too?

What the heck?

"I have a guesthouse if she'd prefer her privacy," he says. "We can do whatever makes you two happy."

"But me? I'd live with you?" I ask, each word measured.

A slow, seductive smile dances along his lips. My gaze is glued to his mouth as I try not to squirm.

If he wants this to be believable, that means our marriage will include things like ... *sex*.

My stomach clenches at the thought. And by the way he looks at me, I think he's thinking the same thing.

"Are we consummating this marriage, Mr. Brewer?" I ask, hoping I'm reading the situation correctly. *If not ...*

"That's up to you." He shifts his weight from one foot to the other. "But I hope so."

My gaze flips to his, and I try not to melt from the heat in them.

"Remember," he says, his eyes searching mine. "I'm happy just to give you the money. There are no strings unless you want them."

I swallow to wet my throat. I'm afraid my words will stick otherwise.

"So my options are to take the money and run ..." My cheeks flush as I meet his gaze. "Or take the money, have a place to stay, *and* have sex with you for six months?"

He pins me to the spot with only a look. If this intensity is a promise of things to come, I'm in. *I'm so fucking in.*

"Option B, please," I say.

A flicker of a smile kisses his lips.

I've made my choice, and it's truly the one I want to make. It's the decision I'm certain he was hoping I'd make, too. But these sinful rewards have risks, and I'm not too turned on not to consider them.

What if this ruins us?

My stomach flips upside down.

"Just promise me that we'll still be friends when this is over," I say. "Tell me I'm not delusional, and this will work out."

"I promise. You have my word. I would never do anything to compromise that, Chloe."

"But you can see why I'm questioning it, right?"

He lifts a brow. "And you understand that if you didn't trust me down deep, you never would've suggested this in the first place."

That's very true.

"So are we doing this?" he asks.

I give myself a moment to reconsider.

I want to do this. I need the help he's more than willing to give me, and I can help him win a bet in the process. And I'll also have the excuse to do something I've wanted to do for years—sleep with my boss. He obviously wants that, too. And this allows us to do that without violating every rule in the employee handbook.

My mind is made up. This feels like a gift, and I'm not one to turn down a present from above.

"We're doing this," I say.

Relief washes over his features. "What happens in our marriage stays in our marriage."

The ridiculousness of that statement makes me laugh.

He clicks around on his computer and types a few things in, then he looks up at me. "How fast do you want to become my wife?"

My wife. Chills zip across my heated skin. Those two words do something to me—and I didn't expect that.

"I need to be out of my apartment by Sunday morning, I think," I say.

"I can get a truck to your house this evening to move you out. Does that work?"

Wow. "Um, yes. I can get our stuff together in a few hours if I can find some boxes."

"I'll put an order in and have some delivered." He clicks around a few more times. "Should I reserve a church?"

"It kind of feels wrong to get married for money in front of God, don't you think?" I ask, laughing.

He laughs, too. "I'm going to Vegas tomorrow. Want to get married there? We could take Mimi and make a weekend trip of it."

All I can do is stare at him. *Why is he this wonderful to me?*

Even in my most hopeful moments, I didn't imagine he'd go to these lengths to make this okay for me ... and Mimi. He has immense responsibilities on his plate between Brewer Air and his family—not to mention the enormous mess of his dad's atrocities—and so many people are counting on him. He doesn't need my mess, yet here he is, asking to help me hold my load.

I don't know how I managed this or if I'm dreaming, but I'll make sure he doesn't regret it.

Tears fill my eyes again. "You'll really do all of this for me?"

There's something on the tip of his tongue, but he doesn't say it. Instead, he shakes his head and grins a shy smile. "You'd be surprised what people will do for you if you let them. Now go home and start packing. I have a few calls to make."

I stay rooted in place. *Should I hug him? Kiss him? Shake his hand like I did Tate's?*

But the idea of touching him sends a bolt of energy through me that makes my knees weak. Brushing against him before today made me tingle. But now, knowing what his arms feel like, the sturdiness of his chest, the feeling of him holding me tight, I can't risk touching him again.

Not now.

Not here.

"Thank you," I say.

"You can thank me later." His lips twitch as he sits behind his desk. "And, trust me, you will."

My insides burn, and it takes everything I have not to drop to my knees and thank him properly right here. But I have stuff to pack and a move to make.

Then I can make the other, more pleasurable moves.

"Looking forward to it, Mr. Brewer," I say.

Before he can respond, I pivot on my heel and leave him sitting there.

Chapter 12

Chloe

"Is your car supposed to make that noise?" Mimi asks, peering over the dashboard as the scenery around us changes.

The city buildings stopped a few miles back, and as we've wound our way deeper into a residential area, the trees lining the road have grown taller. The homes behind the pines and strategically placed shrubs are harder to see. Still, their grandeur is unmistakable.

The evening sun's rays filter magically through the vegetation and create a muted glow over everything in their path. It would make a perfect scene in a movie. A granddaughter and her Mimi, traveling into the sunset to start a new life.

Ha.

I let off the gas a bit, and the thumping stops. "There? Is that better?"

"You really need to get that checked."

"I'll add that to my to-do list."

The box truck in front of us stops at a gate more ornate than the one we passed through to enter this neighborhood. It's copper colored, the metal twisting and turning into elegant arches and bends. A *B* for *Brewer* is situated in the center.

It swings open, and we follow the truck through.

I can barely sit still as we crawl down an extended driveway lined with beautifully sculpted hedges and pops of colorful flowers. The landscaping is immaculate. I can only wonder how gorgeous the drive is at night when the path is lit by the solar lights dangling from posts every few feet.

It gives storybook vibes. And it doesn't feel real.

For the next six months, this is where I'll live.

My stomach bubbles with anticipation as we grow closer to Jason's house. Mimi's curiosity intensifies, too. When I got home, I realized I didn't know what to tell her, and I didn't feel capable to get through the conversation alone. So I picked the easiest of the two options and decided to wait until we made it to Jason's in hopes he would help me break the news.

She always takes news better from handsome men. *But don't we all?*

"Where exactly are we going, sweetheart?" Mimi asks, squinting into the sun.

"You'll see soon. We're almost there."

"I can't wait to see where *there* is, considering this is nothing like what I imagined."

Oh, just wait ...

I've labored over how to explain this to her because the last thing I ever want to admit to my grandmother is that I'm marrying someone for money. Hell, that's hard enough for me to admit to myself, and the more I think about it, the more nauseous I become. But it's not just for money—it's for a life-changing amount of money. And I'm not just marrying any man. I'm marrying a man I trust and respect, and who seems to be into this ruse to benefit himself, as well.

If you take the religious element of marriage out of the picture, this is really no different than him loaning me the money and having me work it off. It's just that instead of paying him interest and maybe defaulting on a few payments when times get hard, I'm helping him with a project of his own by playing a role.

I'm being paid to play the role of his wife.

That doesn't make me any less queasy.

"Are we consummating this marriage, Mr. Brewer?" I ask.

"That's up to you ... But I hope so."

I've dreamed of having sex with Jason more times than I can count. But it was just that—a dream. We may have flirted and teased each other, but we've been careful to stay in our lane. Our professional relationship and private friendship were on the line.

But now? Those lines are blurring, and even though I'm the one who proposed this, I'm still nervous.

"Are we staying here?" Mimi grips her seat belt and gawks at the house in front of us. "What the heck is this place?"

Oh wow.

My mouth hangs agape at the sight looming before us. I had no idea people really lived like this.

The home is a deep, tobacco-colored wood with two stories and many windows. A long porch extends down one half of the house with a swing drifting back and forth in the breeze. On the other side is an attached garage deep enough and with enough bays to hold more cars than I'll probably ever own in my whole life. The driveway circles in the front around a flagpole, and the landscaping is immaculate. It's clean and sophisticated. Yet I can see Jason's brothers on the front lawn playing football on Thanksgiving.

I smile at the idea.

"I think you're supposed to go that way," Mimi says, her bony finger pointing toward the side of the house.

I follow the box truck along the side of the house and stop alongside it. Then I cut the engine.

My hand trembles as I drop my palm to my lap.

The car is quiet as my grandmother looks at me skeptically. "When do I find out what's going on?"

My anxiety rises as the movers spill out of the truck and raise the door in the back of it. Before I can gather my wits and explain what's going on to Mimi, her gaze shifts over my shoulders. And the skepticism in her face turns to excitement.

I know that look. She's seen Jason.

Her lips part into a smile as he appears, pausing to talk to the movers. He's changed from his suit into a pair of dark denim jeans and a green polo shirt that matches his eyes. His hair is damp. His face freshly shaven.

Those delicious tattoos are on full display.

Jason laughs at something one of the men says, then he turns to me, his smile growing wider as our gazes meet.

My stomach tumbles as he comes to my door.

"Mimi, will you give me a second? Just sit right here," I say, unbuckling myself.

"Sure."

There's a question buried in that single word, but I don't stop to address it. Instead, I grab the handle just as Jason pulls my door open.

As I step out, the air is warm and sweet-smelling, filled with the sounds of the moving crew prepping to unload our boxes. I texted Jason and asked about our furniture. He said we could bring it, store it, or leave it.

I chose to leave it. It was junk, after all, and I'll have the funds to replace it when this is all over.

"Hey," I say, a lot breathier than I'd like. It's hard to speak clearly when your heart is racing.

"Hey." His unabashed smile is one I haven't experienced before. There's no hint of our professional relationship. This isn't a smile you give a friend.

This is the smile a man gives his woman.

Breathe, Chloe.

"What did you tell Mimi?" he asks quietly.

"I told her that I had a surprise that I knew she'd like, but she had to wait until we got here for me to tell her." I blush. "She'll take this better if it comes from you. Your charm easily sways her."

"My charm, huh?" He grins, satisfied with that response. "What do you want me to say? I don't want to complicate this for you. You're in control here."

I've been so busy focusing on moving and fighting myself about this whole plan to really think too much about the reality—we're moving in with Jason.

I glance around, taking in the opulence. *Don't panic, Chloe.*

"Well," I say, tucking a strand of hair behind my ear. "First of all, do you really want us here? I mean, this all happened so fast, and it really is kind of ridiculous, so if you want to just bail—"

"I want you here. *Both of you.*"

I lean against my car and blow out the longest breath. His kind eyes sweep away my second thoughts. His sincerity soothes my nerves.

"If you just need a place to stay, you can stay here," he says. "But if you want to go through with the marriage thing, I'm in."

"Really?"

His grin is lopsided. "Do you want the truth?"

"Of course."

"I think it might be fun, and it's been a long time since I've had any fun in my life. I've had something besides bullshit to think about all afternoon." He pauses. "And I really want to beat Tate and Renn."

I bite my lip to keep my smile from stretching entirely across my face. I think the last part of that sentence was an afterthought for my benefit. And if that's true, that means one of two things: either he wants to make me happy and let me feel good about his help, or he wants me to feel good in many ways.

I shudder a breath.

"Tell me the truth," he says, as if he's almost afraid to finish his thought. "Do you want to go through with the marriage part of this?"

The words are careful—*loaded*. And the anxiety I've felt about this when I was away from him is hard to remember.

"I think it might be fun," I say, my tone playful as I give his words back to him. "I don't think it's wrong for two friends to have a good time as they work together to achieve their goals."

His smile could light up a dark room, and that makes my legs wobbly.

"I'll fly us to Vegas tomorrow afternoon," he says. "You'll be my wife by bedtime, which is convenient."

My body clenches at the proximity of *wife* and *bedtime*. The weight in my belly and the ache between my legs is nearly unbearable.

"How do you want to tell Mimi?" he asks.

"Let's tell her we've been seeing each other secretly for a while," I say. "And that you proposed today, and we didn't want to wait."

"We were planning on telling her, but then this thing happened with the building, and we felt like it was kismet."

"That works."

He lifts a hand and brushes the back of his knuckles down the side of my face. I gasp at the contact. My breath comes out in a pant.

The corner of his mouth twitches. "If we've been seeing each other a while, you can't jump when I touch you. No one will believe I've never touched you before."

My face flames.

"And you can't turn red every time I say something." He chuckles.

"This is a lot for me."

His smirk settles against his lips as his eyes crinkle in the corners. "If you think this is a lot, just wait."

Oh God.

"Mr. Brewer! Where do you want these things?" a man shouts from the truck.

Jason holds up a finger, his attention still on me. "Are you ready to do this?"

I nod.

"Then let's go."

He moves gracefully around the car with me a few steps behind.

He opens Mimi's door, whispering something to make her laugh, and then helps her to her feet. Her eyes are wide and bright as she takes in her surroundings.

"Meems, we have something to tell you," I say.

She laces her arm through Jason's, patting his bicep. "Is this your house, Jason?"

"It is. And the men over there need to know if you'd like to stay in my house with Chloe and me, or if you'd like to stay in the guest-house over there." He points at a quaint, one-story home on the other side of a glittering pool. "The choice is absolutely yours."

She looks at me, narrowing her eyes with a sly smile. "And you're staying with Jason?"

"I haven't told you this," I say, glancing at Jason, "because there's been so much going on. And we wanted to wait until we could really celebrate the occasion. But—"

"Oh my God, you're pregnant, aren't you?" she asks, gasping.

"*What*? No!" I shriek.

Jason laughs, completely unbothered by Mimi's reaction.

"I'm not ... *no*," I say, shaking my head fervently. "I'm not pregnant, Mimi."

She tilts her chin so she can see Jason's face. "You two would make beautiful babies."

"*Stop it*," I say, blushing.

Jason's amusement is written all over his face. "While that isn't our news, we would like to tell you that we're getting married."

She clasps her hands together and looks at the sky. "Oh, thank you, sweet Jesus. Thank you so much." She turns to my "fiancé" and pats his face with both hands. "I couldn't be happier about this. I really couldn't. I was praying you came to see me about something like this and Chloe interrupted us when she got home. I just knew something was going on. I knew it." She looks at me, pointing. "You can't hide things from your grandmother. I always know."

Glad one of us did.

"When I married my husband, we had sex like rabbits for a full year," she says, shrugging. "Sometimes several times a day."

Jason's eyes connect with mine over Mimi's head. We exchange a secret grin that somehow feels like the most intimate thing we've exchanged all day.

"That being said, I'll take the guesthouse," she says, chuckling.

"But are you sure you can live alone?" I ask, snapped back to reality. "You fall and—"

"*Chloe*." She speaks my name as a full sentence. "I'll be fine. I'm certain there are no broken tiles for me to trip over in that cute little place."

Jason pats her hand. "If anything isn't to your liking, you say the word, and it'll be fixed. I want you to be comfortable. Whatever you need or want, all you have to do is say the word."

Well, I guess that answers that ...

"Can you walk me in?" Mimi asks Jason. "I really need to sit down."

"Absolutely. Let's get you inside and then you can direct the movers where to put your things. Chloe and I can help you get it all put away."

She waves a hand through the air. "I'll let them know where to put it all, but let's put it away later. This old woman needs a rest."

"I'll be right back," Jason says, moving slowly across the driveway with my grandmother clinging to his arm. He's unrushed and comfortable, chatting away with her like they've known each other for a lifetime.

Whether he knows it or not, I think he just stole my heart.

He's definitely stolen Mimi's.

But what about when she finds out it was all a lie?

Chapter 13

Chloe

"Welcome to our humble abode," Jason says from my side.

I flush at the use of *our*—as in this is my home now too—and step beneath the oversized ferns hanging from along the edge of the patio.

The patio is bigger than four of my apartments put together. Ceiling fans swirl silently overhead, and a sauna is seamlessly tucked into the back corner. An outdoor kitchen complete with a built-in grill is nestled along the other side. Sitting out here in the evenings, looking across the pool and hot tub while reading a book, must be so relaxing.

I glance across my shoulder at Jason. *Or doing other things ...*

My heart thumps steadily as he reaches ahead of me and opens a door into the house. I try not to breathe in too deeply so the scent of his cologne doesn't trigger my body's automatic response to him. I need to keep a clear head.

"Humble?" I ask, giggling. "With all due respect, there's nothing humble about this."

The door closes softly behind us.

"This is magazine-worthy." I turn in a circle, taking it all in. It feels like I've stepped out of my world and into another universe. "Did you design this?"

He shoves his hands in his pockets. "Yeah. Most of it. I had a good idea of what I wanted."

"I like your style."

This seems to please him. "Let me show you the rest."

He leads me through the family room with a gigantic fireplace that burns real wood and a television screen that transforms from a piece of art with the touch of a button. The shiny hardwood floors are so clean I can almost see my reflection, and pictures in simple frames are peppered around the room. They complement the perfect shade of soft white walls.

Nothing is out of place or even slightly askew.

Except me.

I glance down at my dirty Coffee and Cream T-shirt the coffee shop was giving away last spring at a customer appreciation event and a pair of cutoff jean shorts I made when my favorite jeans got a hole in the knee. I'm undoubtedly dusty, and I wouldn't be surprised if there are cobwebs in my hair.

This is not the Chloe I usually present to Jason. And as he looks at me over his shoulder, explaining something about his quartz countertops in the chef's kitchen, I consider what he must be thinking.

What is she doing here?

I know I'm wondering how the hell I got here ... and how, despite every convenience known to man, I'll ever be comfortable in a place like this.

We round the corner, and he shows me the pantry, which is big enough to live in. Down the hall is the laundry room, a bedroom with a small desk and a bathroom that he says is Mara's office, his housekeeper, whom I'll meet later. The dining room, with a wall of windows overlooking the backyard, has a long table that seats fifteen.

It's incredible.

It's a lot to take in.

"My goal was to create a space where I could relax at the end of the day," he says. "I never really felt that way in any other home, and I really wanted a place that felt like me."

"Your mother's house, the one you grew up in, was always so untouchable, if that makes sense," I say, remembering the home with actual busts of philosophers placed on tables. "My mom threatened me every day not to break anything. She'd tell me not to even breathe on it."

We make it to the landing, and he ushers me to the left.

"Oh, Mom would tell us the same," he says. "Our childhood was interesting. We were a tactile bunch—wrestling and whatnot. And Mom is a big hugger. But our house didn't really match that vibe. Renn's friends used to call it a museum, and they weren't wrong."

He points out three bedrooms, all with their own bathrooms. Then we retrace our steps and pass the staircase.

"I can see what you're saying," I say. "Your mom was always so warm and sweet. But your house was so ... cold."

"I have lots of theories about that." He opens a set of double doors. "But we can save that for another time."

"Yeah. Let's save that for later."

I gasp as all thoughts of Jason's childhood home become distant memories.

Jason's very adult bedroom is moody. Relaxing. *Sexy*.

It's an oasis from life outside these doors. And it's very different —*so much better*—than I visualized late at night while I imagined lying in his bed.

But now I'm here. And I'm going to be lying in his bed very, *very* soon.

My mouth goes dry.

The walls are the deepest green—so dark that they're almost black. The bed sits high off the floor with four posts and a headboard that's padded in leather. The bedding is black, and as I drag my fingertips across it, I note how silky it feels against my skin.

It sends a shiver up my spine.

He presses a button, and the blinds open, displaying French doors that open to a terrace. Beyond the railing are treetops. It's as if we're in a tower, secluded from the world.

"Do you like it?" he asks, a thread of hope in his tone. "This is a closet." He pulls open a door I didn't notice. "And the en suite is through the doorway."

"Do I like it?" I chuckle, moseying my way through the arch toward the bathroom. "What's not to like?"

The en suite is beautiful and masculine, with no expense spared for luxury. The floors are stone. Two sinks are positioned atop a cabinet suspended off the floor, with mirrors behind each one. A massive, sleek, square tub with a brass faucet is mounted on the wall. A shower big enough for a small party lines the back wall.

I think about my thread-bare towels packed in boxes in the driveway and want to laugh. *And cry.*

"Can you imagine yourself in here?" he asks, leaning against the wall.

"I can imagine myself in this tub for sure." I sit on the edge. The material is cool against my behind. "I might get in and never want to get out."

This makes him smile.

I take a deep breath as a moment of peace settles in my soul. For the first time today, I'm calm. The tilt-a-whirl has stopped.

"I'm not sure if I said thank you or not," I say. "This day has been one for the record books."

"It's not a problem."

I grin up at him. "I mean it, Jason. I'm sitting here in your personal bathroom with my grandmother occupying your guest-house." I laugh softly. "Mimi was on the floor bleeding this morning, and I was in a state of panic. My life was falling apart one six-hundred-dollar error and broken tile at a time, and I felt alone and helpless ... and I don't know which I hate more."

He presses off the wall. "You're the least helpless person I know, Chloe."

"It doesn't feel that way when every time you try to take a step in the right direction, the world somehow pushes you back three spaces."

"Why didn't you say something to me? I know we went over this earlier, and I don't want to get into it too much now because I don't want to be angry. But why in the world didn't you mention your situation?"

I swallow around a knot in my throat and choose to ignore his questions. "Thank you for taking us in."

"You aren't foster animals."

I grin, my heart swelling.

"I want you to promise me something," he says.

"What's that?"

He stops by the shower and takes a breath. When he speaks, his words are soft yet serious. "Promise me you won't worry—about anything—for the next six months."

"That's easier said than done."

"*Promise me.* We'll be married. Your problems will be mine, and there can be no secrets between us."

"I'll try." I exhale and smile through it, though it's wobbly. "I know you have the bet to win, but I also understand that you're the one being put out by all of this. We're invading your home. I'm inserting myself into your personal life. I didn't really think too much about it before I blurted out to Tate that we were getting married like it was a foregone conclusion. That probably makes me a bad person."

A flash of irritation sweeps across his face. "You are absolutely not a bad person."

I shrug because I'm not so sure. "Either way, I want you to know that I see your sacrifices, and I know you're choosing to make them, and I appreciate you. More than you will ever know."

We exchange a grin.

"And I want you to know that I respect the hell out of you for trying to juggle all of this on your own—even though it irritates me," he says. "And marrying you might seem crazy to some people, but it makes sense to me. Just remember that I make deliberate decisions. I wouldn't do this if I didn't want to."

I stand, my hands shaking. I need to say this—I need to be clear.

"Marriage isn't a big deal to me because I don't put a lot of value on it," I say. "For reasons I don't want to discuss, it's not sacred in my world. But I realize it might be for you. Marrying *me* might stain something that matters to you, and I need you to know I don't want you to do that. Not for me—even if you want to."

My words are uneven, filled with fear that he'll back out. Maybe he got caught up in the moment, in the stress of Tate's shenanigans, and agreed too easily. And, because he's my friend, maybe he can't backtrack without fear of hurting me—something I know he'd never do.

My heart pounds as he cuts the distance between us. He stands directly in front of me, peering down, with energy rippling off him so hard that it steals my breath.

"I don't do anything I don't want to do," he says, focusing on my lips. "And I don't want to be questioned about it again."

I gasp a quick breath as his gaze crashes into mine.

"Do you want to be my wife? Is this really what *you* want?" He licks his lips, hesitating. "Because marriage *is* a big deal to me, even if this one has special circumstances. But I will expect complete exclusivity. I will be your husband—and I will take that honor seriously. You need to understand that. This is going to be very real to me."

His pupils dilate in the dimly lit room. The muscle in his jaw flexes as he waits for my answer. His mind is going a million miles an hour—I can see it behind the gold-flecked jade of his irises.

My mouth goes dry as I imagine his hands on me, removing our clothes and then guiding me to my knees.

The only thing sexier than the look he's giving me is the care he's taking to get my consent—to make sure I know what I'm agreeing to and that I want it.

I want it.

I want him.

In every way.

The thought makes me shudder.

"So no fucking anyone else?" I ask coyly.

The vein in the side of his temple throbs. "Absolutely not."

I'm playing with fire here. I can already feel the heat. Even though it should make me nervous, it does the opposite. I feel safe and absolutely turned on.

"I told you once I'd do anything for you," I say, staring into his eyes. "And I don't want to be questioned about it again."

His smirk is foreplay.

I move backward against the tub until the edge hits the backs of my knees. Jason takes a step forward until his chest nearly touches mine. His cologne envelops me in pheromones, and if he asks me to strip right now, I will.

His feet are on the other side of mine, caging me in. His cock brushes against my stomach, and all it would take is one touch, and I'd explode.

"So that settles it then," I say, my chest rising and falling quickly. "I'm going to be your wife in every aspect of the word."

His Adam's apple bobs in his throat. I want to rise up and lick it—grip his muscled shoulders and pull him into me. He must read my mind because he pulls a minuscule distance away.

"For the next six months, you're mine," he says, his voice rough. "If you want out, all you have to do is ask. But until you do ask, I will treat you like I think you should be treated."

"How's that?"

The twinkle in his eye is divine.

"With respect." He brushes a strand of hair off my shoulder, making me shiver. "With attention." His hand wraps around my neck under my hairline. "With kindness." He leans in and kisses me just under my earlobe.

Oh. I moan softly. *I might melt right here.*

His lips hover over my ear. "And I'm going to give you so many orgasms that you'll be begging me to stop," he whispers.

I've kept my attraction to Jason in check for years, but nothing will stop me from acting on it now. The light is most definitely bright, glaring green.

I reach between us and cup his cock in my hand.

He gasps, then grunts as he flexes against me, his eyes hooding.

"While I'm going to hold you to that promise, I'm also going to reciprocate," I whisper back. "As a matter of fact, I'm thinking about taking you in my mouth right now and showing you just how grateful I am for your kindness."

He grips my face with both hands, his mouth hovering over my lips. I sink against the tub as my pussy aches, begging for relief.

Begging for him.

"I'm not touching you until we're married," he whispers back, grinning deviously.

I gasp. "*What*?"

"I have to be sure you aren't agreeing to this now just because you want my cock."

My laughter is thick with frustration. "You're really going to make me wait?"

He blows against my lips, making me moan. "You're going to wait." Then he pulls away without making contact.

"I'm glad it's so easy for you." Even I can hear the need in my voice. "Maybe I don't want to marry you after all."

"Chloe, I've wanted your pussy since the day I saw you in Coffee and Cream. Every day, I climb into that shower and jack off while imagining your mouth covering my cock, and I climb into that bed and think about how you'd feel stretched around me."

He lifts a brow as his words land.

"You can find out right now," I say, my insides vibrating with need.

"I've shown an enormous amount of restraint for three years. Waiting another day or two to get what I want, even if it's only for six months, is not that hard." He grins devilishly. "It'll make that pussy even sweeter."

Holy shit.

"Now let's go," he says, walking away without waiting for an answer.

I pick my jaw off the floor and follow him, too mind-blown to find a proper retort.

He's been thinking about me all these years? Holy shit.

We move silently through the house and out the back door. He pauses to instruct the movers about where to put my things, then he guides me into the guesthouse—all without so much as brushing against me accidentally.

I glare at him as he enters the guesthouse behind me, ensuring to keep his distance. *Bastard.*

"Oh, Chloe," Mimi says, beaming. "You should see this place."

I take in the sweet, simple casita with smooth tile, a tidy little kitchen, and a door opening to a bedroom. It's exactly what I would dream for her. It's perfect.

I glance over my shoulder at Jason, the hunger in my eyes telling him I'll be thanking him for this, too. He winks.

"Thank you for letting me stay here, Jason," she says, reaching for a hug. "You're a good boy."

My chest fills with warmth as they embrace.

"Now, when are you two getting married?" she asks.

"Um, I think we're still working out the details," I say, uncertain.

"Saturday," Jason says. "What do you think about Vegas, Mimi?"

She wrinkles her nose. "Vegas? I don't want to go to Vegas. You two go and enjoy yourselves. I'll be fine here."

"You can't miss our wedding," I say. "You have to be there."

"Your wedding day is about you, not me. All I want for you is to enjoy yourself. Even if I'm there, I'll worry I'm in the way. I'll be too tired to be out doing shots with you at two in the morning."

Jason chuckles.

"Meems," I say, shaking my head.

"Go on," she says. "Have fun. Have lots and lots of sex."

"*Mimi!*"

"I'd be riding that man like a pony, Chloe."

My eyes are wide, and I don't dare look at Jason even though I know he's looking at me.

"Can we not do this right now?" I ask, fanning my face. "Besides, we can't leave you alone. I don't want you to fall."

"*Yes, you can.* I'm not going to fall here. And I love you, Chloe, but I think I'm going to like having a bit of time alone for a change. And I can go sit outside." She rests her head on the back of the recliner. "Greta isn't here to drive me crazy. I can watch my shows in peace. You go marry that stud and work on babies and let me relax."

I steal a glance at Jason. He's looking at the floor, chuckling softly.

"I can't just leave you," I say, my stomach stirring at the thought of having Jason all to myself.

"My housekeeper, Mara, could check on you," Jason offers, lifting his chin. "She's worked for me for ten years. She's practically family. I can even ask her to stay while we're gone." He looks at me. "She does that sometimes for various purposes and usually doesn't mind. I can ask."

"Ask." Mimi says it too quickly for me to get a word in. "I want you two out of here."

"Mimi, he'll have to pay her. Let's not be too quick to ask for things."

She laughs. "Sweetheart, he has the money. And if you haven't noticed how he looks at you, I'm pretty sure he'd sell the moon to have you all alone."

Jason's grin knocks me sideways.

"Chloe, I've wanted your pussy since the day I saw you in Coffee and Cream. Every day, I climb into that shower and jack off while imagining your mouth covering my cock, and I climb into that bed and think about how you'd feel stretched around me."

With that visual in my head, there's no way I can say no.

So I shrug. "Ask her."

Jason takes his phone out of his pocket and makes a call.

Chapter 14

Jason

"Will advise when I have the weather. November-Four-Four-Five-Whiskey-Xray," I say before taking my thumb off the radio button.

Chloe giggles, and the sound is like music through my headset. "In English, please?"

"I'm telling the guy on the approach frequency that I'll let them know when I've listened to the radio broadcasting the weather."

Her face is lit up, as bright as it has been since we arrived on the tarmac earlier tonight. The previous couple of hours were hectic. Mara's excitement over my engagement was palpable. She offered to come immediately so I could whisk my fiancée away. I started to decline her offer, figuring Chloe and Mimi had had enough excitement for one day. But Mimi interjected, something I'm discovering happens often, and Chloe held her breath. I took my chances and here we are.

On our way to get married.

I fight against the smile tickling my lips as the thought runs through my mind again and again.

This situation is against everything I am in so many ways. Yet … here I am.

Chloe peers into the night sky, more relaxed than I've seen her in a long damn time. Her skin is smooth and her shoulders slack. I kick myself for not noticing how stressed she must've been lately. While she was worrying about me—scheduling massages and ordering me dinner to arrive once I was home—she needed someone to be worrying about her.

I tell myself it was because I had no reason to believe she was struggling. But that's just an excuse.

And it'll never happen again … although it seems I have a habit of not seeing what's in front of my face. *Thanks, Dad, you fucker.*

"Are you doing okay over there?" I ask.

Chloe rolls her head to face me, her thick lashes fluttering. "This is pretty incredible. I've dreamed of this a million times and knew it would be something to see, but it's better than I imagined."

"It's pretty dark out there. Wait until we fly home. It'll be light out, and you'll see some beautiful landscapes."

Her lips twitch. "I'm not talking about landscapes, Jason."

I smirk as her gaze travels over my jaw, down my shoulders, and along the length of my arms.

"Just when I think you can't get any hotter, I get to watch you fly a plane," she says, grinning.

"That makes sense," I say, bracing myself for her reaction. "Every woman who finds out I'm a pilot is instantly turned on."

She gasps. "Hey! You can't talk about other women now. I'm about to be your wife, Mr. Brewer."

She's only playing, but I'm not.

I lift a brow. "And hearing you call yourself my wife is, *by far*, the hottest thing I've ever heard."

Her playfulness switches to lust, and I feel the heat in my cock.

Our connection has shifted seamlessly from friends to soon-to-be lovers, a term I'm ready to unhyphenate as soon as possible. I've tried to play it cool and ensure I'm not taking advantage of her. But she brushed her hand against my groin when getting into the car, swiped her ass against my cock when boarding the plane, and wore the lowest-cut top she owns.

She wants this as much as I do.

And I'm here to help ... and please.

God, I want to please her.

"I thought the hottest thing you've ever heard would be something like *the safety reports are all on your desk, and there are no violations,*" she jokes, pulling her sweater tighter. The movement causes her breasts to press together and amplifies her cleavage.

I chuckle. "That *is* pretty hot."

Her laughter's quick, and I want to reach out and touch her. Stroke the side of her face. Let my fingertips dance up her thigh. Press my hand into the small of her back and guide her to me.

But I can't. Not yet.

If it kills me, and it might, I will show her respect. I'll wait until she proves this is what she wants by going through with it. *By marrying me.*

"What are you thinking?" she asks.

I hide a smile.

"Tell me," she says.

"I was just thinking that you were my assistant yesterday, and today we're on our way to get married—and we weren't even in a relationship."

"It's kind of perfect, huh?"

My brow furrows as I look at her.

"Relationships are a pain in the ass," she says. "What's the point of them? To get to know each other?" She shrugs. "Well, I know you better than I would've had we been dating. I've seen you every day for years, and I've seen you at your best and not so best."

That makes me laugh.

"We skipped the getting-to-know-you and are going right to the fun," she says, her grin mischievous.

She has a point.

"Do you think anyone in the office will believe we've been secretly dating?" she asks. "I'm kinda worried it'll be weird on Monday."

"What can I do to make it less weird?"

She shrugs.

"Well, first, I don't give a fuck what anyone believes," I say. "My private life is none of their concern. Second, I'll fire anyone who makes you feel uncomfortable. And, third, if you really don't want to be there, you can work from home. Or quit. Or go work for Tate."

"Yeah. No thanks on that last option."

I chuckle.

"Can I ask you something else?" she asks.

"Sure."

"Why did you agree to this so quickly?" She nibbles a fingernail. "You didn't even think about it."

"Because I know what I want."

Her eyes narrow, but she doesn't speak. She keeps biting her nail.

"I told you we can't have secrets between us," I say, adjusting our altitude. "So, in the spirit of transparency, when this opportunity came along, it wasn't hard to agree to it because I've known for a long time that if I were ever to marry anyone ..." I settle back and face her. "You were the only choice."

She gasps, her lips puckering into the sweetest pout.

"I know this is for six months." I drag my gaze away, my stomach churning. "And that's fine. But I'll know what it's like to be married because I'll likely never do it again."

"Jason ..."

She says my name as if it were a question and a statement. I don't dare look at her because I'm unsure what to say. I told her the truth—*well, most of it, anyway. Six months won't be enough for me.* I'll never be sorry for telling her what I think she can manage. I only hope the truth doesn't scare the shit out of her.

"I had no idea," she says, stammering.

I shrug. "You weren't supposed to have an idea. You were my

good friend and my excellent EA." I grin. "But, come on. You had to know I think you're beautiful. How many times have we been seconds away from crossing lines?"

"A hundred." She shifts in her seat. "But okay. This is good information."

"It is?"

"Yes. It is." She takes a breath, releasing her grip on her sweater. "This should add pressure to the situation, but it really takes it off."

"How do you figure?"

"Well, we're going to be married anyway. I know we said we'd treat it like a real marriage, but that was still under the guise of the bet. But if we look at it like we're curious about marriage, even if we don't really want it, we may as well experience it."

I like where this is going.

"I'm going to be your wife, Mr. Brewer," she says, her voice filled with a naughtiness that constricts my entire body. "We're marrying because of the bet. We're going all in because we want to."

Fucking hell.

She lays her palm on my leg precariously close to my groin. There's enough pressure to send bolts of electricity rippling through my veins but not enough to feel satisfied.

Her hair is pulled back from her face, and the front of her shirt scoops just above the top of her bra. Her nipples are hard, pebbling through the thin fabric of her T-shirt that she leaves bared for me to see.

I fight a swallow, reminding myself I'm flying an airplane.

The tips of her fingers tease my cock. I snatch her hand in a snap and then bring it to my lips. Her hand is tiny, fitting easily inside mine as I press the slightest kiss to her palm. She moans softly, her eyes fluttering closed as I release her.

"Were you being serious earlier?" she asks, opening her eyes. "When you said you thought about me in the shower?"

"And in my bed. And this plane. God knows how many times I've imagined you on your hands and knees under my desk with my cock in your mouth while I do business."

"All you had to do was ask."

My insides burn as she toys with me. "That's illegal, I'm pretty sure."

"Not if I'm willing. What about blow jobs on airplanes? Are those illegal?"

I laugh—a mix of frustration and need—as the lights of Vegas come into view. I've never been happier to see a destination in my career.

"November-Four-Four-Five-Whiskey-Xray, cleared to land," Tower says. "Runway Two-Five-Left. Winds are Two-Seven-Zero at Fifteen."

I repeat the information back.

"I take it that means we're almost there," Chloe says.

"We'll be on the ground in a few minutes."

Our gazes connect, and her smile pulls at the corners of my mouth.

She's going to be my wife.

And I have six months to convince her to make it forever.

Chapter 15

Jason

"This is Renn's penthouse?" Chloe asks, spinning in a circle. "Holy crap. This is crazy."

I tip the bellman—cash is king—and then lock the door behind him.

Renn's apartment *is* something to see.

Chloe moves through the sitting area, mouth agape, and passes the spiral staircase. I follow her into the atrium. High ceilings open to the loft above, and floor-to-ceiling windows give an unobstructed view of the Strip. A white marble table has been placed in the center of the room. I can only imagine what Renn has used it for over the years, considering he doesn't exactly host dinner parties.

"If this were mine, I'd just live here," she says, taking in the twinkling lights below us. "I mean, look at this view. It's like you're a princess perched in your castle, looking across your kingdom."

I sink into a leather sofa beneath the loft and watch Chloe.

"Renn doesn't even come here much anymore," I say. "Hell, he's never really used this place."

"Then why does he have it?"

"Gannon convinced him to invest in real estate a few years ago.

Renn had more money than he knew what to do with, and Gannon was trying to make him more responsible—think ahead and plan." I sigh. "Dad said something to piss Renn off, so he bought this place."

Chloe turns to me. "Why would this make him mad? Who wouldn't be proud of their son for owning this?"

"Well, Dad and Gannon were thinking of a family home in Nashville or a ski château in Aspen. Renn bought a penthouse in Sin City."

"*Oh.*"

"Yeah. *Oh.*"

She looks up at the loft. "Does Renn not get along with your dad and Gannon?"

I catch my response before it rolls off my tongue and rethink how to phrase it.

Our relationships with our father are complicated, but Renn's was the most contentious, especially at the end. I'm still surprised that Renn didn't put Dad in the hospital after what he did to Blakely. Maybe Renn has more self-restraint than we give him credit for.

"Renn and Gannon are okay now," I say. "Gannon has always been a little harder to deal with than the rest of our siblings."

"Why?"

"I don't know. I guess because he's good at everything but not exceptional at any of it. He's the oldest, and the only thing he can do better than the rest of us is golf. Bianca is the smartest of us. Tate's the funniest. Ripley's the most charismatic. I could kick the shit out of all of them."

Chloe grins.

"Renn's the most athletic, and Gannon is second or third in all those categories except that he was supposed to take over the Brewer empire—but he *couldn't*. Wouldn't. Bianca stepped in and filled that void."

Her grin falters.

"Dad saw a lot of himself in Gannon, especially when he was younger," I say, wondering why the hell I'm talking about this with her. But the thought doesn't stop me. "He said it all the time. I think as Gannon grew up and saw more of who Dad was, the perceived similarities bothered him. I think that's why Gannon didn't take over. He could've. Maybe not as well as Bianca, but he could've done it. Yet he didn't."

I've never admitted that to anyone—not even my siblings. But it's a thought I've always held.

She leans against the table, her face serious. "Did it bother you growing up to think Gannon was your dad's favorite child?"

I stretch until the pull of my muscles makes me wince. "I don't know if I would say it bothered me. But I probably have a lot of second-child complexes."

Chloe smiles softly.

"Dad and I didn't get along," I say. "Ever, really. I don't know if it was because I was the second born or if I was just a different kind of child than the rest of them. But I remember thinking all he cared about was money and reputation, and I hated that."

"That makes sense. You're still like that now."

I smile at her. "I was also pretty hardheaded."

"*I'm shocked.*" She grins. "How is your relationship with your mother? Can I ask that? Or is that pushing too far?"

It would be pushing too far, and I'd shut anyone else down for asking. But I'm strangely okay with talking about it with her. It's no surprise, really. I've shared more of myself with Chloe over the years than with anyone else. It's why I've valued our friendship so much, and why she's the only person I could ever see myself marrying. This, talking about the hard shit, *the ugly shit*, is what we've always been able to do.

"Our relationship now is great," I say. "I love my mother. I can understand why she did a lot of the things she did that bothered me as a kid."

"Like what?"

I blow out a breath. "I don't know. Like, she always wanted us to think the best of our father, which I get. It's important for kids to have someone to look up to, and for boys, that's generally the dad. But I never wanted to be like him." My stomach twists. "He wasn't the man I wanted to emulate. I found my heroes in books, and Mom and I often fought about that. She wanted me to be like him, and that's the last thing I wanted. Then you factor in that she had five other kids. I either had to pretend to be something I wasn't, like interested in business, or behave badly, which I didn't like to do, to get their attention. There wasn't space for me to just be myself—to be real. Someone was never just cheering for me because they were all too busy. I see that now, but I didn't then. I carried that with me for a long time."

Chloe shoves off the table and sits next to me. She pulls her bare feet up and under her, her knee brushing against my arm. The contact lights me up. I want to draw her closer ... but I don't.

"Do you want to be a dad?" she asks, her eyes searching mine.

I nod, holding my breath. I don't want to scare her off, but I can't lie to her. Omitting the truth or being vague is not being honest.

"I do," I say slowly. "The older I get, the more fucked up life becomes, and the more I want a family of my own. Just my own little family to pour my energy into, you know?"

"I understand although I've never really wanted kids."

My stomach drops.

"My father ..." She sighs. "He wasn't very nice to my mother. And the last thing he said to me was that he loved me, and I never saw him again. That'll screw with you. And then my grandfather wasn't a nice man. My first memory of him was yelling at me for spilling my drink at dinner. And the last memory I have of him is telling Mimi she caused his heart attack." She sighs again. "I guess I've always felt like having more people to love is a burden because, eventually, they'll disappoint you. I do a good job of disappointing myself."

She grins, but I can't return it.

"You'll be a good dad someday," she says.

"You never know. You might meet a man someday and want to have kids."

Her shrug is noncommittal. "I've wondered what that kind of love would *feel* like. It may be the only form of real love that exists."

"Why do you say that?"

"I've seen it between my mom and me, and I've experienced it with Mimi. That's all. Because from what I've seen, love between two adults is so transaction-based. It's all about filling a role in the other person's life and not this undying selflessness toward someone. At least, I've never seen that in real life."

My breath stalls in my throat as I focus on her words. *"It's all about filling a role in the other person's life and not this undying selflessness toward someone."* That's exactly what we're doing here. We're filling a role in the other person's life via a transaction.

The idea that she sees me like every other man in her life bothers me. A lot. I don't want to feed into her wound. I want to fix it. I want to heal her by loving her sacrificially and by showing her that love isn't a burden.

Loving her is the easiest thing I've ever done.

"I think that kind of love exists," I say.

"Well, it doesn't matter what all the men I've encountered have done," she says. "I'm only concerned with one man right now."

Her tongue darts along her bottom lip, leaving a glistening trail behind.

Fuck.

She stretches backward until her shirt slips up her stomach, displaying her smooth skin just below her tits. As she lowers her arms, she catches me watching her and grins.

"What do you say we call it a night and go to bed?" she asks coyly.

I chuckle. "There's no way I'm getting in bed with you right now."

"Why?"

I place my hand on my lap and squeeze my jeans around my hard cock. Her gaze drops to it and then back to me.

"And how is that a problem?" she asks.

"Because I'm not touching you until we're married. I told you that."

She groans. "We're not taking serious vows, for crying out loud. What does it matter?"

It matters to me because I don't want her to look back on this and think it was a joke. Even though it is technically a bet, and the premise of this isn't exactly love, if I can figure out how to make her fall in love with me, I want her to reflect on this day and know I was in love with her even now. And if that doesn't happen, then it doesn't.

"Fine," she says, standing. She faces me and slides her sweater off her shoulders. "You don't have to touch me. But what if I touch you?"

I want to tell her no—to hold firm to my decision not to make this physical until tomorrow after we're married. But the way she's looking at me makes it really fucking hard.

My knees spread farther apart, and I reach up, unable to help myself. I keep my hands on the outside of her skirt and grab her ass, guiding her to sit on my lap.

I hiss as her pussy sits against me, and her tits are in my face. *This was a terrible, amazing move.* She pushes her weight down and smiles as if she won a battle.

A battle, maybe. But not the war.

"This is the closest you're going to get until tomorrow," I say, groaning as she rocks against me. The heat of her pussy radiates through the denim covering me. I grab her hips and try to hold her still. "You should stop."

Instead, she leans forward, breathing against my lips. "What if I don't want to?"

Dammit.

Before I can talk myself out of it, I take the hem of her shirt and drag it up. She lifts her hands as it rises and tosses it to the floor.

"Who knew you'd be such a troublemaker?" I ask.

The tops of her breasts round above the cups of her bra, jiggling with every move she makes. The white lace covers her dark nipples. It's a good thing, or else they'd probably be in my mouth.

"Is this a dream?" I ask as she grinds against me. I clench my teeth and try not to come in my pants.

Her fingers wind through the hair on the back of my head, and she presses my face forward—into her cleavage.

"It could be a wet dream if you let it," she whispers.

My body buzzes. My cock strains so hard against my jeans that it hurts. With every push, circle, and slide of Chloe's pussy against it, it threatens to burst.

"I'm dying to know how wet you are." I drag my tongue beneath the lace and over the top of her chest. Her skin is silky and sweet, making me crave her taste elsewhere.

She moans, pulling her bra down to expose her hard buds.

"Fuck, Chloe," I say, my restraint faltering.

She moves my head toward her again, and I drag one nipple into my mouth. She rocks harder against me, tilting her clit to move against the rough denim.

I palm her other breast, feeling the weight of it in my hand. The heat of her skin. The scent of her arousal.

My head spins as I try to keep grounded, but it's impossible. Her sweet pants whisper through the air. The taste of her body on my tongue. The feel of her moving against me, her hair brushing my face, and her breath on my cheek.

The pressure inside my cock builds higher than I thought possible.

"I can't wait to feel you inside me." She throws her head back, her eyes closed—giving me access to as much of her as I want. *And I want it all.* "I need to get off, Jason. I've needed it for so long."

It would take a second to bury myself in her, but watching her like this is erotic.

My hands drop to her ass again—this time, under her skirt. She gasps at the contact and then grinds even harder.

"Can you come like this, beautiful?" I ask, taking in every whisper of a breath.

"I think so."

"Come for me. Let me watch you."

Her eyes fly open as reality hits her.

I smirk. "Don't be shy now." I spread her cheeks apart. "I want to watch you fall apart."

She hesitates, her face flushing. For a long moment, I'm not sure what she'll do. Her hips lift as if she's going to say something. As she adjusts her position, my fingers find her seam, and I swipe a finger through the wetness.

"*Oh*," she says, exhaling.

I move my knees farther apart. "Is that a yes?"

"Yes."

She moves again, her chest bouncing in my face. Her juices coat my hands as she works against me.

"You are fucking gorgeous, Chloe," I say, squeezing her ass. "Watching you like this makes it hard not to get off."

"Jason ..."

I grit my teeth, so close to coming myself, and will myself to hold on.

She shrieks as she falls apart spectacularly.

A flush colors her face, and heat pours from her pussy. Her head falls back, her hair swishing against my arms, and her lips form the perfect O.

"I want all of it," I say, moving her hips as she slows.

"I can't. I can't, Jason," she says between ragged breaths. "*Please*."

She falls to my shoulder. I press a kiss to her clavicle and then move her to the side.

I can't wait anymore.

My zipper falls. My cock is in my palm. I shake as I pump myself, holding her gaze as I do. A bead of precum is already on the tip.

"You did this to me." I stroke it once more and then stop.

Reaching over, I drag my fingers through her slit. She moans again, and it only makes me harder. "I want you so fucking bad."

My teeth are clenched as I spread her cum over my length and then run my hand up and down my shaft.

"I'm yours," she says softly.

And that's all it takes.

I tense as her words throw me over the edge. My entire body shakes. My eyes squeeze shut. Cum spews from the tip in thick, hot ropes.

Before I know what's happening, Chloe's between my legs, covering the head of my cock with her mouth, taking every drop down her throat.

The sight of her positioned like this—of her doe eyes looking up at me with my dick in her mouth—is more than I can take.

I grab the back of her head and flex into her mouth, my orgasm wracking my body with such force that I think my head might explode.

"*Fuck!*" I groan, trembling as the last waves of pleasure wane.

I release her, and she sits back, grinning as she licks her lips.

I laugh in disbelief.

"Do me a favor?" she asks, fluttering her lashes.

"Right now? I'd do anything you ask."

"Is this a life hack?" She grins. "Suck you off and then ask for favors?"

"You now know my secrets."

She laughs, rising off her knees. "Can we get married tonight? Surely, you can do that in Vegas, right?"

"Your wish is my command."

And right now, that's a dangerous place to be.

Chapter 16

Jason

For the first time in my life, I wish Renn were here.

The King and Bling Chapel off the Strip was his suggestion, to put it lightly. It's where he accidentally married Blakely on her thirtieth birthday, and he argued with me for twenty minutes this evening when I mentioned getting married on a gondola.

At least if my brother were here, he could make a joke, and I'd want to throttle him instead of concentrating on how fast my heart is beating.

Chloe fidgets with a bouquet of pink roses I had delivered to the apartment before we left.

"Hey," I say, nudging her with my elbow. "Having regrets?"

"Only one."

My brows furrow.

"I wish Mimi were here," she says softly. Tears spring to her eyes. "I didn't think I was going to get emotional." She laughs, sniffling. "I'm just ... ignore me."

I step to the side to allow a newly married couple to pass. "I will never ignore you, Chloe."

"You know what I mean."

As the couple before us enters the staging room, a woman with a name tag reading *Corbin* arrives at our side.

"Are you two lovebirds ready?" she asks, shoving a pair of black-rimmed glasses up her nose. "You make a gorgeous couple."

"Thank you," Chloe says, accepting a tissue from Corbin.

"Yes," I say, keeping an eye on my bride. "We're ready."

"*Not yet*!" a voice shouts.

We all look over our shoulders as a commotion erupts in the lobby. The couple behind us steps quickly out of the way as a barrage of bodies—ones I know very well—charge into the room.

"Did we make it?" Tate asks, panting. "Tell us we made it."

"If you wouldn't have been taking selfies with the stewardesses, we wouldn't be cutting it so damn close," Ripley says, smacking me on the shoulder. "What's up, brother?"

Chloe's fingers lace through mine, and she gives them a tight squeeze. It's almost as tight as the one in my chest.

These bastards.

"What in the hell are you guys doing here?" I ask, laughing.

"Do you really think you're getting married without us?" Tate asks. "I had to see this with my own eyes."

"And Mom sent us to FaceTime." Ripley holds up a phone. "She basically threatened to give Bianca my inheritance if I didn't get here in time. She couldn't get to the airport quickly enough, and Bianca didn't find out the news until about twenty minutes ago. So prepare yourself. She's pissed."

"How did you get here so quickly?" Chloe asks.

Tate grins. "We have a brother who owns an airline." He looks at me. "You paid for that flight, by the way."

I roll my eyes as my brothers each pull my fiancée into a quick hug.

Chloe's cheeks color the same as her flowers as she accepts their congratulations. They tease her, joking that she's now fair game. And although she pushes back, she has a smile on her face. If I'm not mistaken, she's enjoying this.

"I also have orders," Tate says, digging his hand into his pocket. "Mimi wants to FaceTime, too."

Chloe's jaw falls open. "How do you know Mimi?"

"I have my ways." Tate winks at her. "She's at home, propped up in bed, watching black-and-white movies with Mara. They're having a girls' night. But Mimi does want to watch you get hitched to the old man here."

I shove my elbow into Tate's side. He bends at the hip and groans for effect.

The couple from before comes out of the staging area, whooping and hollering. We all clap as the groom picks up his bride and throws her over his shoulders. She loses a shoe in the process.

"You're up!" Corbin says, her red lips parting into a wide smile. "Go on in. Do you have any questions? Or do you remember how we went over everything?"

I glance at Chloe. She's beaming up at me.

"We're good," I say. "Thanks, Corbin."

"Of course. Now, go get married!"

Ripley holds the door open, and we enter a white room. White tile floors, white fabric draped over the walls and ceiling, and a white chandelier streaming a bright white light.

"What do we do now?" Tate asks.

"I go on inside and wait by the floral arch," I say. "Chloe stays here until she hears the wedding march. You guys can go on in with me, I guess."

Ripley starts toward the door into the chapel but stalls. He looks over his shoulder at Chloe.

She grips my hand, tears filling her eyes again. Her gaze darts around the room until it lands on Ripley.

"Hey," he says, flicking his attention to me for approval. I nod. "I know I'm not your father or anything, but would you like me to walk you down the aisle? If not, that's okay. I just thought you might need someone to whisper in your ear on the way to Jason and remind you of all his good qualities so you don't realize what you're doing and bail."

She laughs, the sound strangled by a wash of emotions. She doesn't speak, only nods.

My heart grows, and I give my little brother a wink.

"Give me your phone," Tate says, holding out a hand. "I'll be the best man and the wedding videographer."

Ripley forks his phone over to Tate. I take one last look at my soon-to-be wife.

She's absolutely beautiful.

Her hair is down, one side pulled over to the other shoulder and fastened invisibly. Her dress hits her mid-calf and has billowy sleeves that make her look like an angel. The fabric tightens at her waist.

I could stare at her forever.

"See you soon," I say.

She grins. "See you soon."

I give her a smile before following Tate down a white pathway to an arch of white flowers.

"At least there aren't any chickens," Tate mumbles, reminding me of Bianca's backyard wedding to Foxx. One of Foxx's brothers has free-range chickens, and they definitely made it an interesting day. It wasn't at all how I ever imagined Bianca getting married.

I glance at the man walking our way with slicked-back hair and a gold jumpsuit.

But I didn't imagine getting married like this either.

"Okay," Tate says, holding two phones aimed at the doorway. "I'm ready to rock and roll."

"That's what I like to hear!" Gold jumpsuit man stands behind the arch. "Are we ready, boys?"

My heart pounds. I slip my hand in my pocket and find the small box I had delivered with the flowers. "Let's do this."

Music plays overhead, and on cue, the doors open.

Chloe's arm is through Ripley's elbow. Her flowers are in her hand. Her eyes are on me.

I struggle to breathe.

Everything and everyone blurs. She's my only focus.

With each step she takes, my blood pumps harder.

They stop in front of me, and Ripley presses a quick kiss to her cheek and then stands beside Tate.

This is really happening.

I take her hand and, as instructed, she faces me. Gold Jumpsuit comes between us and signals for the music to end. It drifts away.

"Are you good?" I ask.

She nods. "I'm really good, actually."

I squeeze her hand.

"We're gathered here in The King and Bling Chapel for the marriage of"—Gold Jumpsuit looks at his notes—"Chloe Goodman and Jason Brewer."

Chloe's eyes shine as she stares into mine.

"Do you, Chloe Goodman, take Jason Brewer to be your husband and to live together in marriage? Do you promise to love him, comfort him, honor and keep him, for better or for worse, for richer or poorer, in sickness and in health, and forsaking all others, be faithful to him, so long as you both shall live?"

"Or for the next six months," she whispers.

I chuckle.

"Yes," she says loudly. "I do."

"And do you, Jason Brewer, take Chloe Goodman to be your wife and to live together in marriage? Do you promise to love her, comfort her, honor and keep her, for better or for worse, for richer or poorer, in sickness and in health, and forsaking all others, be faithful to her, so long as you both shall live?"

"I do."

"Are we exchanging rings?" Gold Jumpsuit asks. "It's not in the notes."

"No," Chloe says.

I pull the box from my pocket. "Yes, we are."

Chloe's eyes widen. "*Jason*. What are you doing? I don't have a ring for you."

"Well, I have one for you." I open the box and remove the ring, saying a silent prayer that she likes it. Then I take her finger. "This was very last minute, so if you don't like it, we can get something else."

"I don't know how you did this." She gasps as I slip on the ring. "*Oh my gosh*. Jason!"

I hold my breath as she brings the jewelry to her face.

"You don't wear a lot of jewelry, so I didn't really know what your style would be," I say, trying to read her expression.

She giggles a short, disbelieving sound and beams. "It's absolutely perfect. I can't ... I don't even know what to say."

"Well, you just said *I do*, so that pretty much says it all," Tate says. "*Ouch*!"

"Behave, Tate," Mom warns over the phone.

Chloe laughs. "I'll get you a ring."

"Don't you dare."

She narrows her eyes. "I'm your wife. I don't have to take your orders anymore."

I grin. "We'll see about that."

"By the power vested in me by the State of Nevada, I now pronounce you husband and wife," Golden Jumpsuit says. "You may kiss your bride."

My brothers clap, Tate yells something, and faraway voices also rejoice through the phones, but none of that matters. All that matters is headed toward me.

Chloe meets me halfway, throwing her arms over my shoulders.

Blood races through my veins as if a dam has burst. Her eyes meet mine.

I wrap an arm around her waist, pulling her into my chest, and her smile widens as our bodies touch.

"Are you ready for this, *Wife*?" I whisper against her lips.

"I'm ready for you."

My mouth captures hers. I intend for this to be a sweet, chaste kiss and make her wait until we get back to the penthouse for more.

It was a good plan.

It was also futile.

She moans as I sweep my tongue against hers. Her body goes limp in my arms, so I haul her tighter against me.

Her head falls to the side, allowing me full access to her mouth.

Her lips are like pillows as I take them, her breath hot and sweet as I breathe it in. She gives as good as she gets with her free hand scratching against my scalp. It sets off a rush of goose bumps across my skin.

"Fuck," I whisper as we pull apart.

She giggles, panting alongside me.

"May I present to you, Mr. and Mrs. Brewer," Gold Jumpsuit says.

Tate and Ripley clap once again, congratulating the two of us. I can hear my mom's sounds of joy, and I love that I've brought her happiness to counter all the shit she's been through lately.

"Yes, Chloe and Jason." Mimi whoops through the phone. "Now, go climb that stud like a tree, Chloe, and make me some great-grandbabies!"

Everyone bursts out laughing. Of course, Mimi would go there.

"Get me back to the penthouse," Chloe says, her words rough and pleading.

Yup. She's going to be the death of me.

"We told Mom and Mimi you'd call them later," Ripley says. "Figured you'd be busy for the rest of the night."

"And tomorrow," Chloe says, much to my brothers' amusement.

"Thanks for coming," I say, nearly dragging Chloe out of the chapel. "It really does mean a lot to me."

"To us!" Chloe adds, laughing.

Ripley laughs, too. "We'll talk about it later. Go enjoy yourselves."

Tate pats me on the back as we step onto the sidewalk. He and Ripley shout their goodbyes as they head off into the throngs of people on the Strip.

I make a mad dash, bride in hand, to our car. I'm done waiting. I want my wife.

Although, I know that will never stop being true.

I'll always want her to be mine.

Chapter 17

Chloe

"I'm glad the building isn't burning down, or we'd be dead," I say, tapping my heel against the elevator floor.

Jason chuckles beside me, a smug grin on his face. "May I point out that if the building was on fire, we should be taking the stairs?"

"Now isn't the time for logic, Mr. Brewer. You know what I mean."

Could this thing take any longer to get us from the garage to the penthouse?

The bell chimes, and the elevator comes to a stop. The doors open onto the landing in front of Renn's door. My heartbeat is in my ears as I step gingerly onto the tile, my knees wobbling with anticipation.

Jason takes his time getting the fob out of his pocket and has the audacity to whistle some silly little tune while he unlocks the door. Meanwhile, I stand behind him, trying desperately not to turn into a pool at his feet—or strangle him.

Finally, the door swings open, so I start to move around him, but he sweeps me off my feet.

I shriek in surprise, wrapping my arm around his neck as my legs dangle over his arms. "What are you doing?" I ask, laughing.

"Carrying you over the threshold."

"I didn't peg you to be so traditional."

He smirks. "You're never going to peg me. Let's get that straight right now."

I laugh as we enter the penthouse. Jason flips on a light in the foyer—and I gasp.

Candles flicker strategically around the space, the light bouncing off the glass in the atrium. The air is warm and rich, scented with a creamy spiciness that stirs something in my belly.

"It was the best I could do since you decided to change plans and get married tonight," he says, kicking the door closed behind us.

I try to respond but can't find the words.

He peers down at me with a reverence that steals my breath.

The weight of the ring on my finger is suddenly heavy, and I hold it up. Even in the low light, it's stunning. Nine small diamonds form a halo around a large transitional-cut diamond in the cluster's center. The platinum band is perfect against my skin. It's understated and eye-catching at the same time.

It's absolute perfection.

"We need to talk about this ring," I say, dragging in a breath.

He readjusts his grip on me. Concern etches across his face. "Do you not like it?"

"Jason, *really*?" I smile up at him. "This is the most beautiful ring I've ever seen, and it's entirely too much. Tell me you rented it or something."

His shoulders fall as he exhales.

"You bought it, didn't you?" I ask.

He carries me into the atrium. "Of course, I bought it."

"I don't want to know how much this cost. It would make me sick."

"That's a good mindset. Hold on to that."

"What do you mean?" I ask as he sets me on the marble table.

He plants one hand on either side of me and peers into my eyes. "Don't ask what things cost."

"It's the first thing that goes through my mind. I can't help it." I glance at the sparkler again. "I'll give this back when this is over. Speaking of that, I haven't signed a prenup and, as your EA, I'm panicking over that piece of missing paperwork."

He grins, the candles reflecting in his eyes. "We need to set a few ground rules, I think."

"I agree."

"I bet you do." He licks his lips, trying not to chuckle. "You promised me you wouldn't worry about anything. Remember?"

"Yes, but—"

"And I warned you that I was going to spoil you."

I hold up a finger. "Okay, yes, but—"

"You're only my EA at work. I don't want to hear a word about the office when we're not in the office. I'm aware that you haven't signed a prenup. It's slightly offensive that you think I've forgotten. Also, you aren't giving me the ring back, as I'll spend my money any way I damn well please, and I expect you to spend it on whatever pleases you, too."

My eyes widen. *Has this man lost his mind?* "I think you're just really horny right now and aren't thinking clearly."

"Have you ever known me to be clouded by emotion and misspeak?"

"Not once," I whisper, my insides quivering at the look he's giving me.

He leans closer, the intensity in his stare causing my heart to pound. My mouth to go dry. My thighs to clench.

"You're Mrs. Brewer," he says, the words brushing against my lips. "Act like it."

Oh fuck.

His smirk sets off a combustion inside me—a wild desperation for this man.

Jason's mouth finds mine, his teeth nipping at my bottom lip. Each pinch has me squirming, panting—ready to beg for more.

"Do you want to know my biggest problem with you?" he asks, pressing kisses across my jaw and down my throat.

I tip my head back and wind my fingers through his hair. "Not really."

He chuckles against my throat. The sound reverberates through me and gathers in my core.

"My biggest problem is that I don't know where to start." He loops his thumbs into the sleeves of my dress and slips them down my shoulders. "I want all of you all at once."

I pull my arms out of my dress. Jason shoves it down until it pools at my waist, the air washing against my exposed nipples.

His mouth's on mine once again. Our kisses grow hurriedly. *Frantic*. His tongue dances with mine as I fiddle with his belt.

"You could've done me a favor," I breathe between kisses. "And not worn this stupid belt. I didn't wear panties to make this easy for you."

"*Fuck*," he mutters between my lips, sliding his hands up my thighs.

His palms are rough. The pressure from his fingertips sears into my skin. The contact has my breath stuttering as he inches closer to my sex.

Finally, the belt loosens, and I quickly work on his pants. My hands fumble with the button—too excited to be smooth—and manage to get them over his hips. I waste no time ridding him of his shirt.

His mouth works against mine, demanding attention despite his touch below. My hands roam over his chest and shoulders, mapping the ridges and valleys. He seizes my hips in his firm grip—his fingers splayed onto my ass, and his thumbs pointed at my groin.

I think I might die.

"You weren't joking," he says regarding my pantyless state, biting hard enough on my lip to make me squeal before releasing it.

He pulls away, leaving me gasping for air.

His eyes are wild, his chest heaving, and my muscles clench with anticipation.

"Lie back." He puts a hand under my back, guiding me flat against the table. His eyes hold mine, taking me in. "My God, you're perfect."

I observe him shirtless for the first time since he wouldn't get ready for our wedding in front of me. It was one of his torture tactics, but I secretly enjoyed it. It was sweet in a frustrating kind of way.

A thick line of muscle extends from his neck to the edges of his shoulders. The taper down to his waist is definitive. His body is hard and mouthwatering, but his confidence has me withering.

His hands leisurely roam up the insides of my thighs, pausing to press his fingertips into my skin midway to my slit. There's no humor, no playfulness in his features. Just something akin to adoration that has me reeling. It makes me think of those incredible, inconceivable words Jason said earlier.

"So, in the spirit of transparency, I've known for a long time that if I were ever to marry anyone ... you were the only choice."

That sentence has rolled around in my mind since he uttered it. You were the only choice.

So this is what feeling special feels like.

And now, with this look of reverence, I'm buzzing with need. It's barely contained desire for the man pulling my knees into a bent position. With his eyes locked on mine, he drags me to the edge of the table with assistance from my dress that is now entirely bunched at my waist.

Candles burn on the table's far side, casting shadows across Jason's face. It gives his handsome features a moody, sexier edge that does nothing to help me from not coming.

He strokes himself a few times, his gaze glued to my pussy, before kneeling between my legs.

"I seriously might come if you touch me," I say, blowing out a breath.

"Then prepare to come."

"I—*oh, my God*!"

My back arches off the table as his mouth covers my mound.

Despite thinking about this moment for the past twelve hours, I'm in shock. Unprepared. Wholly in over my head as Jason licks through my wetness and toys with my clit.

My knees fall farther apart, giving him access and permission to take what he wants. Preferably all of me.

"You have to tell me what you like," he says, kissing my bud.

"All of it." I barely get the words out before I hiss as he slides a finger deep inside me.

"I'm going to need you to be more specific." He adds another finger. "My first job as your husband is to learn how to please you."

I groan, the room starting to spin. "This works."

His chuckle is deep and gravelly—and hot as fuck. "Then how about this?"

He pulls my clit into his mouth, sucking lightly enough to almost sting.

"That's *so good*," I say as clearly as I can through the tension in my throat.

"You taste sweet." The sound of his tongue against my wet flesh makes me shiver. "I can't wait to watch you come on my face."

"Keep going, and you're going to get your wish."

"I've already gotten my wish," he whispers before licking along the inside of my thigh.

I tremble under his touch, two seconds from exploding. I've waited too long for this to hold back much longer.

The pressure builds inside me, assisted by the steady rhythm of Jason's fingers.

"Look at me," he demands, giving me no chance to object.

I lift my head to watch his face lower against my pussy.

"I want you to watch me enjoy you," he says, his eyes burning into mine. His hands slide beneath my ass. "Watch me enjoy *my wife*."

I reach for him, threading my fingers into his hair as he lowers his mouth to me again. I brace myself, knowing he's going to let me fall apart.

The assault between my legs is immediate and glorious. And the sight of Jason framed between my thighs is like nothing I could've imagined.

The roar of an orgasm hits me fast and hard. I buck against Jason's face, unable to contain a scream that pierces the air. The intensity is too much. The fierceness of the climax more than I can take. I try to wiggle back, to push on Jason's head, but his grip on my bottom is too strong.

"Jason!" I moan, my eyes squeezed shut. "I can't take it!"

His tongue flicks against me, sending shocks of powerful jolts through my body. "Yes, you can."

"I can't." Tears fill the corners of my eyes. "I can't, Jason. *Dammit.*"

He sits back, slowing his fingers until every wave of pleasure has been milked from my orgasm. Then he slides them out. I shiver.

His lips are shiny from my cum. He drags a finger over them and grins devilishly.

I think I might like this marriage thing just fine.

"All of that," I say, laughing softly. "I liked all of that."

"I could tell."

His chuckle mixes with mine as he stands. He makes quick work out of finding a condom and rolling it down his length.

"Come here," he says, offering me a hand. He helps me up and onto my jelly legs. "I need to fuck you right now."

"Please."

I swipe a thumb across his lips, earning a smile from him. Then I place a kiss against him before allowing him to turn me around.

He bends me over the table. My breasts are flat against the cool stone, and my arms are stretched across it. Our reflection shines back at us in the oversized windows.

Seeing Jason's naked body positioned behind mine with his cock in his hand, looking at me like I'm a prize, makes my mouth water.

"What are you waiting for?" I ask, smiling at him through the reflection. "Fuck me."

He hooks his fingers around the front of my hips and angles my ass to him. I look for something to hold on to and brace myself against, but there's nothing.

I'm at his mercy.

The head of his cock parts my swollen lips and sits at my opening.

"Remember to tell me what you like," he says, swirling his cock around my hole. "I want to hear you, Chloe."

"I'm sure you—*fuck*!"

He thrusts into me in one long, hard stroke, completely filling me. I sink back against him as he plunges inside me again. Then again.

"Watch us in the glass," he demands, his fingertips digging into my waist. "Look at how fucking gorgeous you are."

I look at our reflection, but I don't notice me. All I can see is him.

He's power and confidence, strength and sex. His muscles flex, a show of their own, as he pounds into me from behind.

"I like that," I say, meeting him stroke for stroke.

"Do you want it harder?"

"Yes."

He grips me tighter and drives into me.

The fire in my pussy. The burn of his hands. The sting of my chest grinding against the table.

The heat in his gaze.

The sensations are too numbered and too intense, and when mixed—it's all too much.

"I'm going to come," I warn as my body begins to tremble. "I can't stop it."

"Don't stop it." He groans, his pelvis hitting against my backside. "I want to feel you on my cock."

My final band of control snaps. Wave after wave of pleasure rolls over me, drowning me in its bliss.

"That's it," he says, sliding into me one last time. He's buried so deep as he groans that I can feel his release. "*Fuck.*"

I force my eyes open to watch him.

Head back. Throat exposed. His muscles strained as he swirls his hips against me.

"Look at me," I say with surprising clarity. "I want to watch you enjoy me."

His eyes open—heated and hooded. A sheen of sweat coats his delicious body. His throat flexes as his orgasm fades.

My God. My heart skips a beat. *I've never seen anyone so sexy, and I've never witnessed a better sight in my life.*

He heaves a breath, growing still behind me. I'm rewarded with a soft smile as he pulls out of me.

I tingle from head to toe.

"You, Mrs. Brewer, are a force to be reckoned with."

I turn, my dress draping down my body, covering me again. "You can reckon me any time you want."

He scoops me up like he did before. This time, he kisses me softly before he moves through the room.

"Where are we going?" I ask, my fingers toying with the hair on the back of his head.

He grins. "To reckon with you again."

Chapter 18

Jason

Dawn begins to creep into the desert.

I glance at the clock and then over at Chloe, curled beside me. The whispers of her sleep drift through the bedroom.

Her hair is splayed across the pillows, and her cheek nestles against my side. Having her this close has caused something to bloom inside my chest.

The contentment that fills me this morning is a feeling I've never believed was real. Life's too busy, too complicated to have a moment without something niggling in the back of my brain. There hasn't been a day in my life—not even as a child—that I remember not being preoccupied with something—a test, contract, or duty.

Until now.

There's only one thing on my mind that I care to be concerned about while in this bed. *Chloe.*

Her ringed finger sits on my stomach, and I can't help but recall her reaction to me placing it on her finger. Shock. Disbelief. *Happiness.*

I'm just happy that it made it on time. It was possible only because my mom's best friend is a jeweler with a boutique in Las Vegas. And Siggy just happened to be in town for the grand opening, understood what I was after, and had it couriered to the penthouse just before we arrived.

My phone chirps on the nightstand, and I grab it without disrupting Chloe. Just as expected, the family text chat is alive and well.

Grinning, I open the thread and catch up.

Bianca: Did anyone bother to get an actual picture last night?

Tate: Yeah, but not sure it's what you want to see. <wincing emoji>

Bianca: Ripley, I'm counting on you.

Ripley: Look, I walked the bride down the aisle and held a phone so Mom could watch a ceremony. I'm skilled, but even those skills are limited.

Bianca: <eye-rolling emoji> How did you two screw this up?

Renn: Excuse me as I squeeze into this conversation since I'm the Vegas wedding professional here. But if you call the chapel today, they probably snapped some shots they'll be willing to sell you for an exorbitant price.

Bianca: What's the name of the place?

Renn: The King and Bling Chapel

Bianca: So classy.

Ripley: YOU HAD CHICKENS AT YOUR WEDDING

Tate: YOU HAD CHICKENS AT YOUR WEDDING

Renn: THERE WERE CHICKENS AT YOUR WEDDING

Gannon: I heard there were chickens at your wedding.

My chest vibrates as I try not to laugh and wake Chloe.

Me: There were chickens at your wedding?

Bianca: I hate all of you.

Bianca: At least I remember my wedding, Renn.

Ripley: Yeah, she got you there.
Gannon: So you're really married this morning, Jason?

Chloe moves against my side.

Me: I am.
Gannon: I didn't see this coming, but congrats, my man.
Me: Thank you.
Bianca: I'm throwing you a party.

A party? What would Chloe think about a party? Would she enjoy it, or would she feel pressured?

My fingers move swiftly over the keys.

Me: Let's give it a while before we start partying, okay?

Bianca: If we didn't have Gannon, you'd be the least amount of fun in this family.

Ripley: Tate and I are heading back to Nashville this afternoon. What are your plans, Jason?

Me: We're flying out tomorrow morning.

Bianca: Take her on a proper honeymoon.

Tate: Where did Foxx take you on a honeymoon again?

Bianca: <devil emoji> Do you REALLY want details on my honeymoon?

Tate: No.

Gannon: No.

Ripley: Abso-fucking-lutely not.

Chloe stirs and flutters her eyes open.

Me: I gotta go.
Tate: Later
Renn: Enjoy.
Gannon: Call me later.

Ripley: See ya.

Bianca: Love you.

My phone chirps in quick succession as they continue. I turn off my ringer and set my phone next to me.

"What time is it?" Chloe asks, yawning.

"It's still early. You can go back to sleep."

She peers up at me with heavy eyelids. "Then why are you up?"

"Because I haven't gone to sleep yet."

"Why?"

I press a kiss against her forehead and nestle her against me again. *Because I was afraid if I went to sleep, I'd wake up and this wouldn't be real.*

That's not entirely true, but it's the essence of it if it were all boiled down.

"Are you having second thoughts?" she asks, holding her breath.

I stroke her back with my fingers, appreciating her delicate dips and curves. "I'm having second thoughts that I let you fall asleep without being inside you."

She laughs against my side, placing a kiss on my ribs.

"What about you? How do you feel?" I ask.

"Sore."

"I like you sore."

"I like being sore." She traces the tattoos on my arm. "Tell me about these."

"What do you want to know?"

"Do they mean anything?"

I bend my arm, and Chloe points at an owl tattoo near my elbow.

"That was given to me by a good friend in London. Owls mean wisdom, and he always jokes about me being wise. But that's only because I've saved him from marrying the wrong woman and potentially a serial killer—in separate incidents," I say.

She lifts her head. "I need details."

"Let's get into those stories later." I chuckle.

She makes a face but settles back beside me once again.

"This one is for a friend I lost in my first military battle," I say, pointing down to the next tattoo. "We called him Root, so I got a tree."

"I'm sorry you lost a friend."

"I've lost many friends." I pull her tighter. "But we honor the fallen by living."

Chloe seems to want to say something but decides to move on instead. I'm thankful. While memories of my friends are good things to have, discussing them carries a sense of sadness. And I don't want anything spoiling this moment with her.

"What about this one?" she asks, tracing a birdcage on my forearm.

"That's a reminder that there's always a way out. If you can't open the door, break through the bars. But there's always a way out."

She touches a simple script. "And this one?"

"All of my brothers have that one. A *B* for Brewer. It was Tate's twenty-first birthday, and the five of us were out together, which is a rarity. Tate had a little too much tequila and was emotional. The next thing I know, we're at a tattoo shop." I laugh. "Tate wanted us to get a knot that looked like a testicle."

Chloe laughs, too.

"But we teamed up against him and settled on a letter instead."

"I think that's cool. If I had siblings, I hope we'd be as close as you are with yours. It's like you always have a friend."

"It wasn't always this way. I couldn't stand Tate most of his life." I shrug, thinking back to his teenage years when I thought he was the goofiest kid on the planet. *And not in a good way.* "And Gannon still annoys the hell out of me most of the time. But I think it comes with age, you know? You care less about those irritations and more about the big picture."

"Maybe when I'm old like you, I'll be more introspective like that."

I grab her, making her squirm. Her giggles almost get her fucked, but I hold back since she's sore. Four rounds in one night are probably enough ... for her. I'll never get my fill of this woman.

"Is there anything you want to do in Vegas?" I ask.

She shakes her head. The blanket covering her slides down until it nests in the small of her back.

"It's not like I had much time to think about it, but no," she says. "It's nice just being away, honestly. What about you?"

"I'm supposed to have a meeting later this morning."

"That's right. You were coming here anyway."

I nod. "If I had an EA who wasn't naked beside me, I'd have her cancel it."

A worried look passes through her eyes.

"I'm kidding." I kiss the top of her head. "I'll cancel it myself as soon as it's a respectable time."

"I can do it."

"Not if you like your job."

She grins. "What's that supposed to mean? "

"It means I'll fire you if you try to work on your honeymoon, Mrs. Brewer."

Her fingers dance over my skin, spraying goose bumps on my arms. "I think you should go."

"What?"

"Go," she insists. "Our lives still have to continue, and I know that meeting was important. I'll be fine by myself for a few hours. I'll check in on Mimi and take a bath. *Really*. Being alone for a little while sounds glorious. Do you know the last time I was by myself? With a bathtub that doesn't leak onto the floor?"

I blow out a breath, considering her questions because my instinct is to be here with her. But the more I think about it, the more I realize she's probably right. She's with me at the office all day, and then Mimi in their cramped apartment at night. She probably does want some time alone. I'd lose my mind if I didn't have time by myself to decompress.

"If you're sure," I say. "But I want to be clear. I'm doing this because you want me to, not because I want to."

She kisses the center of my chest. "I'm sure. I'll feel less guilty about you getting behind on work."

"May I remind you that you aren't my assistant right now?"

"You brought work up. Not me."

"That's true."

"And it's really hard for me to just *not* think about it. Your work isn't only important to Brewer Air. It's important to *you*."

I smile, watching the sun begin to rise. "It's a good thing you married me."

"Why?"

"Because you would've quit in the end, or you would've been single forever."

She laughs. "What do you mean?"

"You weren't going on that date with Thomas."

Her laugh grows evil.

"You weren't," I say, the thought making my stomach tighten. "I was going to find a reason to make you work over."

"You wouldn't have."

"Oh yes, I fucking would've."

"Fine. I wasn't going anyway. I canceled it the night you called me. He came by to check on Mimi, and it was just ... sparkless."

"Sparkless, huh?"

"*Sparkless*." She moves her leg over the top of mine. "This feels pretty sparky, though."

We lie tangled up in the sheets, our bodies connected in every way but one. Chloe is so still, so peaceful, that I think she's fallen asleep. But when I look down, I notice her eyes are open.

I'd be happy staying in this apartment with her forever, and God knows I could come up with things to entertain us. But something about that doesn't quite sit right with me. She deserves more than to be kept inside this gilded cage. I want her to enjoy herself in ways besides sex.

I want to show her off and make her feel special.

"I want to take you to dinner tonight," I say softly.

She takes a deep breath. "I don't know what you have in mind, but I didn't bring anything too fancy to wear. Not that I have anything fancy, but the point remains the same."

"Don't worry about that."

"I'm not worried about it," she says. "I just want to limit your expectations."

She has no idea that she exceeds them at every turn.

"I'd be proud to take you to any restaurant in this town wearing sweatpants," I say. "You do know that, right?"

Her breath is hot against my neck. "That's very sweet of you to say. But even if that were true, that doesn't mean I'd be willing to do it."

"Why not?"

"Because I'd be embarrassed."

I peel her away so I can look her in the eye. "What do you have to be embarrassed about? If anyone judges you over sweatpants, they can fuck off."

She resumes her position with her arm draped over my stomach. "It's childhood trauma. I've been working for years to erase it."

"May I ask what happened?"

"It's nothing too complicated. It's just that when my parents were married, things were great. But then Dad left us, and Mom and I went from having a very comfortable life to having virtually nothing. I was the daughter of a banker and then the daughter of a woman who cleaned houses for a living. It was a total one-eighty."

My heart sinks. "Didn't she get a settlement?"

"His assets were all tied up in trusts. Dad was clever, I'll give him that. I think Mom did get child support, but the system screwed her." She sighs. "It just brought Mom and me closer, as we did everything together. She cheered so loudly for me that I didn't even notice Dad wasn't there until I was older."

My jaw flexes as I imagine Chloe's father walking out on her and her mother. *How could he do something like that?* It's beyond comprehension. Then again, my father has done things beyond comprehension, too. It's even more of a reason to prove to Chloe that good men still exist.

And she has one, if she'll accept me.

"Things got harder as I got older, and life became more expensive," she says. "Our situation caused cracks in my friendships because teenagers are mean. I'd be teased over my clothes and that I didn't get a car for my sixteenth birthday. I couldn't go to camps with my friends. Honestly, I didn't even ask because I knew we couldn't afford it. I still hear those voices laughing at me when I'm underdressed or self-conscious about my makeup."

"You feel that way now?"

"Sure. I never feel like I'm quite doing things right." She tenses. "I felt that way coming here. I thought, *Women always have lingerie for their honeymoon, and here I am once again without the bare essentials.*" She laughs nervously. "It is what it is, I guess."

What the fuck?

"Hey," I say, trying to lift her chin to look at me. She resists. "If that thought even crossed your mind, I'm doing something wrong, sweetheart."

She clings to me. It's a knife in my heart.

"Do I ever make you feel inferior?" I ask, worried.

"Never. It's one of the things I love most about you. You never make me, or anyone around you, feel less ... even though you're the most."

My chest constricts as I think of this complicated yet simple woman, and I realize how much I have left to learn—and not a lot of time to do it.

I roll her onto her back and hover over her.

For the first time, her guard is down. She's completely vulnerable with me. There's no shield, no joke on the tip of her tongue to distract me from a topic she doesn't want to discuss. She's open to me.

I almost can't take it.

"It's funny you say that," I say, my voice thick. "Because when I'm with you, I'm aware that I'm batting way out of my league."

Her smile is soft and sincere.

I brush a lock of hair off her forehead. "If you ever feel those types of things sneak up on you, just remember how beautiful I think you are." I slide a knee between her legs and spread her thighs apart. "And if you keep feeling that way, let me know so I can spank that delicious ass of yours."

Her eyes twinkle as her hands slide up my chest. "I'm feeling that way right now, as a matter of fact."

"Do you want a spanking?" I ask, a smile teasing the corner of my lips.

"I want whatever you'll give me."

My whole heart? Done.

Chapter 19

Chloe

"M*imi*," I say, smiling at the sound of her voice. "Hi, how are you?"

"Probably not as good as you are right about now." Her laugh is mischievous. "How are things over there?"

I glance around the bedroom, my cheeks aching from smiling so much.

"It's good, Meems. Really good."

"I knew it would be. He has hands that—"

"Can we ... not?" I ask, giggling.

"We share everything! Don't bail on me now."

That's true—I do share everything with my grandmother. I don't know why it's different this time, but it is. *Very different.*

"And I'll share with you later," I say, hoping it'll satiate her need for knowledge. "But tell me about you. How do you like your new digs? How's Mara? Are you two hitting it off?"

I've been worrying about her in the back of my mind, hoping she's settling in well. Last night, she texted me to congratulate me on the wedding, and her spirits seemed high. Jason also swore that Mara had everything under control. Between the two of them, I'm a lot calmer about being away from her than I thought I might be.

Mimi sighs happily. I imagine her in the living room recliner, a blanket on her lap, and her head resting against a pillow. I imagine her smile stretching across her wrinkly skin.

"First things first, I adore Mara," Mimi says. "We like the same kind of movies. She's one hell of a cook. She made homemade chicken potpie last night. Can you believe that?"

I laugh. Mimi is easily won over by two things—handsome men and good food.

"This little place is so damn cute, Chloe. I have my own kitchen. Mara went to the store for me this morning, and I made my own oatmeal, then sat outside by the pool and enjoyed it with a cup of coffee."

I smack my forehead. "Shit, Mimi. I brought my credit card with me. I left you there with no money."

"Honey, wise up. Your new husband took care of it, just like he had an adjustable bed delivered this morning because Mara told him I was having trouble getting in and out."

Tears well up in my eyes, and the bridge of my nose burns. *This wonderful, over-the-top, thoughtful man. How did he even have time to talk to Mara, let alone arrange for a new bed for my grandmother?*

Mimi breathes softly. "I don't know what happened between the two of you, Chloe, but I know one thing—that boy is crazy about you. I hope you see that."

I bite my lip, afraid the lump in my throat will cloud my voice if I try to speak.

Is he crazy about me?

My stomach flip-flops at the idea, but I don't want to think about it too much. This is only for six months. There's no use in getting my heart broken. I just need to enjoy what I have while I have it and not get greedy.

"Mara is supposed to be by this afternoon," Mimi says. "She's going to take me out in the golf cart looking for hot guys."

I snort. It quickly dissolves into a fit of giggles. "Oh, Mimi."

"What? I'm old, not dead, Chloe."

"Well, good luck. I hope you find one."

"Or two. Hell, let's go out with a bang."

I don't know what to say to that, so I just laugh.

"Where's your husband?" she asks. "Can I thank him for my new bed?"

"He's actually at a meeting right now. It was scheduled before we decided to get married, and I asked him to go. He didn't want to, but I really wanted some time alone."

I don't have to explain that to Mimi, and I doubt she'd comment about it, anyway. But I felt the need to defend Jason's absence, just in case.

"Okay, then. Tell him I love it, and if I'm feeling up to it, I'll bake him a pie when you get home."

Her hopeful and optimistic attitude makes my day. She's stronger than I've heard her in a long time, no longer frail and defeated. And that's how I know I absolutely made the right decision to marry Jason. *For so many reasons.*

"I will. I love you, Mimi."

"I know you do, pumpkin. I love you, too. Now go enjoy your alone time while you have it. I suspect your hubby will be home soon to invade every inch of your privacy."

"Goodbye, Mimi," I say, giggling again.

"Goodbye, Chloe."

I hold the phone against my chest. My robe hangs open, the air caressing my skin covered only by bra and panties, as I enter the atrium. The candles are in their respective spots where we blew them out before we went to bed. Our clothes and shoes litter the floor where we shed them last night. The bottle of champagne we shared after our bath sits empty on the table.

It's the aftermath of a night that will stay with me forever.

I open my phone and find Jason's name.

Me: Thank you for sending Mimi a new bed.

Jason: Of course.

Me: How did you know she needed one? And how did you have time to get her one in the midst of the craziness of the past day?

Jason: I know everything. See you soon, beautiful. Enjoy your morning.

Me: <heart emoji>

I wait for a response, but nothing comes.

I blow out a breath and traipse to the kitchen. I find a bagel and cream cheese that seems fresh enough and make a quick breakfast. As I move around the kitchen, finding snacks and drinks and fresh kitchen towels, I can't help but wonder if Renn leaves this place stocked all the time. If he never comes here, why is there food? Do his brothers visit often enough to warrant groceries?

Or did Jason have a few things delivered before we arrived?

The thought makes me smile. I haven't been taken care of like this in a long time.

My heart aches as I think of my sweet mother. I wish so badly that I could call her and tell her what I've been up to. What would she think of this whole situation? Would she cheer me on like Mimi? Or would she be disappointed in my lack of ethics?

Something tells me if I'm not hurting anyone and I'm happy, she wouldn't care. And I know she'd be over the moon that I married a Brewer. She thought so much of their family—except Reid. Mom never liked him too much.

I nibble the bagel and curl up on the sofa in the living room. The television looks too complicated to work, and I don't want to break anything, so I pick up my phone instead. Instinctively, I consider checking my email, but Jason's warning about not working this weekend rings loudly in my head.

Yet the idea of going back to work has now entered my mind, and I can't shake it. There are too many unknowns and too many variables.

I set the bagel down and dial Nickie. She answers in two rings.

"Hello," she says.

"Hey. It's Chloe."

"Hey, you. I came by your office yesterday afternoon, but Brandi said you were already gone. Is everything okay?"

I glance around the penthouse and then at the giant rock on my finger. "Yeah. Things are going okay."

"Good. I was worried something was wrong. So what's up?"

A flurry of excitement bubbles through me, and suddenly, I can't wait to tell someone my news.

"Remember when I told you that if I got a secret boyfriend, you'd be the first to know?" I ask, my cheeks flushing.

"Yeah." She pauses. "And?"

"Well, I don't exactly have a secret boyfriend. But I do have a husband."

"*What*?"

I giggle. "I got married last night, Nick. In Vegas."

"*You what*? Oh my God. You little liar! You've been seeing someone this whole time, and you lied right to my face." She laughs happily. "It's a good thing I'm a forgiving friend. Now fill me in. Load me up with details."

I sigh. "I ..." *Don't know how to say this.* "We hopped on a plane yesterday evening and flew to Vegas. Then we decided to head to a little chapel on the Strip and get married last night."

"Was this planned or an impromptu thing?"

It was a bet. "Planned. We knew we were getting married when we came here."

"So, you're still in Vegas, I assume."

"I am."

"With your husband." She laughs. "That sounds so wild. *You have a husband*. Do I know him?"

I'm glad she can't see me because I can't hide my smile or my blush. As excited as I am to tell her and share it with my only friend, it also feels a little bit like losing a precious secret. But it has to be done, and I know I'll feel better about it once I break the news. At least I'll be able to gauge her response and hopefully worry less until Monday morning.

"You do know him, actually," I say carefully. "It's Jason."

"Jason who?"

The silence is deafening.

"Wait ..." She sucks in a breath. "You don't mean ... *There's no way.*"

"Way."

"You're telling me that you married Jason Brewer?"

"I am."

"*You married your boss*?" Her voice is just below a shriek. "Are you shitting me? Are you serious right now? Don't play with me, Chlo."

My laughter fills the line.

"You are serious. *Oh my God.* How did I miss this? How did I miss the signs? There had to have been signs?" It sounds as if she smacks her head. "And I've been drooling over the man, and he's been your fiancé? I'm humiliated."

"Don't be. I can't blame you. I *don't* blame you."

She sighs as if she's in disbelief. "So how? Why? When? Tell me all the things."

I'm not sure what I'm supposed to say or how much I'm supposed to divulge. I don't want to outright lie to her. Then again, I'm not about to say anything that would hurt the Brewer image. And if word spreads that Jason married his assistant in a bet, that's not exactly a good look for him—or me.

"We didn't really want it to get out," I say, dancing through the fire. "If things didn't work out between us, we would still be friends and coworkers. So we didn't want the potential drama, you know?"

"Understandable. I just can't believe I didn't notice. I think if I were fucking Jason Brewer, I'd be telling the whole world."

Which is probably why he'd never sleep with you. The idea of her betraying Jason like that rubs me the wrong way. But before I can respond, the doorbell rings.

"Hey, I have to go," I say. "Someone's here."

"When are you coming back to town?"

"Tomorrow, I think. I'll see you Monday at work."

"Can we at least do lunch? I need details, you little minx."

I laugh. "Lunch for sure."

"I'm so happy for you. Congrats!"

"Thanks, Nickie! Bye."

"Bye!"

I end the call, then I tie my robe tightly around me and head for the door.

"Who is it?" I ask, peering out the peephole.

A bellhop stands on the other side and identifies himself.

I make sure I'm presentable and then open the door.

"Mrs. Brewer?" he asks.

"Yes." I giggle. "That's the first time I've been called that by anyone besides my husband."

My husband. A flutter of butterflies takes flight in my stomach.

"This is all for you," he says, motioning to the cart behind him. "Would you like me to bring it into the suite or leave it here?"

The three floral arrangements alone are as tall as I am. There's a box, too.

"Would you mind bringing it in?" I ask, perplexed. *What is all of this?*

"It would be my pleasure."

He scoots by me, and I direct him to the table in the atrium.

"Just set them all right there, please," I say, realizing I must tip this man. "I need to grab my wallet."

The smile he bestows upon me is kind. "Thank you, ma'am, but Mr. Brewer has already taken care of everything."

How does he think of everything? "Are you sure?"

"I'm sure." He sets the box by the vases. "Have a great rest of your day, Mrs. Brewer."

I'll never tire of hearing that.

He lets himself out quietly as I investigate the delivery. The first arrangement is a massive selection of the prettiest pinks, whites, peaches, and coral flowers with eucalyptus and sprigs of greenery. I pluck the card from the center.

Welcome to the family, Chloe! I'm so excited to have another sister and can't wait to celebrate!

Love,

Bianca

"Wow," I say, pulling in a shaky breath. "I didn't expect this."

I move to the apothecary vase next to it, which is filled with purple orchids and pale pink roses.

Dearest Chloe,

Congratulations on the start of something beautiful. I wish you and Jason the happiest ever after.

Welcome to the family, sweetheart,

Rory

I laugh softly. "At least I know where Jason gets it."

I return Rory's card and then slip out the one attached to the garden of roses. There must be a hundred or more of them in the deepest, sexiest red.

Chloe,

My wife. Here's to an adventure we'll never forget.

Jason

I swipe my finger over his name, my heart filling with a warmth that radiates from head to toe.

"It's going to be an adventure, all right." I smile, placing his card on the table. I then turn to the box. "Now, what's this?"

I pull the satin ribbon from around the box and then remove the top. Black tissue paper hides the contents below. My heartbeat pounds as I push my way around. As my fingers skim the fabric, my core tightens.

"He didn't." Although, I know he did.

Three lingerie sets are in the box, each in a different style and color. The black one is racy—practically see-through, with the tiniest panties and a barely-there bra. The wine-colored one is a corset-style bodysuit with a thong in the back. The lace is dreamy, and the boning gives it structure. It's beautiful. The final one is a pleated baby doll set with an empire waist and a bow that sits just below the breasts. It's soft and feminine, with a thong bottom.

A card has been placed below them.

Wife,

For you. Well, really, for me, as I'll enjoy taking them off your delicious body. I'll be thinking about you wearing these all day.

There's a store downstairs called Halcyon. They're expecting you. Pick out whatever you want and something to wear to dinner. They've been instructed not to let you leave empty-handed.

Enjoy yourself today, beautiful.

Jason

I exhale, my body instantly craving him again. I reach for my phone and tap his name.

Me: Thank you, you crazy man.

Jason: I'm crazy about you. And you're welcome.

I glance at the box of underthings. The quality is exquisite. I don't even want to know what that cost him.

Me: This is over the top. You know that, right?

Jason: Let me spoil you.

Me: You're ridiculous. And there's no way I'm going downstairs to shop. It's too much.

Jason: You think this is ridiculous?

Me: Absolutely.

Jason: Then don't go downstairs today. See what happens. <winking emoji>

I laugh.

Me: Don't you have things to do, like run an empire?

Jason: Lucky for you, I'm a good multitasker. I'm sitting in a meeting with four attorneys, arguing with my wife about gifts, and sporting a hard-on as I imagine you in the black lace.

So he did pick this out himself. The thought sends a spiral of giddiness through me.

He likes the black one best. Noted.

Me: Go work so you can come home sooner.

Jason: Take a selfie of yourself in the store so I know you're there.

Me: And if I don't?

Jason: Then the store will come to you.

Me: I don't even know what that means, but you wouldn't dare.

Jason: Try me.

A part of me wants to do just that because I think I'll like how it ends. But another part of me wants to make him happy, and something tells me that he'll be happy if I act on his request.

I stand in the middle of the atrium and laugh. *How did this happen? How is this my life?*

Instead of bothering him again, I take my gifts and go to the shower. Apparently, I'm about to go shopping.

A grin touches my lips.

And I'm crazy about you, too, Jason Brewer.

Chapter 20

Jason

Jason

I step into the elevator and punch the button for the door to close.

My hand immediately goes to my tie, loosening it from around my neck. The air is stifling. The elevator is too small and far too fucking slow. I watch the floor numbers increase at a snail's pace.

The morning drew on much longer than I anticipated or wanted, but I couldn't just cut it short due to the nature of the conversation.

Someone has to negotiate with Dad's attorneys. And that someone is me. And I couldn't think of anything further from what I'd like to do on my honeymoon.

I hate that he's had any space in my time with my new wife. It only makes me angrier at him, if that's possible.

The bell rings, and the doors open, and I step into the foyer on a mission. I make quick work of the lock and enter the penthouse.

Blood rushes past my ears as I look for my wife.

I've thought about her all day. Her texts broke my aggravation and helped me relax. They gave me something to look forward to, a reason not to lose my shit and tell the attorneys to go fuck themselves.

"Chloe?" I call out into the silence.

"In the kitchen."

I set my briefcase down and shed my suit jacket, tossing it over an armchair as I make my way toward her voice.

"Did you have a—*holy fuck*."

"You tricked me," she says, pressing her pink lips in a sexy pout.

I'd object to that ... if I could remember how to speak.

The black lingerie I ordered in the middle of the night while she slept fits her like a fucking glove. It accentuates her hips, gorgeous tits, and delicate shoulders. She turns to set her champagne glass down on the counter, giving me a glimpse of her round ass and the thin strip of fabric lying between her cheeks.

"What's the matter?" she asks, sauntering my way. "Do you not have anything to say for yourself, Mr. Brewer?"

Her heels click against the floor until she stops in front of me. Her eyelids are smoky, and her lashes are thick. Her lips are a pinkish hue that I'd love to see on my cock. *Fuck, I'm one lucky man.*

She leans to me, pressing her mouth roughly against mine. The taste of champagne is on her breath as her tongue swipes against my lips. I open for her, and she deepens the kiss, her tongue stroking mine like she owns it.

Like she owns me.

How quickly she learns.

She breaks it far too soon with a devious look in her eye.

"Is something wrong?" I smirk, knowing exactly what she's worked up about.

She gives me a pointed look over her shoulder and returns to the bottle of champagne.

"Imagine my surprise when I arrive in Halcyon this afternoon intending to take a picture in the store to send to you and then leave," she says, pouring us each a drink. "Only to discover that Nadia, the store manager, was not only waiting for me but had already pulled quite a selection of things for me to try on."

I take the glass and nod as if this is new information. "This Nadia must be good at her job."

"That or she was enticed to do a good job by a certain billionaire with far more money than sense, it seems."

I hum, taking a sip of my drink.

"Do you know how many things they sent back with me?" she asks, lifting a brow. "They didn't even ask me. I tried something on, and Nadia decided whether she liked it. Then I was handed the next thing. Everything that passed her inspection—twenty-two items, Jason—was delivered to this room." She blinks. "Did you hear that? Twenty-two overpriced garments."

"How curious."

"How curious, my ass."

I grin. "Your ass does look amazing tonight. How would you feel if I played with that a little?"

Her eyes widen, and her cheeks flush. "Don't distract me."

"Sorry. As you were saying ..."

She sighs in exasperation. "That was almost *forty thousand dollars*."

"I can't wait to see it all on you."

"You're not listening to me."

I roll my eyes and set my glass down. "Do you not like it?"

"Yes, but—"

"Does it all fit you well?"

"Yeah, but—"

"Does it not feel good on your body?"

"That's not the point."

I smile at her fledgling objections. "Then what is the point?"

"Maybe that's not a lot of money to you, but it's a lot of money to me. Like *a lot*. And I'm not comfortable spending that much cash on clothes."

"Good thing it's not your cash, then." *It's ours.*

I swipe my glass off the counter and refill it.

It's a good thing I haven't mentioned that what's mine is hers because I know exactly what her objections to that would be.

"Jason …"

I keep my back to her. "I work very hard, Chloe. I spend little time doing anything other than work. And I find one thing that gives me joy, and you want to steal that from me."

Her silence lets me know I'm on the right track.

"I was just in a meeting with attorneys over a threat against my family. My father has decided to point the finger at Gannon and me —something Gannon doesn't know yet. While the action in question was absolutely done at his request, it's a little murky and will, at the very least, cost us an exorbitant amount of time and even more stress."

I turn to her. She's standing like a vixen in the middle of the kitchen, watching me warily.

She's so damn beautiful that it takes my breath away. It's not even her traditional beauty, although it's that, too. It's her sincerity. Her openness and honesty. The way her heart shines as brightly as her eyes.

I'm falling in love with her and falling fast and hard. And there's nothing I can do about it.

"Do you know what got me through the morning?" I ask before taking another drink. "*You.* I imagined you shopping and having lunch inside the store. I knew they'd fawn over you and care for you." I drink again, holding her hesitant gaze. "I don't give a fuck about money, Chloe. I have it. A lot of it. I've worked for some of it, and some I had given to me. But I watched my father and my mother, to some degree, waste their lives in a quest to have more of it. And I can't help but think that if they'd spent some of that energy and money on each other, things would've worked out differently."

She narrows her eyes, as if she's mulling that over.

"I told you I was going to spoil you and treat you like I think you should be treated," I remind her. "If you don't like this, say the word, and I'll stop. But don't say you don't like it because you think you're taking too much. Because coming in here tonight and seeing you like this—confident and sexy—is worth every fucking penny to me."

She lifts her chin as a slow smile draws across her lips. She takes my hand and pulls me through the penthouse and, naturally, my attention is glued to her ass as she pulls me behind her.

I have no idea where we're going or if she's still pissy. But her ring is on her finger, her hand's in mine, and we're entering the bedroom. All good signs.

The closet door is open, and bags line a bedroom wall.

She leads me to the foot of the bed and then stops. I lift a brow. She grins.

"I'm sorry," she says, reaching for my tie. "This is just taking me a little bit to get used to, and I'm afraid to get too used to it."

"Why?"

Her gaze flips to mine briefly before it drops back to my neck. "Because this isn't my actual life. It's my temporary one."

Only if you want it to be. But I don't say that. It feels like pressing my luck.

"I should say thank you," she says, pulling my tie off and tossing it on the bed. Then she goes to work on my shirt buttons. "You've done so much for me and my grandmother. I can't begin to understand where you find the time to pull all of this off—my ring, the gifts, Mimi's bed. It never ends with you."

I grin. "Do you know one thing that's bothered me all day?"

"What's that?"

"I forgot your coffee this morning."

She laughs, pushing my shirt over my shoulders. "Totally ruined my day."

"You can believe I won't forget again."

"I'll forgive you if you do."

Her hands move at my groin, her knuckles grazing over my cock. I hiss a breath as she pulls the zipper down. She grins in return.

"So are you going to keep the clothes?" I ask, slipping off my shoes, socks, and pants.

"Do you want me to?"

"Of course, I want you to." I lean forward, kissing the spot where her shoulder meets her neck. "I want to be inside you right now."

She steps away, turning in a circle—toying with me with her eyes as she moves. I notice every dip of her waist, every curve of her hip, the swell of her breasts, and the way her thighs touch in the center.

Every piece of her is perfect. Just like I knew it would be.

I grab myself, stroking slowly from root to tip.

"You made me feel like a princess today," she says, moving close enough for me to touch her with my free hand. "I want to make you feel good now, too."

I slide my hand between her legs, slipping my finger through her wet pussy. The feel of her slick slit makes my cock pulse.

"You can stand right there and let me touch you. I'll come in a minute," I say, teeth gritted together.

She places her hands on my shoulders and pushes me back on the bed. "Lie back."

I scoot back until I'm lying completely on the bed. I grab a pillow and fashion it under my head. Chloe crawls onto the mattress, loose tendrils of hair falling into her face, and she makes her way up my body.

I take her face in my hands and bring her mouth to mine. Her lips are soft, molding against mine as I press kisses to them.

She straddles me, setting her pussy directly on my cock. The contact elicits a hiss from deep in my throat, and she groans, rocking herself across my length.

My hands fall to her chest, freeing her tits from the confines of the lingerie, making her moan as I roll her pebbled nipples between my fingers. She moans again as I lift my hips against her.

Chloe pulls away, her breaths ragged, and smiles. She climbs off me and faces away. "Unhook me, please."

I do as she requests, brushing my knuckles down her back. She shivers against my touch, biting her lip as she watches me over her shoulder.

"I have one more request," she says, letting the material fall forward. It slides down her arms slowly.

My hands follow the fabric, skimming her arms. *Needing contact.* Her heels fall to the floor, and then she stands on the bed, shimmying out of the lingerie. From my vantage point, I have a clear view of her pussy.

Her thighs glisten with wetness. The dimples in her ass are so real, *so fucking sexy*, that I can't help but stroke myself again.

"You can have anything you want," I say.

"I'm on birth control," she nearly whispers. "And I'm good to go."

Oh, fuck. I suck in a breath as my body trembles at the idea of being bare inside her. *Is that what she's asking?*

Her grin is full of mischief.

That's exactly what she's asking.

"Just had my aviation physical," I say, my heart pounding so hard that I'm glad I'm lying down. "I'm good to go."

She casts a provocative grin over her shoulder. "So can I ride you without a condom?"

I've died and gone to heaven.

I take her hand as she climbs onto me, facing the other way. I grab her hip with one hand and my cock with the other as she sinks all the way down on me.

She breathes heavily as I fill her, her tight cunt squeezing me so hard I groan.

Chloe begins to move slowly, her hips grinding against me in slow, sensuous circles.

Watching her like this is so hot that I struggle not to come already.

This. *Her.* This is what I've been waiting for. She's a vision, a vixen, a sweet soul who I'm so glad I get to love on—*hopefully forever*.

"There you go," I say, gripping her hips. She adjusts to my size, freeing up her mobility. "God, you feel good."

"This is my favorite. It hits every spot."

She wiggles around until she's bouncing up and down on my

cock. Each rise and fall is a wash of pleasure, and watching her ass is a bonus.

"Do you like this?" I ask her, massaging her backside as she moves. "Because I think you'll have to do this every time now."

She laughs, her head falling back as she moans. She cups her tits, holding them from jiggling as she takes me all the way in—*hard*.

I grit my teeth. "I can take that about five more times, and then I'm coming."

Instantly, she stops.

I groan. The intensity building inside my balls is so powerful they ache and, as if she can read my mind, she slides her hand between my legs and plays with them.

"Fuck, Chloe," I say, laughing through clenched teeth.

"I love feeling you inside me like this." She swirls her hips. "Does it feel better to you without a condom?"

"It feels so good that I'm struggling not to fill you full of my cum right now."

She grins over her shoulder. "Is that so?"

"What are you doing?" I ask, smiling at the wicked look in her eyes.

She leans forward until she's holding my ankles. If I thought the view was good before—*holy shit.*

I slide a finger through her pussy and drag it to her ass. She flexes her hips and begins to move.

"You're going to kill me," I say, parting her with both hands. "Every inch of this body is perfect."

"You've not had it all yet."

"No, but I plan on it."

She moves harder against me, releasing little moans as she grinds on my cock. I lift my hips and thrust into her as she moves.

"If you want to know what I like," she says, gasping, "this is it. Remember this."

"Noted."

I rub her wetness around her puckered opening, trying to concentrate on it so I don't come too soon. My thumb massages the rim, pressing just hard enough to make her yelp.

"Ride me," I say, thrusting even harder. Her little sounds make it impossible to stay in control. "Ride the fuck out of me."

She sits up, moving her hips like a belly dancer. Around, up, and down. Harder. Faster.

A sheen of sweat coats her back as she moves. My fingers dig into her skin, pressing her down as I shove my cock into her.

Every movement is heaven. She's sleek and smooth, each rotation of her hips a stronger sensation than before. Her pussy is hot, and her juices cover my groin. I get a glimpse of her tits bouncing, and that does it.

"I'm coming," she says, just as the first wave of cum shoots inside her.

"*Fuck!*"

Her cries pierce the air as I pick up the pace. She hungrily accepts my release as the sounds of our bodies enjoying each other ring through the room. I empty myself fully inside her—deeply inside her—not stopping until I'm sure she's spent.

She gasps a breath, sagging against me, and I reach up and guide her back onto my chest.

Our pants sync. We look at each other at the same time and laugh.

"Did you say we had dinner reservations?" she asks, still catching her breath.

"Yes. In about two hours."

"Want to take a bath with me?"

I'll do anything with you. And maybe, just maybe, I'll show her how precious she really is to me. How she was meant to be mine all along.

I pull her into my side and press a kiss to her forehead. Then I release her. "That sounds like a plan to me."

Chapter 21

Chloe

"Would you like more wine, ma'am?"

I shake my head, offering the server a smile. "No, thank you. I've had enough."

"Very well," he says, turning to Jason. "What about you, sir?"

"I'm good. Thank you."

The server nods and disappears into the rest of the dining area.

Ciro's is unlike any place I've ever eaten. It's sophisticated and moody, with shadowy corners and low lighting. I fully expect that celebrities and dignitaries are tucked into the booths lining the walls and sitting at the tables surrounding ours. It's *that* kind of a place—opulent—that makes me wish I knew the difference in all the forks.

If Jason notices my inability to choose the right eating utensil for each course, he doesn't mention it. His smile hasn't left his face since we climbed off the bed a couple of hours ago.

"What did you think of your meal?" he asks, sitting back in his chair and lacing his fingers against his stomach.

He's regal and debonaire in his suit, easily the most handsome man in the room. Every female in the building, and some males, took notice as soon as we entered. I doubt it takes three people to service one table, but that's been our experience this evening.

"This was incredible, actually," I say, surveying the remnants of my dinner left on my plate. "I've never had Wagyu beef before, but I'm a convert. Total fan."

This pleases him.

"How was yours?" I ask.

"I preferred my appetizer over my main course. Now I'm looking forward to dessert."

The heat in his eyes makes it clear what's for dessert. *Me.*

"I believe you had two appetizers before we got here," I say, grinning. "Aren't you full yet?"

He smirks. "I have a feeling I'll never be full of today's particular menu."

My cheeks flush, and I reach for my wine.

"Have I told you that dress looks stunning on you?" he asks.

"Only five times." I laugh. "But you can tell me again. I don't mind."

"You are the most beautiful woman in this room, and it has nothing to do with your dress. It's lovely, of course. But you are the star of this show."

I shake my head adoringly at him. "I hope you like this dress. You bought it."

He grins, sipping his drink.

The dress *is* beautiful with short sleeves and a modest back slit. The sheer mesh gathers to a V-back neckline, giving it a vintage vibe. Vertical seams streamline the crepe sheath. It's classy but comfortable. But when Nadia insisted that I *needed it*, I disagreed—especially with the price tag. Nadia, however, takes her orders from the man with the credit card, and that's not me.

I guess she was right, after all.

"We go home tomorrow, right?" I ask, a sense of dread filling me.

Jason's eyes narrow. "Yes."

I nod.

"Are you okay?" he asks.

"Yeah, of course." I slide a strand of hair behind my ear. "It's just that this weekend has been ... phenomenal, really. And I worry that returning to Nashville is opening the door for real life, I guess."

"This is real life."

I scrunch my nose. "But is it, though?"

He leans forward, folding his hands before him, but doesn't say a word. Something about the look on his face compels me to explain.

"You have made this weekend extraordinary in every way," I say softly. "And not just the gifts, or the sex, or the attention you've given me. But I've just felt ... alive, I guess. And I haven't felt like this in a long time."

"Like what?" he asks with genuine curiosity.

I shrug. *Like I've finally managed to adult without feeling like I'm on the verge of failing.*

"I feel like I'm a whole person," I guess. "Like I can breathe without feeling strangled. I took two baths today and didn't feel guilty about it." I laugh. "I don't regret any decision I've ever made regarding Mimi. But I do wonder late at night sometimes what my life would be like if she was healthier or if my mom was still here to help me care for her." I sigh, letting the thoughts go. "But it doesn't do any good to wonder, does it?"

"Can I ask why you didn't get Mimi into an assisted living of some sort?" He holds a palm up. "I'm not saying you should have. I'm not saying that at all. It's just an interesting choice for a twenty-five-year-old woman."

"I don't know. It's what I do, I guess. It's what my family does. It's how we're built. You know, when my mom got sick, Mimi and I took care of her. We washed her. Dispensed her medications. I made her food." Tears fill my eyes. "The last coherent day she had, she asked me to make her hot mashed potatoes. They had to be *hot*. She kept saying that for some reason."

The words catch in my throat. I look away from Jason as I battle back a wave of pain that I didn't realize was sitting so close to the surface. It's heartbreak and desolation all wrapped up in a big mess of misery.

It's been seven years, but some days it feels like it was only yesterday.

My husband reaches over, places his hand on mine, and rubs his thumb against the back of my hand. The simple, sweet gesture causes a single tear to slide down my cheek.

"I'm sorry," I say, swiping it away.

"Don't be sorry, Chloe."

The tenderness in his voice catches me off guard.

My heart strums as I absorb the kindness in his gaze, the warmth of his hand, and the peace found in his proximity.

"Anyway," I say, "we took care of her, and then she passed. And then Mimi and I took care of each other." I sniffle, clearing my throat. "My mom died with dignity—at home, with her daughter and mother beside her. I'm so grateful to have had the privilege of doing that because not everyone does. I sang her favorite songs to her. I held her hand. I bathed her body before the funeral home came to get her. And, once she was gone, I realized how important that was ... not just to her, but to me. To Mimi."

"You're an incredible human being."

I shake my head, laughing softly through the new round of tears. "We have very little in life that means anything. Our connections to each other and our dignity are all there really is at the end of the day. And to be able to give that to someone is really the best gift in the world."

I pat my eyes with the edge of my napkin and settle myself.

"You have me now," Jason says earnestly. "You're not in this by yourself anymore."

"My problems aren't—"

"Why do you do this?" He leans back again, surveying me carefully. "Why are you constantly poised to throw up a barrier between us?"

I grin. "I just let you fuck me without a condom. So your words don't really hold water, but thanks."

"You know what I mean."

I want to argue with him and pretend I don't know what he means, but the argument would be futile. This is a look I've known for years. It's a silent expression that says *don't push me too much further because I will take this to a place you don't want to go ... and I'll win.*

"I've told you this before," I say, pausing as a couple walks by our table. "Every time I've sucked it up and allowed someone access to that part of my life, it's bitten me in the ass. And not like the thought that just ran through your head."

His brows shoot to the ceiling.

"I can read you like a book," I say, laughing.

He chuckles, too. "Eventually, you'll realize you're wasting a lot of energy fighting me. I'm here, Chloe. I'm not going anywhere. And if you won't tell me what you want or need, I'll cover all my bases."

My heart swells. "Like the insane amount of clothes in my closet?"

"Oh, sweetheart. That's just the tip of the iceberg."

"The last time you promised me it was just the tip, you lied. My ass still hurts."

His laughter is quick and loud as I remind him of round three last night.

"Then I guess you better not push it," he says, smirking. "Trust me or don't. I'll win you over eventually."

You're well on your way.

The server comes back, and Jason requests a check. We sit quietly, sipping what's left of our wine, waiting for him to return.

"I talked to Nickie today," I say. "And I told her about us."

"You did? How'd that go?"

"She has a laundry list of questions I'm going to contend with on Monday, but she's really happy for me."

"What did you tell her?"

"We'd been dating quietly because we didn't want to make it weird in case it didn't work out."

He takes the check from the server and scribbles on the paper before handing it back. Once we're alone, Jason stands and offers me his hand. I take my new purse from the seat next to me, place my palm in my husband's, and rise to my feet.

"I want to fuck you right here in front of all these men watching you so they know you're mine," he whispers in my ear.

"There are men in here?"

He grins, pressing a kiss against the curve of my neck—a spot I'm learning is one of his favorites—then he guides me out of the restaurant.

The evening air is still thick and hot, and my dress sticks to my skin. When the valet brings our car to the front, Jason opens my door, settling me in my seat, before hopping in the driver's seat and jetting away.

Lights flicker from all directions as we roar down the Strip. It's a menagerie of sounds, advertisements, and offers of everything from shows to prostitutes. It's much, *much* different from Nashville. Brighter. Louder. More exciting.

But the most exciting thing in all of Las Vegas is the man sitting beside me, driving a car with the same finesse that he uses to fly planes.

I lie back against the seat and feel the engine rumbling around us. The sound lulls me into a peaceful haze, and I think about all the things Jason has said to me tonight.

I'm not alone anymore.

He's not going anywhere.

He'll cover all of his bases to ensure I have what I want and need.

A smile ghosts my lips as a warmth spreads through me like wildfire.

Maybe Mimi is right. Maybe Jason is crazy about me.

Is that really possible?

I look across my shoulder at him just as he looks over at me and gives me the sweetest, shyest, yet most confident smile I've ever seen.

My heart wobbles, and my head spins.

In my wildest dreams, Jason is the hero of the story. Gorgeous. Kind. Brilliant. And he looks at me in a way that makes me feel like the only person in the room.

Mimi might be right. He might be crazy about me.

And I might be crazy about him, too.

Jason winks and downshifts, the engine roaring as we speed down the road to our hotel.

Chapter 22

Jason

"I would've been much happier had we not walked out of there with a threat still hanging over our heads," I say into the phone.

Towlin sighs.

I gaze across the desert as the hot morning sun hits me through the windows. Sunshine usually lifts my spirits. But not today. Not about this.

"We're confident we can navigate this situation, Jason. And, if it does become a legal issue, we're prepared to pull out all the stops to halt it in its tracks."

"That's good. That's very good. Because if I'm left to explain to Gannon that our father is pinning fraud and extortion charges on the two of us, I'm going to be fucking pissed."

My jaw pulses, clenching so hard it hurts. The pain is welcome, though, because it takes an ounce of focus off my problems at hand. Namely, Reid Brewer.

Towlin babbles on about strategy and how Discovery should help us in the long run, and the claimant knows that. He assures me that they're probably aware it was Dad, but we're targets since Gannon and I are the major controllers of the Brewer finances. And with Dad pointing his finger our way, they're all too happy to agree.

"If you don't mind me saying this," Towlin says, meaning I'm absolutely going to mind what he's about to say. I brace myself. "But you should tell Gannon and take the air out of the argument. Let him know."

"And you should mind your business."

"Jason ..."

"Reid Brewer has torn our family apart," I say, the words hot as they pour from my mouth. "He has gone out of his way to try to dismantle our businesses, our relationships, and each of us individually."

"I know that."

I chuckle angrily. He's known on paper what my father has done. But he doesn't fully comprehend the emotional toll this has taken.

The stress and angst we've had to live with daily. The pain his lies deliver. The brutality of the betrayal.

"May I ask why you want to protect Gannon?" Towlin asks. "If it were Tate, or Ripley, I'd understand. But it's peculiar that you're working so hard to protect your eldest brother."

It's none of his damn business why I do or don't do anything. But I'll tell him anyway. Maybe then he'll follow along.

I slide my free hand into my pocket. "Gannon has idolized our father since the day he was born. He played baseball because Dad did. Went to the same business school. He has intentionally or otherwise picked up most of Dad's mannerisms over the years." I stop moving, my heart pounding. "He took our father's betrayal harder than any of us, even if he doesn't show it."

Towlin is silent.

"If Gannon knew that the man he'd put on a pedestal his whole life cared so little about him that he'd orchestrate for him to go to prison for something he didn't do, Gannon would be devastated." I frown. "He'd be absolutely crushed, Towlin. And that would destroy my mother. Again. Bianca would blame herself for stepping down as the president of Brewer Group. Ripley would probably try to climb the walls of the prison to slice Dad's throat. Ripley isn't going anywhere without Tate. And do you know where that leaves me?"

I pause to see if he responds, but he doesn't.

"That leaves me figuring out how to do it because I'll be damned if my family takes any more pain because of that motherfucker," I growl, running my fingers across my scalp. "I'll figure this out. Gannon finds out as a last resort."

"You don't have to carry this all on your own."

The bedroom door opens, and I turn at the sound. Chloe's wrapped in a new robe from yesterday, and she smiles, hesitating, as she observes the situation.

I exhale sharply, my heart softening as I take her in.

I'm not carrying this alone because I have her.

"Are we done here?" I ask Towlin. "I have a few things to take care of before we head to the airport."

He lets the insinuation of my marital status go. He wasn't thrilled about the news this morning, although he didn't have the balls to bring it up to me. His argument against me marrying Chloe would be that it adds another layer of complication, and it's distracting to the topic at hand.

His argument doesn't fucking matter. Not when it comes to her.

"One more thing ..." He takes a deep breath. "I do have something to run by you."

I hold up a finger to Chloe. She nods, understanding my need for privacy, and disappears into the bedroom.

My insides pulse, preparing for a bomb to land in my lap. It's coming. I can feel it.

"What's up?" I ask, placing a palm on the table.

"Reid's attorneys approached me on Friday. I haven't said anything to you because I needed to clear a few hurdles to see if it was even possible, and it is."

"What's possible?"

My fingers flex against the stone and around the phone, waiting for his next words.

"He wants to meet with you," Towlin says, his voice uneasy.

"Who?"

"Your father."

I snort out a laugh, my eyes popping in surprise. "Tell him to go fuck himself."

"He's willing to sign the plea deal if you sit down with him."

My face burns as I struggle to contain myself. "He doesn't get to call the shots. He doesn't get to ask me for *anything*," I growl into the air. "He doesn't want me anywhere near him, I can promise you that. I'll rip his fucking head right off his shoulders."

"I understand you're angry." *That's an under-fucking-statement.*

"A little bit," I say, shoving away from the table.

"Why don't you think about it and get back to me in a couple of days? Jason, I know it's not what you want to do, but there are silver linings."

The doorbell rings, and I march to the foyer. I hand the delivery person all the cash in my pocket, which is probably enough for a day's worth of coffee deliveries but fuck it. I take the coffee and close the door.

"I need to go," I say, heading for the bedroom. "I'll call you later this week."

"Goodbye."

"Goodbye."

I slide my phone across the table as I walk by and enter the bedroom. Chloe's sitting on the edge of the bed in a long white and pink dress. Her brows lift warily as I approach her.

"Is everything okay?" she asks. "I tried not to listen, but when your voice is that loud, it's hard not to hear."

"Nothing new. Nothing for you to worry about." I hand her a vanilla iced latte and kiss the top of her head. "You look beautiful this morning."

She smiles. "You say that so often that I'm starting to think it's just a line."

"I should've known. You do like creativity."

Her smile darkens as we share a memory of last night after dinner.

She stands and presses a sweet kiss to my lips. "Thank you for the coffee. I was going to say I can't believe you remembered, but that's untrue. I'm not the least bit surprised."

"Good."

"Good?"

"You should expect your coffee in the morning. Maybe we are making progress."

She rolls her eyes before her attention settles over my shoulder—at the ringing phone I'm trying to ignore.

Chloe's words last night regarding returning to reality, about how this weekend has been amazing, and she didn't want to leave it, come drifting back to me. Suddenly, I understand what she was saying. I don't want to go back, either.

"I bet Renn would sell me this place," I say, only half kidding. "We could move here, bring Mimi, and just live out the rest of our lives."

She smacks my chest, sipping her coffee as she heads for the closet. "You'd be bored out of your mind."

"I think you could keep me entertained."

She pauses in the doorway and giggles. "I could for a while. It might be a fun experiment for a few months."

"Wanna try it?"

She shakes her head and rummages around in her bags, the sound crinkling through the room. "Be a good little CEO and check your phone. Make sure the office isn't burning down. I just need a few more minutes to gather the rest of the store you bought for me yesterday, and then I'll be ready to go."

"I know you're being sarcastic, but thanks for the reminder."

"Of my frustration with you?" she calls.

"No. Of the way you looked in that skimpy black thing last night. I think we'll try the white one when we get home."

Her head pops around the corner, grinning. She holds my gaze for a few moments and then ducks back inside.

"Fine," I say, groaning. "I'll be out here when you're ready."

"Good boy."

I chuckle, walking out of the bedroom. Has she ever not handled me?

Leave it to Chloe to make me laugh, even when I'm in a terrible mood.

Mom's name's on the screen, and given she's the only person I'd call back right now, I press her name and listen to it ring.

"Hey, Jason." I can hear her smile through the line. "How are you?"

"Good. Getting our stuff packed to head home. Thank you for the flowers for Chloe, by the way. They're going to be a pain in the ass to get back to Tennessee."

"I'm sure you can handle it."

"I'm sure I can, too," I say, grinning. "What's going on?"

"Well, I was in Savannah a couple of weeks ago and had dinner with Rodney and Siggy Mason. A few of their friends joined us at this fabulous restaurant. You should take Chloe there the next time you're down that way. *Anyway*," she says, earning an eye roll from me, "I met a man."

Whoa.

I recoil from those three little words. "You met a man?"

"I know it's sudden and—"

"Mother."

She hesitates. "Yes?"

"I think that's great." I laugh softly. "I mean, get Ford to run a background report on him and send me his name so I can look him up."

"You are not parenting me, Jason Brewer."

I grin. "No, you're right. I'm not. I'm using my specific skill set and the avenues available to ensure you won't be taken advantage of."

"Hold up, child. I might need to be taken advantage of. It's been a while."

My jaw drops. It lowers even farther as my mother, one of the most prim and proper women I've ever known, finds humor in this situation.

"Who have you been hanging around with?" I ask, chuckling.

"Foxx's parents, actually." Her laughter is loud and free. For the first time in my adult life, she sounds happy. "Damaris and Kixx Carmichael are hilarious—*and dirty*. You should hear them. It's no wonder their children are all little firecrackers. They come by it honestly."

I know Foxx's family, and she's right. The Carmichaels are as lively as they are good people. I just didn't expect my mother to fall into their shenanigans.

Oh, how things change. Or maybe this is who she really is. After all, none of her children could be called shy and withdrawn. Maybe she's only just finding her true self.

I can only respect this resilient woman.

"Who is this man?" I ask.

"His name is Joseph Dallo. His daughter is married to—well, a guy who works for Ford Landry, actually."

"Troy Castelli?"

"Yes. That's him. The dark-complected one who—you know what? Let's move on."

I look at the ceiling. "Yes. Let's."

"Anyway, Joseph was in town to see his daughter and we hit it off. I've seen him a couple of times since. I haven't found the courage to tell you, but I figured you should be on a honeymoon high this morning. So I took my chances."

I grin at her light and airy tone. She's come a long way in the past few months. And even if what happened to her was one of the worst things I could imagine, I'm starting to think it's for the best. Because even if this helps her separate from my father, something I don't think she would've done had he not gone off the rails, it's also given her life back.

This Rory Brewer would not be here had she not experienced everything she has lately.

In a way, I'm grateful for it all—and that's an uncomfortable feeling to wrestle with.

"I expect to meet him sooner rather than later," I say.

"I hoped you'd say that."

"Have you told the others?"

She laughs. "No. Bianca suspects something so she won't be surprised. Gannon and Ripley will be fine with it. But Lord knows I don't want to deal with Tate."

My laughter joins hers. "He's going to give you so much shit."

"I might be loosening up, but I'm not at the point in my life when I can take Tate's debauchery."

I snicker, shaking my head. "He's your child."

"That he is. And I'm proud of that boy, just like I'm proud of you." She pauses. "And maybe you'll know that feeling soon."

My gaze flickers to the bedroom, catching a glimpse of Chloe packing the last of her things. The idea of her being pregnant with my child—her stomach swollen with our baby—makes my cock hard. But it also makes my heart skip a beat.

"Maybe, Mom," I say. "We'll see."

She sighs happily. "Okay. I just needed to get this off my chest. Let me know when it's okay to come up and visit with you and your beautiful bride."

"Thank you for giving us a bit of space. I appreciate that."

"Of course, Jason. I love you so much."

"I love you so much, too."

"Call me."

"I will."

"Goodbye, son."

"Bye, Mom."

I end the call and slide my phone into my pocket, my gaze settled on my wife. She looks at me with a tilt of her head—my beautiful wife.

I love you, too, Chloe. Maybe I always have.

And maybe I'll get to tell you that soon, too.

Chapter 23

Chloe

"Look at her," I say, beaming as Jason navigates his car into the driveway. "She's sitting outside with her coffee and crossword puzzle book."

Jason stops the car by the side of the house and shuts off the engine.

He's been quiet since we got into the car at the airport. Typically, he keeps me engaged in a conversation or a story. Over the past hour, he's focused on the road with his right hand resting on my thigh.

Mimi waves. Even from here, I can tell she has color in her cheeks. The sunshine and fresh air are doing her good.

I glance at Jason. He's doing me good, too.

"Are you okay?" I ask, touching the side of his face. His stubble is rough against my hand, and I immediately wonder what that would feel like between my legs.

"Of course, I'm okay." He leans over and kisses me. "And that thought you just had? You'll find out tonight."

I flush, forgetting that he knows me too well.

"Let's check on your grandmother," he says, climbing out of the car. He says something to Mimi as he rounds the front and then opens my door for me. "She's feisty. I'm warning you."

I laugh, getting to my feet. "When is she not?"

My ring catches the light as we walk hand in hand to the patio outside of the guesthouse. Mimi tosses her book aside and prepares for our arrival with a big smile.

"Jason, you get more handsome every time I see you," she says, holding her arms out for a hug.

He envelops her without hesitation. "You look like you've been enjoying yourself. Mara told me you've been romping the streets in the golf cart."

Mimi gives me a quick hug. The fact that I'm an afterthought in her new life is amusing.

"So," she says, as if discussing war strategy. "There's a man who lives two streets down and four houses to the right. Samuel Hickman. Do you know him?"

"Oh, Sammy. Yeah," Jason says. "I know him. Why?"

She wiggles her brows.

Jason snorts, shaking his head. "I'm going to leave the two of you alone."

He pulls me to him, pressing his lips softly to mine. The tenderness in his kiss makes my knees go weak.

"I'll be inside soon," I say.

"Take your time, beautiful."

He pats me on the butt before waving at Mimi and walking toward his house.

I pull out a chair and sit with my grandmother. "You look good."

"You know what? I'm feeling good, Chloe." She grins. "I'd forgotten what it was like to have a friend like Mara. Someone upbeat and energetic who doesn't care how old we are. Old women can still have fun."

"Of course, you can."

"How was the honeymoon?"

I'm not sure what my face does, but Mimi cackles. "As expected."

Mara heads for the door. "I'm going cruising with Mimi for a while, then I'm heading home, Jason. Unless you need anything, that is."

"No," he says, wrapping his other arm around me. "Thank you, Mara, for everything. I couldn't survive without you."

She stops just short of the door and faces us, a grin splitting her face. She smiles at me and then focuses her attention back on Jason. "I don't think that's true anymore."

Jason and Mara exchange a look I don't quite understand before she slips outside.

The house is not quiet; it's peaceful. It's as if we're locked in a castle away from everything and everyone. I understand why Jason loves it here so much. This would be heaven after what he goes through on a normal day in the office.

It's heaven for me just because he's here.

He laces his fingers through mine, stroking the top of my hand with his thumb, and leads me upstairs. I follow him quietly, lost in my thoughts.

An odd sensation fills my chest. It's heavy and weighs nothing. It's wobbly yet so amazingly still. I could run a race or take a long nap, and I don't know what to make of that.

The only thing that makes any sense is that I'm falling in love with Jason.

I squeeze his hand as the idea cements in my heart and then my brain.

This must be what it feels like. This must be what people search for.

A smile ghosts my lips as I sit with this revelation.

Of course, I fell for him. He's patient and thoughtful, humble and protective. He's honest and hardworking, a nurturer by nature. A lover by design. He's a rock in storms, and a soft spot to land when I fall. It's as soothing as it is terrifying.

"Want to see our wedding pictures?" he asks, guiding me into our bedroom. "They're pretty epic."

"I'd love to."

He goes into his closet, so I sit on the bed, and he returns moments later, carrying a poster-sized picture frame.

"What is that?" I ask, curious.

He tries to hide his amusement. "We need to decide where to hang this—over our bed or above the fireplace downstairs?"

"Let me see it, and I'll let you know."

He twists the frame around and waits.

I burst out laughing. "*Oh my gosh.*"

"Above the fireplace, right?" He laughs, too. "I mean, who are we to keep our guests from enjoying this picture?"

"Don't you dare hang that anywhere." My laughter turns to giggles. "That's the worst wedding photograph I've ever seen."

He peers around the corner. "I don't know. I kind of like it. My eyes are closed. I'm guessing I'm dreaming of the life we'll have together. Your face looks like you just sucked a lemon. Not sure what that's about. Gold Jumpsuit is gyrating, I think." He stops. "Did his penis touch you?"

"No."

"Good." He studies the image again. "Tate's engrossed in a conversation with Mimi on the phone, and it looks like Ripley just saw a ghost." He nods. "I think that covers it."

I pull my legs up and shimmy until my back's against the headboard. I take a moment to appreciate the softness of his bed. It's a freaking cloud—a million times better than the mattress in the Pliny apartment.

"Is that the only picture they got?" I ask. "Tell me there are others. *Better ones.*"

He leans the frame against the wall. "I don't know. Ripley has them, from what I hear. He had this one printed and delivered for our enjoyment."

"It's ... enjoyable."

He flops on the bed beside me, pulling me on top of him. "I'll show you enjoyable."

As I lean down and kiss him, he holds my face between his hands like I'm a treasure. My heart does a cartwheel right across my chest.

"Are you going to tell me what was bothering you today?" I ask, sliding off him and cozying up against his side. "You said no secrets."

He doesn't answer me immediately, and a pang of guilt hits me hard. He doesn't have to tell me everything that happens in his life—I don't expect him to. I only want him to feel how he makes me feel: I'm never on my own.

"Okay." He sighs. "You're right. I've been a little thrown off today because my father has agreed to take responsibility for the fraud and extortion charges being levied at me and Gannon, as well as pleading guilty to the murder charges and all that entails."

What is he talking about? I pull away to see his face. "Whoa. Hang on." My heart pounds. "You told me there was a threat aimed at you but made it seem like it was being handled. And I didn't ask you about it because you didn't appear to want to discuss it." I shift my weight to sit up, my brows pinched. "There are fraud and extortion charges against you and Gannon?"

His gaze grows weary as his palm finds my thigh. "Not yet."

Wow.

"But it has nothing to do with me or Gannon," he says quickly, his eyes searching mine. "I mean it, Chloe. It's—"

"*Shh.* Of course, it doesn't. That's not where I was going with this."

He sinks into the mattress and catches his breath.

I caress the side of his face. "For what it's worth, even if those charges were against you, we'd beat them."

He stills. A small breath leaves his lips as he jerks me into his arms.

I giggle as he rolls me onto my side, my back to his front. "Hey, what's this for?"

"Just let me hold you here for a while."

"Okay." I hold on to his hands locked at my waist. "But you said he's taking responsibility for it all, right? So it's done?"

He kisses the back of my head. "Not exactly."

"And why not?"

He sighs, resting his chin on me. "There's a condition—one I don't want to meet."

"Which is ..."

"He wants to meet with me."

Oh. I know how much he dislikes his father, and rightfully so. I hate the man for what he's done to Jason and his family. There's no way Jason would want to face him. Not after everything that's happened.

But I also know Jason's sense of loyalty and his need to protect those he loves. And if he thinks this is the only way to protect the others from dealing with the mess of a trial, I know he'll do it.

It'll hurt him, even if he doesn't admit it.

"Want me to go with you?" I offer softly.

He smiles against my hair. "No."

"Are you sure?"

He kisses me again. "The fact that you'd even offer is more than enough for me." This time, a third kiss touches me in the crook of my neck. "I'm not even sure I'm going yet. The fucker doesn't deserve a soundboard to rattle off whatever venom or excuse he has. Quite frankly, I'm not sure I could look at him and not kill him."

I hum, pressing my back against him.

I have my thoughts on the situation, but my opinion doesn't matter now. What matters is that Jason knows I'm on his side regardless of his decision and the outcome. I'm doing what he said—acting like Mrs. Brewer.

"Can I help you?" I ask sweetly.

"I don't know how you can."

I laugh. "We haven't been home from our honeymoon for a couple of hours, and have you already forgotten how distracting I can be? Damn. I guess you didn't enjoy—*ah*!"

I'm on my back, sundress bunched at my waist, and Jason's hands are elevating my ass before I know what's happening. His eyes twinkle with mischief.

"Don't you ever, *ever* insinuate that I forget any part of you. And I never want to hear you suggest that I don't enjoy you either."

"What if I do?"

He blows against my swollen clit. "Then I'll have to spend the next few hours ensuring we're clear."

I sink into the bed, my insides quivering with anticipation of his mouth on me. "It'll take at least that long because I think you don't remember—*Jason*!"

I'm unsure if I'm distracting him or if he's distracting me. What I am certain about, however, is that I'm Chloe Brewer, a name I never expected nor did I want. *But I absolutely love it.*

But only forty-eight hours since we said "I do," and I already dread the day when it will be over. This just feels ... right, and if I truly am in love with this man, will I be able to keep our arrangement? Will I be able to walk away and leave this—*leave him?*

What if Jason asks me to stay? What if he wants more than six months?

Despite my initial easy acceptance of the lack of permanence, I'm now terrified. I'm not sure I could live without him anymore.

Fuck.

Chapter 24

Chloe

"Good morning, Brandi!" I practically float off the elevator and into the executive floor lobby. "How was your weekend?"

She stands behind the desk with a hand on her hip. "Not as good as yours, it seems."

I stop, my stomach churning. *Did word get out already? How?* The office just opened.

"Did you and Jason get married, or is this a joke?" She watches me curiously. "I've been thinking about it for the past twenty minutes, and the more I think about it, the more I believe it's probably true. You two have always had a thing for each other. But it does feel very much like a fantasy, so if it's not true, pretend I didn't say a thing."

I grip my bag, feeling the leather slip around my suddenly damp palm. "Well, it's true."

"*Oh my gosh. What?*" Her eyes nearly fall out of her head. "*You married Jason?*" She rushes around the corner of the desk and hugs me. "Congratulations."

"Thank you." I take a step back, frazzled. I knew word would get out. I didn't think it would get out before I got here. "How did you know?"

"Flowers were delivered before I got here. I don't know who set them on my desk, but I read the card because I didn't know what to do with them, and it ..." Her cheeks heat. "Let's just say it made things clear."

Oh shit. What did you do, Jason? I flush.

"I won't say a word until you do," she says. "And I'll pretend I didn't read that card, so please don't tell your husband I read it. Let's not make things weird."

"Thank you, Brandi."

I'm not sure what to say, so I hurry down the hall to my office. I flip on the light and, sure enough, Thomas's arrangement is long gone. In its place is a circular black box stuffed with hot pink roses.

I drop my bag and find the card.

Chloe,

These remind me of the color of your ass after the other night. Let's do that again, my beautiful wife.

Jason

My head falls forward as I imagine the look on Brandi's face when she read the card.

"We're going to have to work on boundaries," I mutter, although a smile is firmly on my lips.

I quickly scan my emails, picking out the important ones and dealing with them. Then I note the number of voice messages awaiting me and decide they can wait. Jason's schedule is manageable today, and there are no surprises. Fortunately. My latte is waiting for me, as it is every morning, but this morning? It's a little more special.

It's from my husband.

I knock on his door, then poke my head around the corner. "Hey. Just letting you know I'm here."

He stops what he's doing and looks at me. A slow grin stretches across his face. *He really is a sexy beast. How did I keep my hands off him for so long?* "Good morning, beautiful."

"You'll give me a complex if you keep calling me that."

"Prepare for a complex, then."

"The roses you sent me are gorgeous," I say, moving to his desk. "I don't know how you had them delivered before we opened, but I'll just chalk it up to yet another thing you do that I can't comprehend."

He taps a pen against his lips, hiding his satisfaction.

"But I will have you know that Brandi read the card," I say.

I'm not sure if he's going to laugh or cringe. That makes me laugh.

"I told her I wouldn't tell you because she doesn't want it to get weird," I say, shaking my head at him. "But maybe next time, don't write something so private."

He shrugs. "It's my company, and you're my wife. I don't see the problem."

"Jason ..."

"Fine." He tosses the pen on his desk. "I'll make sure they put a disclaimer on the envelope next time. Then if she looks, it's on her."

I roll my eyes. "Okay, let's move on. Florence Systems will be coming by at two o'clock to meet with you and Tate. Don't let Tate take over because you have a three thirty call with Ford Landry and a four thirty call with Brunston Aeronautics. Also, there seems to have been a slight issue last night at our gate in Philly. I flagged the email for you if you haven't seen it yet."

He says nothing, only grins.

"What?" I ask.

"You're my wife."

I laugh. "Yes, I am."

"Come here."

"I know that look in your eye," I say, pointing at him. "We can't be messing around in the office."

"It's my office."

"And we have things to do."

He narrows his eyes. "Did you come in through the front door this morning?"

I nod. "Of course. Why?"

"What did it say just above the door when you walked in?"

"Brewer Air ..." My shoulders fall as I realize what he's getting at.

He smirks. "Brewer Air, as in Jason Brewer. Now get your sexy little ass over here so I can hold my wife before this day turns to shit."

This is highly inappropriate and probably against the handbook in a hundred ways. But I'm not saying no to him—and not just because I'm completely turned on when he gets all bossy with me. I don't say no because I want him to hold me, too.

I never understood cuddling. I was firmly in Team Don't Touch Me After Sex and Respect My Personal Bubble. But that was before I knew what it felt like to be in *his* arms. It's my favorite place to be. I don't feel violated or suffocated by him. Instead, I feel cherished—and I love it.

I perch on his knee, but he drags me back into his lap. He finds his spot in the bend of my neck and presses long, sweet kisses there.

"What if someone walks in?" I ask, my eyes fluttering closed.

"They better knock, or I'll fire them."

I smile as his kisses reach my jaw. "You can't just fire people."

"Why the hell not?"

"Because you'd feel bad," I say, laughing.

He grins against my lips. "You don't know me as well as you think you do."

Yet I do.

I hold my breath just before he does exactly what I expect him to do. One hand splays against my stomach, and the other slides up my thigh. I inhale, holding it as his fingers reach my already soaked flesh.

He growls in my ear, nipping at my lobe.

"What?" I ask coyly, tilting my head to the side. "No panties shouldn't be a problem because no one should know but me."

He turns his chair so that if someone does open his door, they won't see anything. Then he slides one of my legs over his lap.

"This is against the employee handbook," I tease, resting my head against his. His cock is rock hard beneath me.

"Probably. But there's probably a clause about spouses."

I snort. "You think?"

"I'll have HR amend it as soon as I get you off."

I sag against him as he slips a finger inside my slit.

"We're going to have to do something about this," he whispers, sliding one and then two fingers into me. "I might have to transfer you after all."

A short gasp escapes my lips as I press down against his hand.

"I love that you're always ready for me," he says, tugging at my earlobe with his teeth.

"Little did you know, but I've been ready for you like this since the day I met you at Coffee and Cream."

He growls again. "Don't tell me that."

"It's true." I moan softly as he forms smooth circles over my clit. "Can we lock the door for just a few minutes?"

"No. I have a meeting in"—he checks the clock—"six minutes."

I bark out a laugh that turns quickly into another moan.

A tingle dances up my spine, drawing with it the weight that precedes an orgasm. I grip Jason's thighs, my nails digging into him, as he pushes a finger deep inside me.

His other hand joins the onslaught, working together to bring me to climax quickly.

"*Ah!*" I gasp, the intensity and pressure so sharp it's almost painful. Jason presses a hand over my mouth as my head pushes against him, my body fucking his hand.

He chuckles, shushing me. "If you can't do this quietly, this won't be able to happen again."

Despite my world falling apart around me, I manage to glare at him.

This only makes him chuckle harder.

Finally, he brings me down slowly until I'm fully satiated. He ends it with a soft kiss to my temple.

"Up you go," he says, helping me off his lap. "I really do have a call in two minutes."

I straighten my skirt, glancing at his pants. I can't help but think about what he said he's thought about at work. *Me, under his desk, his cock in my mouth.*

"Later," he says, winking as if he reads my mind.

"Well, then don't stand for a while."

He grips his cock and groans. "Noted."

"Oh, one more thing," I say as I'm headed to my office. "Fika texted me this morning, and they have a shift open tomorrow night."

"The restaurant?"

I nod. "Yeah. I pick up a couple of shifts there a week if I can."

"You used to, you mean." His lips twitch as he goes back to his computer. "Don't forget to get the report for the gates in San Francisco and Salt Lake City."

"They're already in your inbox."

"I wish I was in your box," he mumbles.

I shake my head and get back to work.

Chapter 25

Chloe

"Mimi, this is the best damn peach pie I've ever had," Ripley says, wiping his mouth on a napkin. "But if you tell my mother, I'll deny I said it."

My grandmother basks in Ripley's attention on her right, and Tate's on her left—both charming the hell out of her.

These Brewer men really are the Trifecta of Power.

I laugh, realizing that it was a different three when Nickie and I discussed this. The fact that it still applies is hilarious—and telling.

I refill my glass of iced tea, pretending that I don't know the pitcher is made of crystal. My plastic one, stained perfectly by years of sweet tea making, was lost in the move. Jason's only pitcher costs a few hundred dollars. He doesn't know why he has it or when he got it. I let him know that we'll be getting a new plastic one because I have anxiety attacks every time I'm forced to use his.

He just laughed.

"The lasagna was delicious," Tate says, holding a forkful up in the air. "Sorry I got here late. My plane was delayed."

"Then hire your own plane next time," Jason says, entering our kitchen. He squeezes my butt before wrapping his arms around me from behind. "What would Sammy say if he could see you now, Mimi? Sitting between two men who clearly have the hots for you."

Tate bumps Mimi's arm playfully.

"Who cares? I'm too old to be monogamous. I'm living it up while I'm still kickin'."

Ripley's dimple sets on his cheek.

It's been a week since our wedding, and every day has only gotten better. Mimi's practically a toddler, buzzing around on her golf cart that Jason had fashioned with a radio. She cruises the neighborhood, listening to Sinatra. You can hear her coming from the street over. And Jason and I have gotten into an easy flow. Our routine begins with a kiss good morning before he leaves a couple of hours before me, and it ends with us cuddled in bed and watching documentaries. *Will it always be this way?* I don't know. But every day that passes, the more my hope grows that it will.

Ripley rises from the table, carrying his plate to the sink. "So are you going to get behind the Royals purchase or what?" he asks Jason.

I peer up at my husband.

"I still think it's a bad idea." Jason sighs. "You all support it, I know. Trust me, I understand. We're always supportive of one another. But I really think we need to let a little time pass before we make big splashes."

"Lincoln Landry has the Arrows charging full speed ahead," Ripley says.

My brows tug together. "Wait a second. Are Lincoln Landry and Ford related? It just occurred to me that they have the same last name."

"They're brothers," Jason says. "Lincoln was a professional baseball player. One of the best center fielders in the league."

"Future Hall of Famer," Ripley adds. "And he played his whole career for the Arrows. It was like coming home for him."

That's great, but I'm still stuck on Ford Landry, Jason's friend and the owner of Landry Security who handles the Brewer family's security, being brothers with Lincoln. *What a small, wild world.*

"Speaking of coming and going, I'm heading to Vegas on Monday," Ripley says. "Peter Zobreski asked me to come out. He has a few new fighters with a lot of potential, but they aren't taking care of themselves. He wants me to assess them and put together diet and exercise plans that they'll actually use."

"That sounds like fun."

Jason pinches me at the hip, making me squirm.

"What?" I giggle, leaning into his hand.

"No fighters for you."

I smack his hands away. "I need to pitch the laundry from the washer to the dryer. I'll be right back."

"What happened to Mara?" Ripley asks.

"Nothing happened to Mara," I call out over my shoulder.

Jason's voice is loud enough for me to hear as I walk away. "Chloe's adamant about doing laundry herself."

"That's cool," Ripley says.

I don't hear the rest of their conversation, but I know what it will be—Jason's frustration that I want to do laundry, dishes, and sweep off the patio. Ripley will be amused but will ultimately take Jason's side because whether Jason knows it or not, Ripley might be his second biggest fan ... behind me.

Flipping the laundry takes two minutes, and I'm back in the kitchen. Mimi's getting to her feet, clinging to Tate's arm like she might topple over at any minute. I give her a look, and she grins, tossing me a wink.

"Where do you think you're going, Meems?" I ask.

"Tate's going to take me out in the golf cart. He volunteered."

"What if Sammy sees you and gets upset?"

"Oh, a little jealousy never hurt anyone."

All I can do is shake my head at her. Seeing her like this makes me wish we could've hung out when she was younger. I bet she was fun.

"Don't be making out with her or anything," Ripley calls after Tate. "Try to control yourself."

"Ripley, you hush your little mouth!" Mimi shouts back just before the door closes behind them.

Tate holds his finger behind his back and flips Ripley off. The three of us laugh.

"Whose phone is that?" Ripley asks, his brows pulling together. "It's rung three times all the way through."

"Mine is on the counter by the sink," I say.

"It's mine. I left it in my office. Let me go turn it off," Jason says.

I watch his back muscles move beneath his shirt as he walks away.

"How's married life treating you?" Ripley asks, rinsing his plate before putting it in the dishwasher.

"Better than I expected."

"Did you not expect to be happy you married my brother?" He laughs.

"I didn't know what to expect, but I'm a very happy woman."

"Glad to hear it." He takes a seat on the counter. "He's been different this past week. Less moody. More pliable. Not saying he's been friendly or anything ..."

I laugh.

"But he seems really happy." Ripley's blue eyes sparkle. "That's pretty cool."

"Yeah, well, he's pretty cool."

Jason returns, pulling a polo shirt over his head. "Blakely's in labor."

"Renn's wife?" I ask.

"Yes. Renn just called me in a panic." Jason grins. "Grey was working security for them and is driving them both to the hospital. I bet Grey's ready to throttle Renn."

Ripley laughs, hopping off the countertop. "Labor can take hours —especially for first-time mothers. I'm going to run home and grab a shower before heading to the hospital."

"I'm heading there now before Blakely divorces our brother," Jason says. "Are you coming or staying home?"

What do I want to do? I take his hand. "I want to go with you, of course."

"Lock up behind you, will ya?" Jason asks Ripley.

Ripley yawns. "Sure will. I'll ensure Tate and Mimi return, and we'll get her situated before we leave."

My heart swells at the kindness of these men. Not only have they embraced me, but they've also extended their warmth to my Mimi. They've changed our lives, and I don't think they even know it.

"Let's go," Jason says, walking beside me to the garage. "We're about to have another little Brewer."

We exchange a look that doesn't need words—which is good. I'm not capable of them right now, anyway.

* * *

"Oh my gosh, Renn," I whisper, pulling back the blue blankets to see the newborn's little face. "He's beautiful."

Renn can't take his eyes off his son. "I just can't believe I'm a dad. I mean, look at him. He has hands for rugby and Blakely's lips. It's so wild."

Jason clasps his brother on the shoulder, admiring his nephew, too.

"How's your wife?" I ask.

The agony of the past twelve hours is written all over Renn's face.

I stayed at the hospital with them for the first few hours—until it was clear the birth was going to take some time. Jason drove home long enough to drop me off, grab his computer, and then returned to stay with his brother.

Jason kept me updated through the night, and as things grew more complicated, the rest of the family began to arrive. Tate and Ripley were next, followed shortly by Gannon. Bianca and Rory flew in around two this morning and sat with Blakely's brother, Brock, and his fiancée, Ella.

I arrived back just as the doctor urged Renn to sign off on a C-section. Arlo Renn Brewer was born just before nine o'clock this morning.

"Blakely's resting," he says, nodding toward the other room of the maternity suite. "This little guy really took it out of her." Tears well up in Renn's eyes. "Thank you for staying by my side last night, Jason. I was scared shitless."

"You know I have you," Jason says, keeping his hand on Renn's shoulder. "Just like you have this little guy."

"Do you want to hold him?" Renn asks.

Jason smiles. "I'd love to."

The baby's transferred between the two men like a priceless heirloom. Renn whispers to his son, explaining who Jason is and promising him his uncle won't drop him. I stand back and watch, trying not to laugh at the sweet moment between the brothers.

"Hey, you," Jason says softly, holding Arlo up so he can see him better. "I'm Uncle Jase. You can come to me to learn everything your dad can't teach you, which is mostly everything besides rugby."

Jason grins, watching Renn out of the corner of his eye. Renn just smiles.

"Don't cry," Jason says, chuckling. "Did Uncle Gannon already say mean things about me? They're all lies." He coos as he brings the baby up against his shoulder. "I got you, little guy."

My heart leaps into my throat, lodging itself there with the force of a hurricane. A fire roars in my chest as I watch Jason and Arlo.

Renn whispers something to Jason, and he laughs. Their conversation is out of my earshot, but it's better that way. Because watching them at this moment—watching them share the sweetest memory—hits me so hard I can barely breathe.

The magic between them touches a part of my soul that's never been uncovered.

Tears fog my vision as I soak in the moment, trying to make sense of my reaction. I'm so drawn to this. I feel a hollowness, an ache inside me that begins so deep in the fibers of my body that I don't know how I haven't noticed it before.

I want this. I want this for myself.

The fierceness of the realization is overwhelming. I'm dizzy from the power of it.

Is this what I really want? Or am I just reacting to seeing a sexy man hold a baby?

It's confusing and baffling because, just last week, I was certain I didn't really want kids. But as Jason watches me with the most tender look in his eye, I remember that just last week, I was certain I didn't want a husband, too.

Maybe it takes this—the right person at the right time—to rip the shields down that protect you from potential harm ... and open you up to the one thing you really need the most. *Love.*

"Do you want to hold him, Chloe?" Jason asks.

"*Oh.* Um, sure," I say as Jason places Arlo gently into my arms.

Oh. My. God.

He's so tiny.

He's so ... precious.

The feeling of the child nuzzling against me makes me reconsider everything I thought I knew about myself. *Because this*? This feels right.

My palms sweat under the hospital blankets. Jason excuses himself to take a call in the hallway.

"Renn, Arlo is so sweet," I say, taking in his little pursed lips and button nose.

"It's wild." He laughs as if the fact that he's a dad is just hitting him. "I've never experienced anything like this before. As soon as I saw him, I loved him more than I've ever loved anything. I'd die for this boy right now. No questions asked." He blinks back tears. "I wasn't prepared. That's all."

"I don't think you can prepare for something like this. How could you?"

He stands behind me, peering over my shoulder. Arlo takes Renn's finger and squeezes it.

"Here," I say, returning the baby to his father. "I think he wants you."

"I don't know what I would've done without Jason last night," Renn says. "He's a really good guy, Chloe. I hope you know that."

My heart swells. "I do. I know that."

Footsteps capture our attention just before Jason appears in the room again. There's a shadow on his face that sends a shot of concern racing through my body.

"Gannon and Bianca are here," Jason says. "If you're good, Chloe and I'll go and let them visit."

"Yeah. That's fine. Thanks for being here, Jase."

Jason nods. "I wouldn't have been anywhere else, buddy." He offers me his hand, squeezing my palm a little harder than usual.

My heartbeat picks up with each step we take toward the elevator. Jason doesn't say a word in the elevator. We walk through the parking lot, the air smelling like fresh bread from the bakery across the street and stop in front of my car.

"What's wrong?" I ask, the breeze picking up the ends of my hair and billowing them.

He runs a hand down his chin. "Dad has until Monday to take the plea deal. He's going to refuse unless I fly to Florida and meet with him."

"Why is he in Florida?"

"Because he was arrested in Florida. He's facing attempted murder charges there."

My spirits sink. "What are you going to do?"

He blows out a frustrated breath and looks at the sky. The struggle is clear, and I hate it for him.

"What do you think I should do?" he asks.

I take his other hand and hold it in mine, too. "I think you should go to Florida and talk to your father."

His face snaps to mine.

"Don't do it for him," I say. "Don't do it because he's holding something over your head." I squeeze his hands. "Do it for you. Do it so when you wake up Monday morning, this can all be put behind you, and you never have to deal with it again."

He holds his breath.

"If you go there and just get closure for yourself, that's a win. And if he follows through on his word, that's a double win," I say. "But the worst solution is you go, and he doesn't follow through, and then you go to court anyway. You won't be any worse off."

"I know, but I just feel like he's winning if I go."

I smile at him. "How is he winning? He's rotting in prison while you're out here, living your life, taking care of your family. You're filling his role better than he ever did. You're winning, Jason. You control all the shots. Don't let your pride get in the way of what's best. You're smarter than that."

"If I go, I need to go now. Towlin can set up a meeting for this evening. Then Dad can sign the plea deal in the morning."

"So go. I'll be here when you get back."

I'm not sure if that's what he needed to hear, or if he needed reassurance, but the relief on his face is undeniable.

"You are the best thing that ever happened to me," he whispers before planting a sweet kiss against my lips. "I love you so much, Chloe Brewer."

Those three little words hit me hard. I gasp a quick breath at *his voice* saying those three little words *to me.*

He loves me.

I know he loves me, and I know I love him, too. I love him with my whole fucking heart. I don't know when it happened or how it happened, but at some point over the past week, it's become clear as a bell.

But saying those words, even though I know them to be true, fills me with a fear in the deepest part of my soul. It feels like I'm slicing myself open, baring my heart to him. And even though I know he'd never hurt me, that doesn't mean I can override the strangulation I feel at this moment.

"Chloe?" he asks, searching me. Prompting me. Begging me to return his words to him.

"Jason, listen, I'm sorry. I just ... I'm struggling over here to get the words to come out." I'm talking too fast, too panicky. But I can't slow down. "Let's go home. I—"

He takes a step back, anger flashing in his eyes. "Go on home. I need to catch a flight."

"Jason, wait."

He takes a deep breath, and the wall I used to see around him all the time—but haven't witnessed since we got married—comes back up.

"We'll talk at home," he says. "But, right now, I have to take care of this other bullshit because, if I don't, there will be hell to pay for us all."

Tears streak down my cheeks at the pain in his face that I caused. Even if I tell him I love him now, he won't believe me. He won't understand. He'll think I'm saying it to make things okay.

I press a kiss to his lips and then back away. "Come home to me. Go take care of this, and then come home to your wife. I have a lot of things I want to tell you."

That I love you ... and that I think I want to keep you forever. And that one day, I want to be the mother of your children.

I need time to process that, anyway. Maybe a day apart will do us both some good.

"I'll let you know how it goes," he says, nodding.

Then he turns and walks away.

Chapter 26

Jason

M*y socks are damp.*

I shake my head at the random thought. Overstimulation causes the mind to focus on the oddest things. *But damp socks?* That's a new one.

It's been pouring since I left Tennessee. The day turned bleaker the farther south I flew, as if in warning that the day would only get worse. I'm taking my chances. After my interaction with Chloe after I told her I love her, I'm not sure how much worse it can get.

I take a seat in the third booth as the guard beside the door instructed me when I came in. The room's clean, yet I don't want to touch anything. The smell burns my nostrils. It's not so much the scent itself that's horrible, but more the lack of anything familiar.

I immediately think of Chloe and how she sniffs every bottle of cologne in my bathroom. She leaves her favorites in the front of the shelf, so I'll choose them over the ones she doesn't favor. If it meant making her happy, I'd toss every one she doesn't love.

But that might mean tossing myself out, too.

My chest pulls tight, and I force my wife out of my head. I must focus on the task at hand. I get one try to get this right. I'll figure out Chloe when I'm done.

A door squeals, and then I see him. Dad shuffles into the room.

His hair is whiter than I remember, and he's much thinner than before. He looks small in the drab-colored jumpsuit as he lifts his eyes to mine.

My hands flex at my sides as I search for humanity in his face—anything to quell this overwhelming need to make him pay for his crimes.

He sits across from me, groaning as he collapses into the chair. On the other side of the plastic wall, he looks like a little old man.

"You look like shit," I say.

Dad nods, sitting up straight. "You look good, Jason."

"Cut to the chase. You didn't ask me to come all this way to tell me I look good."

He sighs. "Can we take this easy?"

"No, motherfucker, we can't."

My tone is sharp and pointed. I want him to know I'm angry and to understand the pain he's caused us all. Not that I think he'll care, but just in case.

"Why am I here?" I ask, resting my elbows on the cool metal table in front of me.

Dad just stares at me, unblinking.

"Okay, fine. I'll say what I need to say, and then I'll go." I hold his gaze and refuse to let go. "I didn't come here for you. I didn't come here to make you feel better, or to give you closure, or to hear your excuses. And you better believe that I didn't come here because you refused to cooperate until you got your way."

"Then why did you come?"

My heart leaps in my throat, my emotions for Chloe clouding my brain. *She's why I came.*

I think about her smile and sweet laughter. The memory of her with Arlo is seared into my mind. I remember the way she slurps her iced tea and the taste of her terrible lasagna, which I don't have the heart to tell her was basically inedible. More than anything, I think about all the memories we have yet to make.

My anger doesn't fade, but it does begin to twist into something else. Seeing my father on the other side of the prison wall doesn't make up for what he's done—not by a long shot—but it does feel ... complete. It's as if the energy I've wasted on this man is now freed. Like I can put it all to bed and move on.

"Do you know what I did today?" I ask.

He shakes his head.

"I stood beside my brother as he became a father."

Dad's brows rise. "Renn?"

I don't dignify him with an answer. "I stood next to him and watched him welcome his little boy into the world. It was one of the wildest experiences of my life. I had the honor of being there, of encouraging him when he was nervous and hugging him when he was scared. I built him up and reminded him what a good man he was and what an amazing father he was going to be—something you should've done."

Dad swallows hard. "Did Renn have a baby, Jason?"

"Then I snuck my siblings and mother into the room so everyone could love on the little guy," I say. "I exchanged a moment of pride with Gannon, watched Ripley's eyes water as he held his nephew, and listened to Tate crack jokes that earned a warning from Bianca to behave."

Tears fill Dad's eyes as he listens.

"I was there as Mom held her grandson for the first time, surrounded by her children, and helped choose the name of her first grandchild. We all celebrated the baby's mama and made plans to take care of Renn and his family for the next few weeks."

A solitary tear slides down his cheek.

"Then I walked my wife to her car," I say.

"When did you get married?"

"And I kissed her and asked her what I should do about you. Should I come and see you? Or should I go home with her?" I pause, letting the wobble in my breathing stop. "And despite knowing she wanted me to go home with her, she told me to come here. And she told me to do that *for me.*"

He wipes his cheek with the pad of his thumb.

"I have a whole life out there," I say. "I get to watch Bianca try to talk Foxx into getting chickens, and I golf with Gannon just to keep his confidence up because it's the only thing he's decent at anymore."

Dad grins through his emotions. I keep going.

"Tate and Ripley come over for dinner and share my wife's grandmother's homemade pies. And Renn calls me to come to hang up televisions in his house because he's suddenly a DIYer who can't DIY himself out of a hardware store."

"That sounds about right."

A surge of emotion ripples through me, and the words lining up on my tongue aren't what I expected them to be. I thought I'd be lashing out at my father—telling him how much I hate him and how pathetic he is as a man. But the truth is that he already knows that. What he doesn't know is that I don't care anymore.

I sigh. "You caused a mess. You did the unforgivable—and I won't forgive you." My breath is shaky. "But I will thank you."

"Jason, I'm so sorry."

"Save it. Don't care. I really don't. Because when I walk out of here today, this will all be behind me. You don't get any more of my energy. You won't take up any space in my head. You can threaten me and Gannon, and you can force the mother of your children and your daughter to testify against you if that makes you feel like a man. But you know what?" I clench my teeth so hard they crack. "We'll still be out there. Together. Tighter than we've ever been. Sure, there may be tears, but we'll be a family—and that's the beauty of this whole thing. You gave us the gift of family." I grin. "Wild, isn't it?"

He shifts in his seat, eyeing me warily. "I asked you to come here for this reason."

"For what reason?"

"I don't even hope for your forgiveness. We both know I don't deserve it. But maybe one day we can have a conversation, and I can try to explain things."

"Or not."

He hangs his head. "Or not." He sighs and looks up again, a broken man in a broken body. *Pathetic. Weak. Imprisoned.* "Of all my children, you were the brightest, Jason. You shined above them all. Hell, you didn't ever need me. You taught yourself to tie your shoes, ride a bike, and drive a car. You could've done anything you wanted and chose what made you happy." He leans forward. "You're a leader. You're strong. You're smart and a protector. And I know if there's any way for me to ever make peace with any of you, I'll have to go through you first."

"You're damn right. And you won't. You don't get access to them."

We eye one another in a strange standoff. It's hard to see any glimpses of the man I once knew, and to some degree, that helps. But, in others, it's harder. It's akin to a death. While we're all better off for that, it still comes with a heaviness that makes it hard to think.

"That's fair," he says quietly. "Thank you for taking care of them. Because I know as I sit here rotting away, deservedly, you're taking care of our family."

"*My family.*"

He grins sadly. "I know they'll be okay because they have you. And even though you hate me, rightfully so, I wanted to look you in the eye and tell you how much I respect you, kid. I've fucked all the way up. And you slid into my spot and became the man I never was."

What? It takes me a minute to process what he's saying. Or to try to, anyway. I'm going to need time to sort this shit out in my head.

"I'm going to sign the plea deal," he says. "And my attorney will settle the rest of the disputes, and I'll admit my responsibility. You have nothing to worry about, son."

"I don't know what you want me to say. Do you want me to say thank you for doing the right thing? Because that's funny."

"I pray for you every night."

"Don't have my name in your mouth to God or anyone." I glare at him. "Maybe He believes in second chances, but I do not."

He balks. "That's pretty harsh, isn't it?"

I laugh, shoving my chair back. It screams as it claws against the floor. "I learned from the best." Then I turn to leave.

"Jason!"

I glance over my shoulder to see tears flowing in rivers down his cheeks. I can't even find it in me to care. I hate that. I hate that I don't have the heart to see through his transgressions and find it in me to still love him.

But I don't.

"I love you, Jase," he says, his eyes red. "I'm sorry for all of this. It doesn't fix it. Nothing can. But maybe you can have a little satisfaction that I'm dying inside."

"Yeah. You're right." I smile at him for the last time. "I do."

I turn away before he calls out again. The guards get me signed out and released from the prison quickly.

The rain pours from the sky in buckets, and the water sloshes in my shoes again. I splash through the puddles to my car and ignore the burn in my chest.

I get inside and don't start the car. My attention goes first to Chloe. I grab my phone from the passenger's seat and call her right away.

My heart pounds as it rings. She's breathless when she answers.

"*Jason*," she says. "I've been waiting for you to call. Are you okay?"

I sink against the seat, water dripping from my hair onto my shoulders. "Yeah. I'm fine." I close my eyes and take a deep breath, letting the soft whisps of her breaths settle my soul. "Thank you for encouraging me to come here."

"Did it go okay?"

"It went as best as it could, I guess."

She hesitates. "Jason, I'm sorry about earlier in the parking lot. I had all of these thoughts running in my head, and I—"

"I don't want to have this conversation over the phone."

"But I need to talk to you."

"And I need to talk to you, too. But this isn't the way to do it, Chloe."

Panic rises in her voice. "This has been such a shock to me in so many ways. I told you I didn't want to get married—"

"But you did marry me. And I fell in love with you." My voice cracks. "*Hopelessly in love with you,* Chloe. I've fallen so fucking hard for you that I can't breathe."

"Jason, I—"

Click!

The line goes dead.

"Fuck," I growl, combing through my pockets and the glove compartment for a phone charger. But there is none.

I throw my phone in the seat beside me, put the car in reverse, and try to get home as fast as I can.

Chapter 27

Chloe

"I have a bad feeling, Mimi."

"What's the matter, sweetheart?" She removes her glasses and sets them next to her crossword on the table beside the recliner. "You've acted strangely all day."

A thunderbolt strikes overhead, sending a rumble through Mimi's house.

I have acted out of sorts all day. *I've been out of sorts all day.*

I've avoided this conversation with my grandmother in hopes that Jason will be back so we can get back on the same page. Today was just too much for both of us. Jason had Renn to take care of and his father's situation on his mind. I was thrown for a loop hearing him say *I love you* and watching him hold Arlo ... and feeling like my world just shifted upside down.

I was caught off guard and didn't mean to make Jason think I didn't love him back. But I know that's what he's thinking ... I just hope he didn't hang up on me a few hours ago.

Things are a mess, and it's my fault.

"What's wrong, Chloe?" she asks.

I can't tell her that Jason just told me he loves me. That would sound the alarm. She'll wonder why he's just telling me now, and I'll have to explain everything. I'm trying to limit drama today, not add a whole mountain of it.

"Nothing, really," I say, folding my arms over my stomach. "We just had our first disagreement. And now he's not here, and the weather's just shitty. I wish Jason were home."

"When should he return?"

I shrug. "I think the flight is like two hours or so. I don't know how far he was from the airport in Florida. He should be getting back soon."

My stomach knots at the truth that I don't share. *He should've been back by now.*

I tried calling him several times, but it went straight to voicemail. I'm sure his phone's probably dead because he spent all night in the hospital. Still, I hate not being able to hear his voice. I hate feeling so disconnected from him.

The situation eats me up inside. The more time that passes, the more panicked I get. I need to talk about it and have someone assure me this will be okay.

"Meems, I might've screwed up today."

"Oh?"

I shift around on the sofa. "I've sort of avoided telling Jason that I love him."

Her brows fly to the ceiling.

"I know it's nuts," I say. "But he seems to understand and didn't say it to me. Until today."

"And what happened today?"

Tears fill my eyes, and pain floods my chest. "I don't really know. We were at the hospital, and Jason was holding Arlo. And I felt this deep shift inside me. I don't know where it came from, and it didn't dissipate through the day. If anything, it's gotten worse."

"What kind of a shift, sweetheart?"

"I've never really wanted kids," I say. "I never really wanted to be married either. And now I'm married, and I think I want kids, but I'm not sure, and I don't even know who I am anymore."

She grins. "Why didn't you want to get married, sweetheart?"

"I don't know." I sniffle. "I told myself that men always screwed up my life—and that's true. They did. But now that I'm on this side of the fence, I think I was scared that I'd pick the wrong guy."

Her nod is telling, as if she already understands what I might not.

We sit quietly and listen to the storm. The thunder's loud, cracking like gunshots left and right, and lightning flashes into the night sky like fireworks. It would be a great night to lie in bed and cuddle.

Instead, I'm wondering where my husband is and if he's cross with me.

"I'm going to take the blame for this one," she says, breaking the silence.

"What do you mean?"

She rocks back and forth in her chair. "I should've left your grandfather long before he died. Maybe if I had, your mother would've had the strength to avoid your father like the plague." She winks. "But I'm glad she didn't because we got you, the greatest thing—besides that golf cart—that ever happened to me."

I snort. *This woman.*

"I set a bad example," she says plainly. "I've carried that around with me for most of my life. I was blinded by what I thought was right, and I cared too much about what was socially acceptable. I should've said screw it all and did what I wanted—and that was to get out of an unhealthy relationship."

"Oh, Meems."

She stops rocking. "But you aren't like your mom and me, little girl. You're strong. You're the best of us. You learned from our mistakes and did better. You *demanded* better for yourself."

I can barely see her through the tears fogging my eyes.

"If I had seen the way love was shown to women the way you've seen it, I would've been scared of it, too. I wish I would've been more leery of it and not just accepted the first man to tell me he loved me. We'd all have been better off."

"That's the thing," I say. "I've always felt that if someone loves you, it gives them a chance to come into your life like a wrecking ball. I didn't want to give up my autonomy. I didn't want to feel stuck or broken like you and Mom. It was better to be alone."

She smiles. "It was. But is it now?"

"Of course not." I laugh softly. "But today, I held baby Arlo, and I felt myself maybe wanting kids. And I'm afraid I'm losing who I am. That or I'm having a super early midlife crisis."

"Or you could just have finally found a soft landing pad and, for the first time, feel safe enough to allow yourself to wish for a husband and babies."

"... for the first time, feel safe enough ..."

That's it. There's the truth.

"You don't have to be scared of love, Chloe," Mimi says. "But you better damn well fight for it when you find it because it doesn't come around often."

My spirits rise as a set of headlights drift across the window. I spring to my feet, ready to throw myself around Jason's neck and tell him a million times that I love him.

Because I do.

I've probably loved him for a long time. I was just too scared to accept it.

"It looks like he's home," Mimi says as footsteps splash outside and a knock raps against the door. "Come in."

"Hey, Jason." I flinch. "Gannon?"

His face is pale, and he's dripping wet. Two more sets of headlights shine up the driveway.

My heart stalls as a chill races down my spine. I can't.

Please, please don't make me do this. Don't make me ask ...

Car doors shut in the distance. Footfalls pound against the pavement. Tate and Ripley stand on either side of Gannon looking as ill as their brother.

I swallow. Hard.

"What ..." I can't get the words out. "Why are you—?"

"Chloe, there's been an accident ..."

Chapter 28

Chloe

Nausea rises in my throat.

"What do you mean?" I ask.

I shiver against the rush of adrenaline blasting through my system. No one talks as Ripley closes the door behind them.

"*Answer me,*" I say, my throat so tight I can barely speak. "What kind of accident?"

My mind shuffles through varied possibilities with his voice overlayed, telling me he loves me. I shake as I point at Tate.

"Answer me, dammit," I say.

"I got a call that Jason's plane went down just outside of Nashville," Gannon says.

I scream inside my head, but nothing comes out. Tears pour down my face. Gannon's lips move, but I can't hear them over my internal cries.

Tate pulls me into a hug and then helps me sit back down. "It's gonna be okay, Chloe. Just breathe."

Ripley hands me a tissue and then tends to Mimi.

"And I need to talk to you, too. But this isn't the way to do it, Chloe."

"Is he okay?" I ask, only able to make out his silhouette. "Where is he?"

Is he alive?

"We don't know yet," Gannon says. "He issued a mayday call and reported engine failure. He dropped off the radar shortly after."

"*Oh my God.*" I shake so hard I think I might puke. "What do we do?" I spring to my feet. "We need to go look for him. Why aren't we looking for him? Why are you here and not out there?"

"His plane had a transmitter that broadcasted his location when he went down. First responders are on their way there now."

My cries fill the room. "How are you not panicking? How are you calm? He could be ... dead out there. Or hurt. Or scared. Or hungry."

"Hungry?" Ripley says.

I glare at him.

He holds his hands up. "Definitely worrying about him being hungry. Ignore me."

Gannon crouches in front of me and looks me in the eye. He's not as confident as Jason, and I don't feel nearly as safe. But there's enough resemblance to remind me that I'm in a room full of Brewers. They love harder than anyone, and this is their brother. If they're calm, I should try to be, too.

"Listen to me," Gannon says. "This is Jason. You could drop the man off in the middle of the ocean, and he'd find his way to shore. And if he was trying to get back to you, I'm sure he could return from the moon."

My bottom lip quivers.

"I know he's going to be fine. I feel it. And I need you to feel it, too. Wherever he is right now, he's thinking about you. He might lose an arm, but he'll just be pissed he can't use it to hold you."

Sobs wrack my body, and I try so hard to keep them in check.

"But you did marry me. And I fell in love with you. Hopelessly in love with you, Chloe. I've fallen so fucking hard for you that I can't breathe."

"What do we do? Just sit here?" I ask, feeling helpless.

"We sit tight and wait on a call," Gannon says.

"And we pray," Tate says, gazing out the window as if he expects Jason to pull up at any moment.

I look over my shoulder to see Ripley sitting on the floor beside Mimi, her hands in his. Tears streak her cheeks, too.

"Where's your mother?" I ask, wondering how she's holding up.

"She's with Renn at the hospital," Tate says. "A doctor there gave her something to keep her calm."

"How's Renn?" I ask.

"He was telling Arlo stories about Jason the last time I talked to Blakely. Jason's going to be a living legend in that kid's mind. I don't know how we're going to even the score," Ripley says.

I laugh through my tears.

Tate turns to us. "Anyone want a cup of coffee?"

"Come help me up," Mimi says. "I'll put on a pot."

It's going to be a long, lonely, terrible night.

You have to come back to me, Jason Brewer. There is no other option here. You can't leave me—you promised you'd always be here.

I need you.

I love you.

Always will.

Chapter 29

Jason

"Has anyone called my wife?" I ask as I'm wheeled into the ER. "Is anyone listening to me?"

"Your family is en route to the hospital, Mr. Brewer," one of the medics says. "We've told you this ten times."

"And I'm now asking for the eleventh time. *Has anyone called my wife?*"

My head feels like it might fall off my neck, and my left shoulder screams in pain. It feels like a hot poker is being jabbed into my clavicle repeatedly, but at least I can walk.

I'm pushed into a secure bay at the far end of the ER. Nurses and doctors come in immediately, hooking me up to lines and machines and getting a game plan in place to check me out.

All I want is to see Chloe.

Once they're sure I'm not going to die on the bed, they begin to filter out, leaving me with one short, dark-headed doctor who can't be much older than Chloe.

Chloe. Where are you, beautiful?

"Where is he?" Her voice rises above the cacophony of the room's noise. "He's my husband, and I will see him now!"

I chuckle. *There's my girl.*

"Hey," I say, wincing as a blast of pain shoots through my head. "My wife's out there causing a scene. Do you think you could sneak her in here?"

"Sure. Just a moment."

He moves silently through the room and disappears into the hallway. He jumps out of the way as Chloe rushes into the room.

Tears stain her face. Her eyes are wild. As soon as her gaze settles on me, she sobs.

"Will you stop it?" I ask, chuckling. I hold my good arm out, and she slides into the bed next to me and throws her arms around me. "*Hey, hey, hey.*" I wince. "That's ... not the shoulder."

She lifts off me and sits up, scanning every inch of my body.

"Are you okay? Please, tell me you're okay," she begs.

"If I'm guessing, I have a concussion, and my left arm and shoulder are royally fucked. But I think I'm pretty good otherwise."

She's not convinced. "What happened to you?"

"Lie with me. I need to touch you. Just stay on my right side, okay?"

She curls up next to me, her hand splayed over my heart. I sigh because *this* is what I need. My beautiful wife. The only woman I'll ever love.

"I'm not sure what happened," I say. "I was flying home and had engine failure. I found a field where I could land, but the winds were awful. The plane was tossed around, and a wing clipped the treetops. That's the last thing I remember for a while."

Her tears are hot against my skin. "I was so scared, Jason."

"I just wanted to get home to you."

She sits up, looking me in the eye. "You didn't call."

"My phone was dead, and instead of stopping to buy a cord or borrowing someone's at the airport, I focused on getting back to you."

I touch the side of her cheek. She leans into my hand as if it's the balm to her wounds. She's the balm to mine.

"Jason ..." She squares her shoulders to mine and grins. "This is not how I was going to do this."

"How were you going to do this?"

"It included me straddling you and wearing the black lingerie you love so much."

I want to take her hand and place it on my hardening cock. Instead, I raise my eyebrows and *tell* her to look lower. And she does. Then she bursts out laughing.

"You almost died tonight," she says. "Simmer down."

"You still turn me on. I'd probably be hard for you in a casket."

She smacks my chest. "No casket jokes, asshole."

"Speaking of assholes, where are Gannon and the others?"

"In the waiting room. Your mom is at the other hospital with Renn. They have her pretty medicated because she was losing her shit." Her grin turns sheepish. "I threatened your brothers and Bianca to let me back here first. They didn't put up too much of a fight."

"Probably because they know I'd throw them out and ask for you."

She presses a kiss to the center of my lips. I try to deepen it, but she pulls back.

"Listen, about earlier ..." Her features sober. "I was scared, Jason. I admitted to myself that I loved you well before today. But hearing you say it as I was trying to wrap my brain around the fact that I had a sudden urge to have your babies—"

"Whoa, back up. Don't talk about this shit unless you can follow through."

She giggles. "I need to say this shit, but you're in a hospital bed Not my fault you can't fly a plane."

"Too soon."

She kisses me again. "I love you, Jason Brewer. With my whole heart. And I told Tate tonight that he could keep his money because you're going to lose the bet."

"I am?"

"You are. You're not staying married for six months." A slow smile splits her cheeks. "I'm thinking since you're old, we probably have a good forty, fifty years left in us."

I pull her down with my good arm, ignoring the searing pain the movement causes in my other arm. Then I capture her mouth with mine.

"I love you, my beautiful wife," I whisper against her lips.

"I do have one request."

"I'll give you whatever you want."

She smiles at the memory. "Will you give me a baby?"

"Shut the door, and you can climb on my dick right now. Fuck."

Her giggles are music to my ears.

"I'm not kidding," I say. "Or leave the door open. I don't care."

"Stop it," she says, laughing. "You can't be this ornery when you're getting ready to be rolled into X-ray."

"New arrangement. Me, you, two babies, Mimi, and the rest of our lives. Deal?"

"Deal."

Chapter 30

Chloe

"He is one grumpy boy," Rory says, descending the stairs. "I don't know how you put up with him, Chloe. But thank God you do."

"It's not as bad as it seems."

She hums. "Do you need anything before I go? I'm going to swing by Renn's and get some baby Arlo snuggles."

And, no doubt, she'll congratulate Renn on securing the bid for the Royals because Jason relented. I knew he would.

"I think we're good here. Jason goes for a checkup tomorrow, and I'm hoping they give him a little more freedom with his arm. If not, he and I might fight."

"Who? You and the doctor?"

I snort. "Me and your son. I keep catching him trying to use it, and he won't listen."

"He didn't get that from me." She pulls me into a warm, maternal hug. "I'm going to see if Mimi's home and tell her goodbye."

"I think she's at Samuel's."

Rory points a perfectly manicured finger toward me. "That woman has it figured out. I wish I had half her game."

I laugh, then wipe off the kitchen counter.

"See you soon, sweetheart."

"Give Arlo kisses from Auntie Chloe."

"I will."

The door snaps shut behind her.

It's a beautiful afternoon in Nashville, with the sun high in a cloudless sky. Mimi and I had breakfast by the pool this morning while Jason did a little work from home. When she jetted off in the golf cart, I came back inside and tidied up.

In the few weeks since the accident, many things have changed, and nothing has changed at all. Our routine has been modified since Jason has needed to take some time off work. He hated it at first, but I think he's starting to secretly enjoy it.

I know I have.

I still go into the office every day for at least a few hours, taking care of the tasks I can't manage from home. But, on the boss's orders, I do everything possible from home—usually while somehow touching my husband. Mara has been coming in every day to help Mimi more than anything since I can take care of our home pretty much on my own. Mara and Mimi have developed a friendship that fills my heart with so much joy.

"Where's my wife?" Jason calls from upstairs.

"Waiting on your lunch to finish cooking."

"What are you making me?"

"Leftover chicken and rice."

"What's for dessert?"

The cheekiness in his voice makes me smile.

The day I thought I'd lost my husband was one of the worst days of my life. Five hours. It took five hours for the search and rescue team to find him, extract him, and get him to the hospital.

Those hours were grueling, but I'm pretty sure the Brewer Trifecta of Power kept me sane. They made it possible to survive the anguish. How? Because they're a unit. They're strong. And they believe in each other.

I haven't stopped telling Jason I love him since.

"I don't know. Chocolate cake?" I ask, waiting for his refusal.

"You better not bring me chocolate cake."

I laugh. "I thought you wanted something sweet?"

"Fuck the chicken and rice and get your sweet little ass up here." He pauses. "Please."

The oven timer beeps, so I take our lunch out and transfer it onto two plates. Then I take the plastic pitcher out of the refrigerator and pour us each a glass of sweet tea. I carry it on a large tray to the upstairs sitting room, where Jason has been holed up for the majority of the past three weeks.

"Here you go, my love," I say, handing him a plate and a drink. Then I bend to give him a quick kiss.

"How was the office?"

"Good. I was only there a couple of hours." I sit on the chair across from him. "I met with Ian Gregory about the catering contract for next year. I told him if his numbers didn't tighten, we'd be entertaining a new provider." I take a sip of my tea. "He's not happy, but neither are we."

Jason beams. "Look at you. A CEO in training."

I scoff. "I have no interest in being a CEO. As a matter of fact, once you're back in the office full time, I might go back to waiting tables at Fika's and let you deal with this yourself. I'm sick of these people."

"Or you could just stay home and do something you love."

"But you're the only thing I love. I don't know what else I'd do until we have babies."

"Well, we could get started on that."

Heat blossoms in my belly at the thought. We discussed having children the night he had his accident, but we haven't talked about it since. With his injuries—a broken collarbone, broken humerus, three cracked ribs, and a broken bone in his foot—our focus has been on his health. But the better he feels and the more active he becomes, the more I think about it.

"Can I talk to you about something?" he asks, setting his plate down beside him.

"Sure."

"When we got married, we did it for a bet. But now, there's nothing funny about it. You're the love of my life."

I swoon at my handsome man's sweet words.

"I was thinking in all my free time that we should get married again," he says. "Let our family be there. Let Mimi see you get married. I want to see you in a dress and let my mother have the experience of a son getting married since she's oh-for-two."

My laughter is soft.

"I want to do it the right way," he says. "Take you on a proper honeymoon. Surprise you with a trip somewhere. The whole thing."

"Who knew you were this sweet?"

He smiles with a small wince. "I think it's less sweet and more obsessed with you."

"I like you being obsessed with me."

"Did I really have a choice?" He grins. "Come here."

I set my plate beside his and climb on his lap, careful not to disturb the entire left side of his body.

For the longest time, I let my fears dictate my life. They were warranted. They usually are. But instead of acknowledging them and working to overcome them, I only deprived myself of something good. And you can't find love if you hide away from it. You still wind up hurt, which is what I was trying to avoid from the start.

And I delayed the best thing that ever happened to me.

"I love you, Chloe Brewer," Jason says, kissing the bend of my neck.

"Not nearly as much as I love you, Jason Brewer."

He sighs contently. "I'm so lucky I have you."

I brace myself. "You're lucky you landed me better than you land planes."

My laughter fills the room as he tickles me, the sound hushed by his mouth over mine. It's how everything ends with us now. We remind each other that no matter what happens, what jokes are made, what squabbles we have—we love each other.

Not for six months.

Forever.

Epilogue

Chloe

One month later ...

"He's starting to get on my nerves." I take a bite off the top of the blueberry muffin. "He's so into this wedding thing that he must dream about it."

Nickie sits across from me in the break room, smiling blissfully. "It's so romantic."

"In theory. I was happy with our little Vegas getaway elopement thing. Now he wants this ... *production*. That's the only word I can think of to come close to what Jason has in mind."

Talk of our new nuptials has taken over my life. It was romantic at first. Now? I have to barter with him to get through the night. For every half hour we talk about the wedding, that's half an hour we do something that I want to do.

That's usually sex, so he wins, too. But at least I can look forward to it as I decide whether I want a cathedral or an outdoor barn vibe. I usually try to determine which way he's leaning and choose that because I don't really care. I want him, and I already have that.

Besides, he's just trying to make me happy. How can I not love that?

"What's been going on in your world?" I ask. "I love that lipstick on you, by the way. Super pretty."

"Thanks. It's called Viper or Vixen or something. It was in the clearance bin at the pharmacy." She puckers for me. "But, yeah, that's about all that's been happening. I miss seeing you."

I laugh. "I have seen you every Thursday night for the past four weeks."

"Yeah, but that's just because I don't get to hang out with you at lunch every day. You had to go snag yourself a super-sexy rich husband that you'd rather screw with than gossip with me." She grins. "But I'm not judging because I'd do the same damn thing."

We sit quietly, eating our muffins and sipping our coffee.

It doesn't feel any different being the CEO's wife. The only difference is I have a better wardrobe, thanks to the shopping extravaganza in Vegas, and fresh flowers are delivered twice a week to my office. I've asked Jason to stop doing that, but he smirks.

You must pick your fights in marriage, I've learned. Flowers aren't going to be it for me.

My phone buzzes next to my coffee, and I swipe it up before Nickie can see the screen—just in case.

It's a text from Tate. But when I open it, there is no message. There's only a picture of him and Mimi in the golf cart flashing peace signs. Tate is shirtless.

Me: Don't give her a heart attack! Put some clothes on.

Tate: She likes me this way. <tongue sticking out emoji>

I snort, shaking my head and closing the screen.

"Who was that?" Nickie asks, plopping a piece of a donut in her mouth.

"Tate. He's cruising the neighborhood with Mimi right now, sans shirt."

"That's it. In my next life, if I can't return as you, I want to be your grandma."

I laugh. "You do realize that only a month ago, I was living in the Pliny Building and you felt sorry for me."

"And you do realize that if I wouldn't have felt a bit sorry for you if I saw how this story was going to end."

"I didn't even believe in happy endings back then."

Her gaze tracks along the glass wall separating the office from the break room. I follow her line of sight to the hallway ... and to Jason. My heart blossoms as our eyes meet.

I never get tired of looking at him. But I also don't get tired of sleeping next to him, fixing dinner with him, or playing a card game while we wait for our frozen pizzas to cook either.

Jason's features have changed over the past few weeks. Despite the pain of his injuries from the crash, his eyes are brighter. His smile is wider. Jason's face isn't as lined as before his father took the plea deal. He's talked a little about their conversation, but I don't push. I know it hurts him to go back to that day.

It isn't comfortable for me either.

But whatever was said that afternoon before his phone died and I thought he died was enough to help Jason let go of so much anger. It refocused him. It's allowed him to give and receive love easier, too.

If there's one thing Jason Brewer does well, it's love on me.

"Excuse me, Mrs. Brewer," he says, grinning. "May I see you in my office for a moment?"

I drop my muffin in the trash can and follow him upstairs.

Chapter 1: Flirt

WANTED: A SITUATION-SHIP

I'm a single female who's tired of relationships ruining my life. However, there are times when a date would be helpful. If you're a single man, preferably mid-twenties to late-thirties, and are in a similar situation, we might be a match.

Candidate must be handsome, charming, and willing to pretend to have feelings for me (on a sliding scale, as the event requires). Ability to discuss a wide variety of topics is a plus. Must have your own transportation and a (legal) job.

This will be a symbiotic agreement. In exchange for your time, I will give you mine. Need someone to flirt with you at a football party? Go, team! Want a woman to make you look good in front of your boss? Let me find my heels. Would you love for someone to be obsessed with you in front of your ex? I'm applying my red lipstick now.

If interested, please email me. Time is of the essence.

Chapter 1
Brooke

My best friend, Jovie, points at my computer screen. The glitter on her pink fingernail sparkles in the light. "You can't post that."

I fold my arms across my chest. "And why not?"

Instead of answering me, she takes another bite of her chicken wrap. A dribble of mayonnaise dots the corner of her mouth.

"A lot of help you are," I mutter, rereading the post I drafted instead of pricing light fixtures for work. The words are written in a pretty font on Social, my go-to social media platform.

Country music from the nineties mixes with the laughter of locals sitting around us in Smokey's, my favorite beachside café. Along the far wall, a map of the state of Florida made of wine corks sways gently in the ocean breeze coming through the open windows.

"Would you two like anything else?" Rebecca, our usual lunchtime server, pauses by the table. "I think we have some Key lime pie left."

"I'm too irritable for pie today," I say.

"*You* don't want *pie*? That's a first," she teases me.

Jovie giggles.

"I know," I say, releasing a sigh. "That's the state of my life right now. I don't even want pie."

"Wow. Okay. This sounds serious. What's up? Maybe I can help," Rebecca says.

Jovie wipes her mouth with a napkin. "Let me cut in here real quick before she tries to snowball you into thinking her harebrained idea is a good one."

I roll my eyes. "It *is* a good one."

"I'll give you the CliffsNotes version," Jovie says, side-eyeing me. "Brooke got an invitation to her grandma's birthday party, and instead of just not going—"

"I can't *not* go."

"Or showing up as the badass single chick she is," Jovie continues, silencing me with a look, "she wrote a post for Social that's basically an ad for a fake boyfriend."

"Correction—it *is* an ad for a fake boyfriend."

Rebecca rests a hand on her hip. "I don't see the problem."

"*Thank you,*" I say, staring at Jovie. "I'm glad someone understands me here."

Jovie throws her hands in the air, sending a napkin flying right along with them.

Satisfaction is written all over my face as I sit back in my chair with a smug smile. The more I think about having a *situation-ship* with a guy—a word I read in a magazine at the salon while waiting two decades for my color to process—the more it makes sense.

Instead of having relations with a man, have situations. Done.

What's not to love about that?

"But, before I tell you to dive into this whole thing, why can't you just go alone, Brooke?" Rebecca asks.

"Oh, *I can* go alone. I just generally prefer to avoid torture whenever possible."

"I still don't understand why you need a date to your grandma's birthday party."

"Because this isn't *just* a birthday party," I say. "It's labeled that to cover up the fact that my mom and her sister, my aunt Kim, are having a daughter-of-the-year showdown. They're using my poor grandma Honey's eighty-fifth birthday as a dog and pony show—and my cousin Aria and I are the ponies."

"*Okay.*" Rebecca looks at me dubiously before switching her attention to Jovie. "And why are you against this whole thing?"

Jovie takes enough cash to cover our lunch plus the tip and hands it to Rebecca. *Perks of ordering the same lunch most days.* Then she gathers her things.

"I'm not against it in *theory,*" Jovie says. "I'm against it in *practice.* I understand the perks of having a guy around to be arm candy when needed. But I'm not supporting this decision ... this *mayhem* ... for two reasons." She looks at me. "For one, your family will see any post you make on Social. You don't think they'll use it as ammunition against you?"

This is probably true.

"Second," Jovie continues. "I hate, hate, *hate* your aunt Kim, and I loathe the fact that your mom makes you feel like you have to do anything more than be your amazing self to win her favor. Screw them both."

My heart swells as I take in my best friend.

Jovie Reynolds was my first friend in Kismet Beach when I moved here two and a half years ago. We reached for the same can of pineapple rings, knocking over an entire display in Publix. As we picked up the mess, we traded recipes—hers for a vodka cocktail and mine for air fryer pineapple.

We hung out that evening—with her cocktail and my air fryer creations—and have been inseparable since.

"My mom is not a bad person," I say in her defense, even though I'm not so sure that's true from time to time. "She's just ..."

"A bad person," Jovie says.

I laugh. "*No*. I just ... nothing I can do is good enough for her. She hated Geoff when I married him at twenty and said I was too young. But was she happy when that ended in a divorce? Nope. According to *her*, I didn't try hard enough."

Rebecca frowns.

"And then Geoff started banging Kim and—"

"*What*?" Rebecca yelps, her eyes going wide.

"Exactly. Bad people," Jovie says, shaking her head.

"So your ex-husband will be at your grandma's party with your aunt? Is that what you're saying?" Rebecca asks.

I nod. "Yup."

She stacks our plates on top of one another. The ceramic clinks through the air. "On that note, why can't you just not go? Avoid it altogether?"

"Because my grandma Honey is looking forward to this, and she called me to make sure I was coming. I couldn't tell her no." My heart tightens when I think of the woman I love more than any other. "And, you know, my mom has made it abundantly clear that if I miss this, I will probably break Honey's heart, and she'll die, and it'll be my fault."

"Wow. That's a freight train of guilt to throw around," Rebecca says, wincing.

I glance down at my computer. The post is still there, sitting on the screen and waiting for my final decision. Although it is a genius idea, if I do say so myself—Jovie is probably right. It'll just cause more problems than it's worth.

I close the laptop and shove it into my bag. Then I hoist it on my shoulder. "It's complicated. I want to go and celebrate with my grandma but seeing my aunt with my ex-husband ..." I wince. "Also, there will be my mother's usual diatribe and comparisons to Aria, proving that I'm a failure in everything that I do."

"But if you had a boyfriend to accompany you, you'd save face with the enemy and have a buffer against your mother. Is that what you're thinking?" Rebecca asks.

"Yeah. I don't know how else to survive it. I can't walk in there alone, or even with Jovie, and deal with all of that mess. If I just had someone hot and a little handsy—make me look irresistible—it would kill all of my birds with one hopefully *hard* stone."

I wink at my friends.

Rebecca laughs. "Okay. I'm Team Fake Boyfriend. Sorry, Jovie."

Jovie sighs. "I'm sorry for me too because I have to go back to work. And if I avoid the stoplights, I can make it to the office with thirty seconds to spare." She air-kisses Rebecca. "Thanks for the extra mayo."

I laugh. "See you tomorrow, Rebecca."

"Bye, girls."

Jovie and I walk single-file through Smokey's until we reach the exit. Immediately, we reach for the sunglasses perched on top of our heads and slide them over our eyes.

The sun is bright, nearly blinding in a cloudless sky. I readjust my bag so that the thin layer of sweat starting to coat my skin doesn't coax the leather strap down my arm.

"Call me tonight," Jovie says, heading to her car.

"I will."

"Rehearsal for the play got canceled tonight, so I might go to Charlie's. If I don't, I may swing by your house."

"How's the thing with Charlie going? I didn't realize you were still talking to him."

She laughs. "I wasn't. He pissed me off. But he came groveling back last night, and I gave in." She shrugs. "What can I say? I'm a sucker for a good grovel."

"I think it's the theater girl in you. You love the dramatics of it all."

"That I do. It's a problem."

"Well, I'll see you when I see you then," I say.

"Bye, Brooke."

I give her a little wave and make my way up Beachfront Boulevard.

The sidewalk is fairly vacant with a light dusting of sand. In another month, tourists will fill the street that leads from the ocean to the shops filled with trinkets and ice cream in the heart of Kismet Beach. For now, it's a relaxing and hot walk back to the office.

My mind shifts from the heat back to the email reminder I received during lunch. *To Honey's party.* It takes all of one second for my stomach to cramp.

"I shouldn't have eaten all of those fries," I groan.

But it's not lunch that's making me unwell.

A mixture of emotions rolls through me. I don't know which one to land on. There's a chord of excitement about the event—at seeing Honey and her wonderful life be celebrated, catching up with Aria and the rest of my family, and the general concept of *going home*. But there's so much apprehension right alongside those things that it drowns out the good.

Kim and Geoff together make me ill. It's not that I miss my ex-husband; I'm the one who filed for divorce. But they will be there, making things super awkward for me in front of everyone we know.

Not to mention what it will do to my mother.

Geoff hooking up with Kim is my ultimate failure, according to Mom. Somehow, it embarrasses *her,* and that's unforgivable.

"For just once, I'd like to see her and not be judged," I mumble as I sidestep a melting glob of blue ice cream.

Nothing I have ever done has been good enough for Catherine Bailey. Marrying Geoff was an atrocity at only twenty years old. My dream to work in interior architecture wasn't deemed serious enough as a life path. *"You're wasting your time and our money, Brooke."* And when I told her I was hired at Laguna Homes as a lead designer for one of their three renovation teams? I could hear her eyes rolling.

The office comes into view, and my spirits lift immediately. I shove all thoughts of the party out of my brain and let my mind settle back into happier territory. *Work.* The one thing I love.

I step under the shade of an adorable crape myrtle tree and then turn up a cobblestone walkway to my office.

The small white building is tucked away from the sidewalk. It sits between a row of shops with apartments above them and an Italian restaurant only open in the evenings. The word *Laguna Homes* is printed in seafoam green above a black awning.

My shoes tap against the wooden steps as I make my way to the door. A rush of cool air, kissed by the scent of eucalyptus essential oil, greets me as I step inside.

"How was lunch?" Kix asks, standing in the doorway of his corner office. My boss's smile is kind and genuine, just like everything else about him. "Let me guess—you met Jovie for lunch at Smokey's?"

I laugh. "It's like you know me or something."

He chuckles.

Kix and Damaris Carmichael are two of my favorite people in the world. When I met Damaris at a trade show three years ago, and we struck up a conversation about tile, I knew she was special. Then I met her husband and discovered he had the same soft yet sturdy energy. All six of their children possess similar qualities—even Moss, the superintendent on my renovation team. Although I'd never admit that to him.

"I swung by Parasol Place this afternoon," Kix says. "It's looking great. You were right about taking out the wall between the living room and dining room. I love it. It makes the whole house feel bigger."

I blush under the weight of his compliment. "Thanks."

"Did Moss tell you about the property I'm looking at for your team next?" Kix asks.

"No. Moss doesn't tell me anything."

Kix grins. "I'm sure he tells you all kinds of things you don't need to know."

"You say that like you have experience with him," I say, laughing.

"Only a few years." He laughs too. "It's another home from the sixties. I got a lead on it this morning and am on my way to look at it now."

"Take pictures. You know I love that era, and if you get it, I want to be able to start envisioning things right away."

"You and your visions." He shakes his head. "Gina is in the back making copies. I told her we'd keep our eye on the door until she gets back out here, so it would be great if you could do that."

"Absolutely," I say, walking backward toward my office. "Be safe. *And take pictures.*"

"I will. Enjoy the rest of your day, Brooke."

"You, too."

I reach behind me to find my office door open. I take another step back and then turn toward my desk. Someone moves beside my filing cabinet just as I flip on the light.

"Ah!" I shriek, clutching my chest.

My heart pounds out of control until I get my bearings and focus on the man looking back at me.

I set my bag down on a chair and blow out a shaky breath. "Dammit, Moss!"

He leans against the cabinet and smiles at me cheekily.

"We're going to have to stop meeting like this," he says. "People are going to talk."

Continue reading here.

Acknowledgments

As always, thank you to my Creator first and foremost.

Thank you to my family for always supporting me and the worlds I make up in my head and live in half the time. I love you guys.

All my love to my husband and sons for understanding what life looks like with a writer. I love you all so freaking much.

Thank you to Kari March for designing the perfect cover. You're brilliant!

Sending love to my friends for their support, laughs, and brainstorming sessions: Mandi Beck, S.L. Scott, Jessica Prince, Dylan Allen, Anjelica Grace, Kenna Rey, and Chelle Sloan.

I'm so thankful for Michele Ficht's friendship and her energy and excitement for my books.

Marion Archer and Jenny Sims—you're the real rock stars. Thank you for always making things work. I love you both.

As always, a huge thank you to the women who help me and my business run smoothly—Tiffany Remy, Jenn Hess, Kaitie Reister, Stephanie Gibson, Jordan Fazzini, and Sue Maturo. I adore you all.

The team at Valentine PR is amazing. Thank you, everyone, for your energy and patience. You are seen and appreciated.

Thank you to my readers for showing up book after book, finding me on social media, and engaging with me. You make this possible and I'm forever grateful for the opportunity to entertain you for a bit.

About the Author

USA Today Bestselling author, Adriana Locke, writes contemporary romances about the two things she knows best—big families and small towns. Her stories are about ordinary people finding extraordinary love with the perfect combination of heart, heat, and humor.

She loves connecting with readers, fall weather, football, reading alpha heroes, everything pumpkin, and pretending to garden.

Hailing from a tiny town in the Midwest, Adriana spends her free time with her high school sweetheart (who she married over twenty years ago) and their four sons (who truly are her best work).

Her kitchen may be a perpetual disaster, and if all else fails, there is always pizza.

Join her reader group and talk all the bookish things by clicking here.

www.adrianalocke.com